french coast

Also by Anita Hughes

Monarch Beach

Market Street

Lake Como

french coast

ANITA HUGHES

 St. Martin's Griffin ≋ New York

This is a work of fiction. All of the characters, organizations, and events portrayed in this novel are either products of the author's imagination or are used fictitiously.

FRENCH COAST. Copyright © 2015 by Anita Hughes. All rights reserved. Printed in the United States of America. For information, address St. Martin's Press, 175 Fifth Avenue, New York, N.Y. 10010.

www.stmartins.com

The Library of Congress Cataloging-in-Publication Data is available upon request.

ISBN 978-1-250-05251-3 (trade paperback)
ISBN 978-1-250-06610-7 (hardcover)
ISBN 978-1-4668-6842-7 (e-book)

St. Martin's Griffin books may be purchased for educational, business, or promotional use. For information on bulk purchases, please contact the Macmillan Corporate and Premium Sales Department at 1-800-221-7945, extension 5442, or write to specialmarkets@macmillan.com.

First Edition: April 2015

10 9 8 7 6 5 4 3 2 1

To my mother

french coast

chapter one

Serena reached the top of Baker Street and turned around to look at the skyline. She had been back in San Francisco for two years but she never tired of the view. It was early evening and the city was bathed in a pink and purple light. The Golden Gate Bridge lay wrapped in fog and Coit Tower rose above the houses like an ancient monument.

Serena smelled the hyacinths and daffodils filling the sidewalk and gazed at the outline of the Transamerica building. She remembered thinking as a child that it looked like an Egyptian pyramid in the midst of steel skyscrapers. Now she had her own office at *Vogue*'s West Coast headquarters on the sixteenth floor. She still pinched herself when she nodded at the receptionist with her long blond ponytail and straight-off-the-runway Tory Burch platforms, when she walked down the hallway with its shiny *Vogue* covers and bright geometric carpet.

Serena flashed on her afternoon meeting with Chelsea Brown, her editor in chief, and the new assignment she offered her. She couldn't wait to tell her boyfriend, Chase, but first she wanted to sift through her mother's boxes of magazines and learn as much as she could about Yvette Renault, editor in chief of French *Vogue* for two decades.

Serena entered the iron gates of her parents' Presidio Heights mansion and saw Chase's car parked in front of the double glass front doors. Chase had bought the car last month: a shiny silver Fiat he had spent weeks agonizing over. Now that Chase was about to announce his candidacy for mayor, everywhere they ate, how they spent their weekends, and what books they read were going to be scrutinized by the public.

"Anything German is too flashy, something American would be too obvious," Chase had said, frowning as they sat at Betelnut one Sunday morning. Betelnut was one of their new rituals: Serena loved the strong black coffee served from an old-fashioned coffeepot and Chase loved the fact that every young Internet entrepreneur, hedge fund manager, and law firm partner passed the big front windows as they collected their Sunday *New York Times* and mocha Frappuccinos.

"My car has to reflect my vision for San Francisco: international, efficient, visionary." Chase drummed his fingers on the Formica table. He wore a yellow Georgetown T-shirt, running shorts, and red-and-blue Nike Air sneakers. His wavy blond hair touched his collar and his cheeks glistened with Tommy Hilfiger aftershave.

"You're going to be a fabulous mayor," Serena told him as she sprinkled salt on scrambled eggs. She had suffered through early-morning Pilates, followed by a two-mile run to Crissy Field, and enjoyed treating herself to eggs and toast and juicy strips of bacon.

"First I have to get elected." Chase furrowed his brow. "We're going all the way to the top, 1600 Pennsylvania Avenue."

"One step at a time," Serena said, laughing. "San Francisco

City Hall is a wonderful address, and I haven't even begun to choose my gown for the inauguration. I picture a red satin dress with a scooped neckline and full skirt."

"You know I love you," Chase said. His eyes dimmed, and for a moment he looked like an eager little boy instead of a thirty-three-year-old corporate attorney perched at the beginning of his political career.

Serena ate a slice of bacon and thought how lucky she was to have found someone who enjoyed the same things she did. They both loved working long hours and getting away on the week-ends. Serena smiled, thinking of the times Chase picked her up from work on Friday night with her overnight bag already packed. He wouldn't tell her where they were going until they arrived at a romantic bed-and-breakfast in Sonoma or a hotel perched on a cliff in Mendocino.

"A Fiat Spider," Serena said suddenly, watching a yellow Fiat maneuver into an impossibly tight parking spot in front of the restaurant. "No one could argue with you buying a Fiat, it's the perfect car for getting around the city."

Serena approached the stone entry and saw her mother stepping outside, wearing Jacqueline Kennedy sunglasses and a pink-and-white Chanel suit with beige pumps. Her strawberry-blond hair was covered with a silk scarf and she carried a soft leather bag.

"Darling, what a lovely surprise." Kate slipped off her sun-glasses. "Chase is here. He and your father are sequestered in the library as if they're planning the invasion of the Bay of Pigs."

"Maybe they are." Serena laughed. "I was hoping to go through the attic; I'm doing some research."

"I'd love to help." Kate checked her watch. "But I'm late for a meeting of the Ladies Auxiliary. I wish I had a real job, instead of planning menus and flower arrangements and fashion shows."

"You're allowed to enjoy yourself," Serena said, and smiled. "You were a political wife for thirty years."

"The problem is I don't know how to enjoy myself," Kate said as she extracted her keys from her purse. "Neither does your father. The only place he's happy is on his boat; otherwise he prowls around like a caged bear."

"You'll find hobbies," Serena replied. "You could learn mah-jongg or Cajun cooking."

"I should be grateful that my daughter has a wonderful job and a lovely apartment and a handsome, caring boyfriend," Kate relented, slipping her sunglasses on her nose. "I like to feel useful; I never thought I'd turn into one of those women."

"You are the most useful person on the planet." Serena pushed open the twelve-foot-tall front doors. "Daddy wouldn't survive a day without you."

Serena walked through the foyer, past the family portrait hanging over the stone fireplace, past the living room with its dark wood floors and Oriental rugs, to her father's library.

She loved to see the house full of fresh cut flowers, the drapes pulled open, the bay shimmering past the stretch of green lawn. All the years her parents had been in Washington the house was closed, and Serena would stop by once a week to open the French doors. Now her mother's perfume wafted through the rooms and her father's newspapers were scattered on glass coffee tables and maple sideboards.

"Serena!" Chase jumped up when Serena entered the library. "I thought I was picking you up at your place at seven?" Serena smiled at her father and Chase, hunched over the polished walnut desk like two boys conducting a science project. Chase wore a navy Hugo Boss suit with a red power tie they had picked out together at Neiman's, and Charles wore his new uniform of dark blazer, khaki slacks, and boating shoes.

"You two look guilty," Serena said playfully. "Are you planning a political coup? Removing a third-world dictator or pushing a new bill through Congress?"

"I still have my uses," her father said as he rubbed his forehead. He had silver hair and green eyes and tan leathery skin.

"Your father was giving me campaign advice," Chase said, then kissed Serena on the mouth. He collected a stack of papers and jammed them in his briefcase. "I have to run, I have a meeting at city hall at six."

"We can eat at Greens another night," Serena said as she smelled Chase's mint shampoo. "I'll get a chicken from Whole Foods and toss a spinach salad."

"It's a perfect night to eat by the water," her father cut in. "There's hardly any fog."

Serena glanced from Chase to her father, sensing an undercurrent running between them. "What's going on, am I missing something?"

Sometimes she felt like Chase and her father belonged to a secret club that only accepted men as members. They loved to watch the Giants game and drink Sierra Nevada Pale Ale. Whenever she mentioned it to her mother Kate laughed and said Serena should be pleased they enjoyed each other's company. Then she'd slip on her oversize sunglasses and suggest she and Serena have afternoon tea at the Fairmont or go shopping at Neiman Marcus.

"Nothing's going on," Charles said as he put on his reading

glasses and attacked the pile of newspapers on his desk. "I was just saying it was a nice evening to eat by the bay."

Serena walked Chase to his car, lingering at the driver's-side door to kiss him slowly on the mouth. She watched him drive out of the gravel driveway down Pacific Avenue, then ran back into the house and up the three flights of stairs to the attic.

Serena heard her father close the library door and smiled. It was no secret that Charles loved having Chase around, that it made him feel thirty years younger, at the start of his own political career. They spent hours going over campaign funding and media strategy. When Chase was in the house, her father's voice was stronger, he walked more purposefully, the lines around his eyes relaxed.

Serena remembered when she met Chase, at one of her parents' salons. Serena had taken the train from Amherst to Georgetown and was holed up in her father's study finishing a term paper.

"You're missing some delicious crab cakes and steak tartar," a man said, standing next to her father's floor-to-ceiling bookshelf. He had blond hair and wore a tweed blazer over a yellow button-down shirt and khakis.

"Not hungry," Serena said, briefly looking up. "I have to finish this paper if I want to ace comparative literature."

"Beautiful and brilliant?" The man raised his eyebrow. "I thought girls who look like you spent their weekends at football games at Yale or Princeton."

"I'm a double French and comparative literature major at Amherst," Serena said, tapping on her laptop. "My studies are very important to me."

"Let me guess," the man said, and he moved closer. "You're

going to go to Harvard Law School and become an international corporate attorney. You'll be the first woman who breaks the glass ceiling and becomes the president of the firm, and your name will be on *Forbes'* Top 100 Most Powerful Women."

"Why would you think that?" Serena blushed.

He stood on the other side of the desk and his mouth formed a slow smile. "Because you have that something special that lights up a room."

"You don't even know me," Serena murmured.

"I'm Chase Barnett." The man grinned, holding out his hand.

"Serena Woods." Serena felt his long fingers brush against hers.

She looked at him more closely. He had brown eyes and long lashes that belonged on a girl. His shirt was buttoned wrong, as if he had been in a hurry and missed a button.

"Serena Woods, born June fifteenth, 1986, at San Francisco Presbyterian Hospital. I've followed your father's career from the beginning: graduated from UC Berkeley with a degree in political science, spent a year backpacking around India, married Kate Chisholm, became the father of a beautiful baby girl, ran successfully for mayor of Santa Rosa, then state senator, and California's youngest treasurer. Followed by a failed attempt at governor of California—the only race he ever lost—four years as the French consul general in Paris, and now the U.S. senator from California."

"You sound like a walking history book." Serena giggled. Chase stood with his hands in his pockets and his brow furrowed in concentration.

"He's my hero," Chase said simply. "He's passionate about foreign policy and on the forefront of energy conservation."

"He drives my mother crazy with his periodicals and newspapers," Serena said, and nodded. "But he wants to leave the world a better place."

"I've wanted to be in politics since I was eleven," Chase said, gazing at the photos of Charles shaking hands with President Obama and Hillary Clinton. "I want to help change the world."

Serena studied him carefully. She had met many of her father's admirers over the years: serious men with short, slicked-back hair wearing pin-striped suits. Chase looked more like an overgrown surfer, with sparkling eyes and a dimple on his cheek.

Serena stood up and walked around the desk. She wore a knit dress she had slipped on because it wouldn't wrinkle on the train, and her blond hair was tied in a high ponytail. She wore ballet flats, and the top of her head reached Chase's chin.

Serena put her fingers on his shirt. She carefully unbuttoned the top buttons, feeling the smooth fabric beneath her fingers, then rebuttoned them and fixed his collar.

"If you're going to be a politician"—she stepped back, admiring her handiwork—"first you're going to have to learn how to button your shirt."

Serena gazed around the attic at boxes separated into neat stacks. The attic took up the third floor of the house and contained furniture, books, clothes, paintings from the cities where her parents had lived. Her mother said there was no point in owning a mansion the size of a city block if it couldn't hold all your memories.

Serena searched until she found the boxes marked "PARIS" and carefully removed the tape. She found French cookbooks and theater programs. There was a yearbook from the International School with a picture of her in a navy uniform and her hair in blond braids. At the bottom of the second box she found a pile of magazines tied with a yellow ribbon.

Serena picked them up and sat cross-legged on the floor. She untied the ribbon and spread the covers in front of her: gorgeous French models with impossibly long legs wearing impossibly short skirts.

Serena flipped to the Letter from the Editor and saw Yvette Renault's picture. She had silky black hair, large brown eyes, and a long patrician nose. She wore her trademark strand of black pearls and an oversize emerald on her finger. Underneath the photo were the words *Vivez la vie au maximum* and Yvette's spider-like signature.

Serena sat back and thought about Chelsea's visit to her office that afternoon. Serena had been choosing photos for her interview with Jennifer Lawrence when Chelsea burst into the room.

"If I ate red meat at lunch I'd nap all afternoon," Chelsea said as she surveyed the remainder of Serena's roast beef sandwich on rye and a sliced dill pickle. "I have a green smoothie chased by a bowl of edamame. I'm afraid I'll glance in the mirror and look like Shrek."

"Hardly," Serena said, putting aside the photos. Chelsea had been a top runway model before she got a degree from Brown. She had long shapely legs and small, childlike breasts. She complained she'd never know the joy of owning a push-up bra, but every outfit she put on—Alexander McQueen dresses, Chloé miniskirts, Jil Sander cigarette pants—looked like a million dollars.

"How would you like to take a break from writing about the best way to wear a bustier and go to the South of France?" Chelsea perched on the edge of Serena's desk. She wore a turquoise Hervé Léger dress and Proenza Schouler wedges. Her brown hair was shaped in a pixie cut and her mouth was coated with dark red lipstick.

"Are you firing me?" Serena asked, flashing on her latest feature, on Cameron Diaz. Perhaps her questions had been too personal and Cameron's publicist called Chelsea in a rage.

"Yvette Renault, the legendary editor of French *Vogue,* is writing her memoir. She is looking for a cowriter and saw your pieces in *Vogue.*"

"She wants me to write her memoir?" Serena gaped. She remembered seeing Yvette's face plastered in *Vogue* when her father was the consul general in Paris. She wore impeccably cut wool suits and towering heels. Serena read she was almost six feet in her stocking feet.

"You're fluent in French and you've written some brilliant celebrity profiles," Chelsea said as she examined her long red fingernails. "Plus she said she'd give American *Vogue* exclusive excerpts. It's going to be juicy. Yvette launched the careers of France's top models and had a relationship with Bertrand Roland. No one knew if she was his personal secretary or his mistress."

"Didn't he win the Prix Goncourt?" Serena frowned.

"He was even more famous for how many women he got in his bed," Chelsea mused. "Yvette was married, to a very Catholic husband."

"It sounds fascinating," Serena replied. "Why the South of France?"

"She's staying at the Carlton-InterContinental in Cannes," Chelsea said. "I'd give anything to stroll down the Boulevard de la Croisette and watch the yachts in the harbor. But I've got a staff of English majors, and if I leave the office they forget how to turn on the coffeepot."

"How long would I be gone?" Serena suddenly flashed on Chase announcing his candidacy.

"Do you have a problem with being surrounded by dark-haired

men wearing white linen suits? I read Cannes has more handsome men per capita than any other city in Europe."

"You made that up," Serena replied, giggling. "I'm not interested in other men. Chase is going to announce his run for mayor soon and I need to be here."

Chelsea eyed Serena carefully. "I didn't take you as a 'behind the podium' kind of woman, I thought you wanted a career."

"Of course I want a career." Serena sat up straight, rearranging her beige Zac Posen skirt. She had worked so hard for this: three years in New York as an editorial assistant, two years in San Francisco as a features writer, and then finally the title of features editor and her own office with a narrow view of the Bay Bridge.

"Then say yes, and I'll reserve a room at the Carlton." Chelsea blew a speck of dust from the front of her dress. "Make sure you write me lots of postcards; I'll put them on my desk and drool over the elegant boutiques and outdoor cafés. I've only been there once, but the window shopping was better than sex."

"Can I let you know tomorrow?" Serena twisted her ponytail the way she did when she was nervous.

Chelsea hopped off the desk and walked to the door. She twisted the door handle and turned around. "Let me know by noon, or I'll have to write someone else's name on an Air France ticket to Paris."

Serena flipped through the magazine, trying to learn about Yvette. She always liked to know her subjects: Did Jennifer Garner advocate public or private schools for her children? What was Gwyneth Paltrow's biggest fashion disaster? When she interviewed Katie Holmes, Serena arrived with a box of Sprinkles salted caramel cupcakes, and by the end of the hour Katie had told her everything about Tom Cruise.

Serena closed the last magazine and twisted her ponytail. She knew Yvette loved the ballet, was an ardent admirer of Oscar de la Renta, and detested the use of fur. But she hadn't revealed anything about her personal life; there was no mention of Bertrand or a cuckolded husband.

Serena walked to the window, gazing at the wide stretch of bay and the sun setting behind the Oakland hills. She imagined sitting on a sun-soaked balcony with Yvette, hearing her stories about legendary French houses: Yves Saint Laurent, Givenchy, Chanel. Then she thought about Chase, straining like a horse at the starting gate to start his campaign, and Chelsea's veiled warning. She taped the boxes shut and hurried down the stairs.

chapter two

S erena pressed the buzzer and waited for Chase to walk upstairs. She wore a pink-and-yellow Kate Spade dress with a
wide leather belt. Her hair fell in a smooth wave and she wore
Brian Atwood flats on her feet.

She gazed at her reflection in the mirror and tamed a few loose
strands of hair. Chase insisted they eat at local restaurants—
PlumpJack, Boulevard, Emerald—at least twice a week. Chase
pumped the hands of the maître d' and the chef and Serena smiled
over glasses of Napa Valley chardonnay and plates of grilled
halibut.

"You look gorgeous," Chase said, and kissed her on the mouth.
"And you smell even better."

"You look pretty good yourself." Serena smiled, musing how
Chase's wardrobe had evolved. The tweed blazers and khakis had
been replaced by Brioni suits and hand-tailored dress shirts from
Wilkes Bashford. He wore his hair a little shorter and had a wardrobe of fine silk ties.

"I want voters to see me as someone who aims high," Chase
would say, glancing at the tie selection at Neiman Marcus.

"Someone who can receive a foreign delegation, woo start-ups, pave the streets of San Francisco with gold."

Sometimes when Chase slept over and they lay in bed, sweaty and elated from sex, she could almost taste his ambition. She would listen to his heartbeat and feel his arm thrown across her waist and wonder what he would do if he lost. Then she'd glance at his firm jaw and his smooth cheeks and knew that wasn't possible. Even asleep, he had winner written all over him.

Occasionally she'd thought about asking her mother what it was like to be married to someone who was consumed by his work. She had watched her mother stand at her father's side at fundraisers, attend endless ribbon cuttings and hospital openings, always dressed in flawless Chanel. But then she saw her father squeeze her mother's hand, watched him rub her shoulders at the end of a long day, and knew he loved her more than anything. They were a perfect couple, like ice skaters skating to their own melody.

Chase drove the silver Fiat down Polk Street and Serena debated how to tell him about Cannes. She decided to wait till after dinner, when they'd be sitting at a window-side table, full of wild mushroom risotto and coconut sorbet. She checked her lipstick in the rearview mirror and felt Chase take her hand. He held it in his lap like a talisman, looking over and smiling his confident, white smile.

"I thought we were going to Greens," Serena said, frowning when Chase passed the restaurant and continued on Lombard Street toward the Marina.

"Your father asked me to check on his boat." Chase pulled into the parking lot of the St. Francis Yacht Club. "He left some papers in the cabin."

Her father's boat was his pride and joy, a sleek white catamaran with SERENA written on it in bold red letters. He spent every free moment polishing her wood, grooming her sails, taking her on cruises under the Golden Gate Bridge to the Farallon Islands.

The main cabin had pine floors, soft leather sofas, and a fridge stocked with California wines and bottles of pale ale. There was a large globe and a mahogany table with a backgammon set and an ivory chessboard.

Serena stepped into the cabin and let her eyes adjust to the dark. She smelled the rich, sweet fragrance of roses. Roses were everywhere. They were scattered over the plank floor, strewn on the sofa, filling the sideboard in crystal vases. There were yellow roses in the fruit bowl and a great bunch of peach roses in an empty milk jug.

"What's going on?" Serena asked, and turned to Chase.

"From the moment I saw you in your father's study, I knew you were the woman I wanted by my side," Chase said, and kneeled on the wood floor. "You're incredibly beautiful, talented, and smarter than I'll ever be. Together we're going to do great things, make the world a better place. Serena Woods, will you marry me?"

Serena felt her knees buckle. Her eyes filled with tears and she saw Chase take a velvet box out of his pocket. He carefully pried it open and displayed a large square diamond resting between two emeralds on a white gold band.

"My grandmother's diamond," Serena whispered.

"Your father insisted I use it." Chase squeezed her hand. "I had it reset with emeralds to match your eyes."

Serena froze, her mind whirring. Their conversations revolved around Chase's run for mayor, his long hours at the law firm, Serena's job. She knew when they talked about his plans for the governorship or the White House that it would be as husband and wife. But that seemed far off, as if it would happen to a more mature, grown-up couple sometime in the future.

For a moment she flashed on Chase's decision to announce his candidacy and a queasy feeling formed in her stomach. She pictured standing beside Chase in front of city hall, the diamond ring glinting on her finger. Could he possibly want the journalists to mention that he was engaged to Senator Woods's daughter when they printed their stories? But then she pictured the giant bunches of sunflowers that arrived at her office, the texts he sent a dozen times a day. Chase showed her he loved her in a million different ways.

Serena looked at the lines that creased his brow, the dark lashes that covered his eyes, and knew she couldn't love anyone more. She flashed on her father proposing to her mother thirty years ago and all the places they had lived, the people they had entertained, the events they had been a part of. She saw her mother in her Chanel suits saying how she loved being a political wife.

"You told my father?" Serena asked.

"I had to ask for your hand in marriage," Chase said, squeezing her hand tighter. "I had to show him I was worthy."

"You're more than worthy." Serena felt round tears rolling down her cheeks. "You're the best man I've ever met."

"Is that a yes?" Chase tentatively stood up. He pushed the ring on her finger and placed his other hand around her back. He pulled her close and kissed her softly on the mouth. He traced the front of her dress, reaching under the thin fabric and brushing her breasts. His fingers stopped on her nipples, squeezing them gently so Serena thought her legs would collapse.

"Yes," Serena told him, nodding.

Chase picked her up and carried her to the smaller cabin, onto the round white bed. He slipped off his shoes, untied his tie, draped his jacket over the captain's chair. He slid his hands beneath Serena's dress and slipped off her panties. He pulled the dress over her head and stared at her full breasts, her flat stomach, the pink curve of her thighs.

Serena smelled the combination of sweat and aftershave as Chase burrowed his face in her neck. She nibbled his ear, running her fingers through his hair. She opened her legs and arched her body to meet his. He lowered himself on top of her, grabbing her hands and carrying her to the edge.

Serena felt his weight shift, his strength build; his body hurtle toward some invisible finish line. She gripped his shoulders and urged him forward with her hips. She held her breath, waiting for the final moment, the hot burst of light that left her sweaty and sated and hungry all over again.

Serena lay against him, listening to his breathing relax, and stared at the diamond ring on her finger. They were engaged and she still hadn't told him about Cannes.

"I thought we could have a combined engagement party and launch party for the campaign," Chase said, biting into a chocolate torte with pistachio ice cream. "Your father suggested we hold it at their house; we could tent the garden and build a dance floor."

Serena pushed her fork around a plate of blueberry upside-down cake. She hadn't been able to eat the first course of wilted spinach salad, and only finished two bites of the mesquite-grilled brochettes. Even the side of polenta and herb butter lay untouched.

All through the meal, as the waiter refilled their glasses of Chateau St. Jean, Serena kept trying to bring up her assignment in Cannes. She saw her career buried under political fund-raisers and wedding planning, and her stomach felt like it was coated in lead.

"Chelsea came into my office today," Serena said, putting her fork on the plate. "Yvette Renault is writing her memoir and is looking for a ghostwriter. She read some of my pieces and offered me the assignment."

"Who is Yvette Renault?" Chase asked, scraping up the last bite of torte. He kept picking up Serena's hand and rubbing the ring as if it were a magic lamp.

"Yvette was French *Vogue*'s editor for twenty years," Serena replied. "She was the doyenne of French fashion and rumored mistress of Bertrand Roland."

"Sounds like a great opportunity." Chase nodded.

"Yvette is staying at the InterContinental in Cannes; I'd be gone for a month."

"Cannes?" Chase sat back, wrinkling his forehead.

"She promised exclusive excerpts for American *Vogue*. I'd have a byline on the cover."

"Cannes," Chase repeated, folding and refolding his napkin. His face took on the expression he used when he was poring over casework or considering tactics for the campaign. He ran his fingers over the rim of his wineglass, gazing out the window at the darkened bay.

"Did you know that women control sixty percent of the vote in a local election?" Chase said finally. "Their own vote and the votes of their fiancés and husbands. If a guy votes for someone his wife doesn't approve of, their lovemaking drops to once a week."

"They have studies on that?" Serena raised her eyebrow.

"They have studies on everything," Chase said, nodding. "Voters are twice as likely to vote for candidates who eat oatmeal for breakfast than cold cereal. Oatmeal reminds them of the breakfasts their mothers made, and makes them feel safe and protected."

"I'll get rid of my boxes of Honey Nut Cheerios." Serena laughed, taking a large gulp of wine.

"I think going to Cannes is a wonderful idea." Chase sat forward. "What could be better than having my fiancée's name on the cover of every woman's bible?"

"You do?" Serena asked, her stomach churning with some new, strange uncertainty.

"We'll have the engagement party when you return," Chase said, and poured the last drops of wine. "It'll give me time to wrap up things at work and focus on the campaign."

"I'm glad you agree." Serena gazed at the square diamond flanked by two emeralds. Suddenly she wanted to ask Chase why he chose now to propose, but the words stuck in her throat. Then she glanced at Chase's chiseled cheekbones and decided she was being childish. Of course he thought in terms of his career, that was one of the things she loved about him.

"I knew we'd be a great team," he said, and squeezed her hand, the diamond chafing between her fingers. "Let's run up to your parents' house, I promised I'd stop by so we could celebrate."

"Cannes," Serena's mother repeated when they were all seated in the grand salon.

Serena sat on the brocade sofa, feeling Chase's fingers press into her back, and a warmth spread through her chest. She glanced around the vast space with its dark wood floors and antique furniture and felt like the luckiest girl in the world. She had all the people she loved in one room, gathered to toast her happiness.

"Of all the places," her mother murmured, sipping her champagne slowly. "We haven't been there in years."

"Do you think this is the best time to go?" her father asked, sitting in a high-backed leather armchair. "There's so much to do."

"Your father's right." Kate wore a Chanel shirtdress and red Gucci pumps. Her strawberry-blond hair was curled in a smooth pageboy and she wore a string of freshwater pearls around her neck. "Planning an engagement party is as complicated as planning the wedding. We need to arrange the caterer and the band and order a cake. We could have a nautical theme. We'll serve oysters and fresh scallops and have goldfish as centerpieces."

"Timing is everything in politics," her father agreed. "In a month it'll be summer, people will leave for their cabins in Tahoe or their houses in Napa."

Serena pictured Yvette Renault's silky black hair, her large brown eyes, and imagined the stories she had to tell. She flashed on the wide boulevards of Cannes and Chelsea threatening to write someone else's name on the plane ticket. She glanced at Chase, silently willing him to support her.

"Serena's career is very important to her." Chase grabbed her hand, curling his fingers around hers. "Isn't the first rule of a happy marriage giving your wife everything she wants?"

Serena let Chase refill her champagne glass, and the tightness in her shoulders relaxed. She heard her father and Chase discussing new energy policies and watched her mother fill silver dishes of macadamia nuts and felt the last traces of doubt disappear. She had picked the perfect partner and their lives were going to be full of exciting people and places. She saw the diamond ring reflected in her champagne flute and sipped the sweet, effervescent bubbles.

chapter three

Serena stepped out of the taxi onto the Boulevard de la Croisette. She had been to New York Fashion Week and the runway shows of Paris and Milan, but she had never seen so many exquisitely dressed people in one place. Slender dark-haired women with sleek chignons wore white Courrèges slacks and crocheted tops. Their waists were cinched by bright colored belts and they wore gold sandals on their feet. Men wore silk shorts and leather loafers and their dark hair was slicked with oil. Everyone talked in rapid French, puffing cigarettes, sipping espresso, pulling apart buttery, flaky croissants.

It was the last week of the Cannes Film Festival and the main boulevard was like a human parking lot. No one seemed in any hurry to get anywhere; they loitered in front of Christian Dior and Yves Saint Laurent waiting for a glimpse of Angelina Jolie or James Franco. Serena saw a dark-haired man with a gold earring descend from a motorboat and was sure it was Johnny Depp.

Serena paid the taxi driver and gathered her bags, turning to look at the bay. The Mediterranean was a shimmering turquoise lake dotted with luxury yachts and peeling fishing boats. In the distance she could see the Île Sainte-Marguerite and the curve of highway leading to Nice and Antibes.

The last week Serena's stomach had been tied in knots. She kept staring at her diamond ring, wondering if she should take the assignment. Her mother kept calling the office asking whether she wanted lilies or peonies, Sonoma or Napa wines, red velvet cake or vanilla custard, at the engagement party.

"I can't believe you're leaving all the decisions to me," Kate said when Serena said she had two stories to file and no time to think. "This is one of the loveliest times in your life; you're engaged! You should be relishing every minute."

Serena would hang up and click on Vera Wang or Valentino on her computer, studying the satin dresses with wide tulle skirts, the long Greek tunics with intricate beading, and think her mother was right. She wanted to choose the most elegant shoes, the sweetest-smelling bouquets, the prettiest bridesmaid dresses. But then she would glance at the piles of tear sheets and photos on her desk and know she made the right decision. She and Chase wanted a year's engagement; there would be months to plan the wedding.

"I don't understand my parents," Serena had said, frowning, when Chase arrived to take her to the airport. It was Saturday and he wore navy slacks and a striped polo shirt. His blond hair was damp and his cheeks glistened with aftershave. "All through college they asked me how I was going to use my English degree. When I was promoted to features editor they took me to Fleur de Lys and my mother gave me her signed copy of Rona Jaffe's *The Best of Everything*."

"Your parents are of a different era," Chase replied, perched on her bed. "Maria Shriver worked for NBC News until Schwarzenegger became governor, and Michelle Obama was an executive director for the University of Chicago Hospitals. I love seeing you excited about your work, it's incredibly sexy."

Serena stopped folding sundresses into her suitcase and kissed Chase on the lips. "I love you, I'd vote for you any day."

Chase pulled her toward him, unbuttoning her Free People blouse, and unsnapped her bra. He lifted up her cotton skirt and stroked her panties with his fingers.

"I'll miss my plane," Serene murmured, feeling his fingers move in deep, confident strokes. She clung to his back, willing him to dig deeper, push farther, make her wet and slick and fluid.

"I want to make sure you miss me," he whispered, wrapping one arm tightly around her waist. She felt her body arching, reaching, pulsing, and then the long sweet release. She rested her head on his shoulder, her heart beating rapidly in her chest.

"There's nothing more important than you and me," he said quietly. "The rest is gravy."

Serena walked along the boulevard, gazing at the long line of palm trees. She had changed into an orange linen jumpsuit and ivory Gucci wedges. She brushed her hair into a high ponytail and tied it with an orange silk ribbon. She sprayed her wrists and neck with Dior, feeling like Grace Kelly in *To Catch a Thief*.

The Carlton-InterContinental had a creamy stone facade and black turreted roof. Serena saw flags flying above the entrance and the yellow-and-white awnings of the Carlton Restaurant, where guests sipped milky cappuccinos and read copies of *Le Monde*.

Serena walked through the gold revolving glass doors into the lobby. She glanced at the thick marble pillars, the gold inlaid floors, and felt like she was inside a jewelry box. Royal-blue sofas were scattered over Oriental rugs and crystal chandeliers twinkled from the lacquered ceiling.

"I have a reservation," Serena said as she approached the reception desk, inhaling the scent of camellias and wood polish. "Serena Woods."

The concierge tapped letters into a sleek keyboard. "I'm sorry, we don't have anyone with that name."

Serena wrinkled her brow, trying again in French. *"Je m'appelle Serena Woods. J'ai un réservation."*

The man smiled stiffly, as if Serena were a stubborn child. "I understand English, mademoiselle, but I do not see your name."

"Try Chelsea Brown." Serena leaned against the cool marble, jet lag and fatigue making her dizzy.

"I have nothing under that name," the concierge said, and shook his head. "Perhaps you are at the wrong hotel; have you tried the Hilton?"

"I'm here to interview Yvette Renault," Serena replied, suddenly desperate. "She is also staying here."

"Madame Renault has been our guest for a week," the man said, nodding. "She is in a suite on the *septième* floor."

"Please." Serena fished some euros from her purse. "I've been on planes for fifteen hours. I have the most important interview of my career tomorrow; I need somewhere to sleep."

"Let me check something," the man said reluctantly, punching numbers into his keyboard. "Serena Woods of San Francisco, California."

"Yes!" Serena exhaled, picturing a queen-size bed with a soft down comforter, a bottle of sparkling water cooling in an ice bucket, an oval bathtub filled with bath salts.

"Your reservation is for May thirty-first. Today is May twenty-fifth," he explained.

"It can't be," Serena exclaimed, her voice echoing throughout the lobby. "It has to be for today."

"It is the Cannes Film Festival, the hotel is completely booked, every room in Cannes is occupied. I cannot help you."

Serena pulled herself up to her full height and squared her shoulders. "I'm a features editor at *Vogue,* and my boss has a bad temper, she's going to be furious if you turn me into the street. You have to give me a room."

The man sighed as if he were tired of dealing with a difficult schoolgirl. He glanced at his notes. "Tell Ms. Brown that she has my sincere apologies, but there is nothing I can do."

Serena walked through the lobby and thought her legs would collapse. Her throat was dry and her head pounded. She stumbled to the bar and sank onto a leather stool, holding the marble counter to stop the room from spinning.

"Can I help you?" the bartender asked.

"Just a glass of water," Serena replied, touching her hand to her forehead.

"You look like you could use something stronger," said a young woman with thick bangs and bouncy brown hair perched on the stool next to her. She ordered two gin and tonics and scooped up a handful of pistachios.

"I'm sorry," Serena said, and shook her head. "Have we met?"

"I saw you arguing with reception," the girl replied. "It's true what people say about the French, they're cold as icicles and just as sharp. I expect they have blue blood running through their veins."

"My reservation is for next week," Serena sighed. "I tried everything, but the man wouldn't budge; I'm going to have to sleep in a fishing boat."

"Hardly." The girl raised her eyebrow. She had hazel eyes and creamy white skin. She wore a cotton sundress and had a silver necklace around her neck. "The fishermen would charge a hundred euros to step foot in a boat. It's the Cannes Film Festival; even the pigeons know how to gouge the tourists."

"I'm here to write a story for *Vogue,*" Serena replied. "If I don't have a room I'm going to lose the most important assignment of my career."

"I came to get that je ne sais quoi, but so far I've gotten a haircut that makes me look like a third-grader and spent a hundred and fifty euros on a dress you could buy at Woolworth's."

"What do you mean?" Serena asked.

"You know, that air that French women have, like some impossibly expensive perfume. I grew up watching old movies with Catherine Deneuve and Brigitte Bardot. I've always wanted to be one of those women with dark hooded eyes who look sexy blowing smoke rings."

"No one thinks smoking is sexy anymore," Serena argued.

"Have you been to the nightclubs?" the girl asked, laughing. "You could get cancer standing at the door. I just want to learn how to hold a cigarette and wear my hair and talk with a French accent."

"Why?" Serena asked, suddenly intrigued. The girl looked vaguely familiar, as if she'd seen her face in a magazine. But she didn't have a model's figure and Serena couldn't remember seeing her on a movie screen.

"It's a long story, perhaps another time," the girl said slowly. "On you that jumpsuit belongs on the catwalk; on me it would look like I just finished finger painting. Some people have 'it,' others don't. I may as well give up and go home."

"If you're giving up your room, I'll take it." Serena finished her drink, feeling a little light-headed. "My editor in chief will kill me if I miss this story."

"How exciting that you work at *Vogue;* you must know everything about fashion," the girl mused. "I bet you know exactly what to wear without going through your closet and deciding your whole wardrobe is hopeless and should be donated to the HOPE Foundation."

"I mainly write celebrity interviews and features," Serena sighed, flashing on Yvette. "I'm here to interview Yvette Renault; she's staying in a suite on the seventh floor."

"I'm staying in the Cary Grant Suite on the seventh floor!" the girl exclaimed. "Six rooms of pink marble floors and ivory silk sofas and a view of the whole coast." She gazed at Serena and suddenly her eyes sparkled. "You can stay with me, I've got an extra bedroom."

"I couldn't do that." Serena shook her head.

"You can share all your wisdom," the girl continued enthusiastically. "You can teach me to be one of those women salesgirls fight over instead of someone they snicker about when I'm in the dressing room."

"Why would you want to share your suite with a complete stranger?" Serena asked curiously. She searched the girl's face to see if she was hiding something. Maybe she ran a drug ring or was the madam for a house of high-class call girls.

"I grew up in British boarding schools and I never learned to wear anything except a field hockey skirt," the girl replied. "I can pick your brain and learn how to coordinate an outfit. You can teach me how to accessorize and which styles flatter my shape."

"Your shape is lovely," Serena said, and smiled, glancing at her rounded arms and small waist.

"I have a fondness for fish and chips and Cadbury chocolate." The girl ate another handful of pistachios. "You can teach me to like spinach salads with tofu."

"I hate tofu," Serena said, grinning.

Suddenly the jet lag washed over her like a wave and she longed to rest her head on a feathery pillow. "Okay, I accept. I'm Serena Woods."

"Zoe," the girl replied, glancing at the marble bar. "Zoe Pistachio."

"Pistachio?" Serena raised her eyebrow.

"It's an old family name," the girl said, and she strode toward the concierge. "Let's get you a key."

Serena opened her eyes and gazed at the scalloped light fixture above the bed. She turned her head and saw beige silk drapes pulled back to reveal white sailboats on a pale blue ocean.

Serena sat against the ivory satin headboard, trying to remember where she was. She recalled taking the private elevator to the seventh floor and entering double white doors. She remembered Zoe ushering her into the second bedroom, showing her towels, robes, and an array of lotions. She vaguely remembered hanging up her jumpsuit, turning back the covers, and climbing under Egyptian cotton sheets.

Now Serena glanced at the canopied bed, at the gold velvet love seat, at the crystal vase of birds of paradise, and thought she was crazy. How could she have accepted the invitation to stay in a suite with a complete stranger?

Serena pulled on a white velour Carlton robe and padded into the living room. She was going to tell Zoe she appreciated her kindness but she couldn't accept her offer any longer. She'd go down to reception and demand the manager call Chelsea's assistant and sort out her room.

The living room had pink marble floors and ivory sofas and a round glass table resting on a stone pedestal. French doors opened onto a marble balcony with chaise lounges and wicker chairs. Serena smelled freshly cut pineapple and dark roasted coffee and saw a sideboard heaped with platters of watermelon, grapes, mini-croissants, and pots of raspberry jam.

Serena suddenly realized she was starving. She piled a plate with English muffins, strips of bacon, and fluffy scrambled eggs. Then she poured a demitasse of rich black coffee and sat in a Louis XVI chair.

"Jet lag is a killer," Zoe said as she entered the living room. She wore a navy one-piece bathing suit and a large straw hat. Her cheeks were smeared with suntan lotion and a pair of sunglasses were propped on her forehead. "The first few days I was here I wanted porridge and toast and marmalade for dinner."

"I didn't mean to eat your food," Serena said, wiping her mouth with a napkin. "It smelled so good and I was starving."

"They refill the sideboard every four hours." Zoe shrugged. "Herb omelets, soufflés, mini-éclairs, and cheesecakes. I keep telling them I'm on a diet and they keep bringing crustless sandwiches and creamy desserts."

"You don't need to be on a diet." Serena shook her head.

"According to fashion magazines ninety percent of women are on a diet their whole lives." Zoe spread a piece of toast with strawberry jam. "I'd stay and eat but I'm late for a waterskiing lesson."

"What time is it?" Serena gazed outside, suddenly noticing that the beach was full of sunbathers lying on white lounges.

"Two P.M.," Zoe replied. "I have a waterskiing lesson followed by a bicycle tour of Cannes and a trip to the outdoor markets. Maybe we can go to a nightclub tonight, and you can teach me to say sexy things in French?"

"Two o'clock!" Serena jumped up. "My appointment with Yvette is at three and my hair looks like it's been attacked by hornets."

"If you need to borrow any clothes or makeup it's all in my closet," Zoe said, grabbing her room key and walking to the door.

"I really can't stay here," Serena replied. "We don't know each other and this suite must cost a fortune."

"You have to stay, you're going to turn me into Katie Holmes. Think of all the delicious fruit and pastries going to waste if you don't." Zoe surveyed the sideboard. "We'll trade our personal information tonight, by morning we'll be BFFs."

Serena unzipped her suitcase and sifted through silk dresses, cotton sweaters, and linen capris for the perfect outfit. She was meeting one of the most important women in fashion and needed to make a good impression.

She selected a yellow-and-white linen dress and white cork slingbacks. She brushed her hair into a knot and secured it with a gold clip. Then she searched the suite for an iron to get the wrinkles out of her cropped Stella McCartney jacket.

Serena walked into the master bedroom, gaping at the king-size four-poster bed and royal-blue love seats. There was a round window like on a ship and a framed Seurat above a ceramic fireplace. She giggled, wondering what Chase would say if he saw her in the Cary Grant Suite of the Carlton-InterContinental. Even with his designer suits and custom shirts, Chase's budget didn't include premier suites at five-star hotels.

Serena entered the vast walk-in closet, searching the shelves for an iron. She glanced up at a row of neatly hung shirts with Peter Pan collars and plaid knee-length skirts. She found an iron and turned to leave and noticed that every shirt had embroidered stitching on the collar. She looked closer, feeling almost guilty for spying, and saw flowery cursive that said "CG."

Serena hurried back to her bedroom, plugging in the iron and waiting for it to get hot. She thought about Zoe's odd last name, her mysterious reasons for being in Cannes, and wondered why all her blouses were embroidered with someone else's initials.

Serena smoothed her hair and rang the doorbell of the Sophia Loren Suite. She clutched a yellow notepad in one hand and a package wrapped in silver paper in the other.

"You must be Serena," a woman said as she answered the door. "Please come in, I just finished my afternoon yoga. I'll open the curtains and let in some light."

Serena nervously followed Yvette into the suite, waiting for her eyes to adjust to the dark. While everything in Zoe's suite was gold and ivory, Yvette's suite was done in pastels, with a window seat piled with green and pink and turquoise cushions. There was a floral sofa and a bamboo table with upholstered silk chairs.

"It's gorgeous, isn't it." Yvette pulled back turquoise curtains to reveal the view. The bay was full of boats and the sand was teeming with sunbathers. Serena saw uniformed waiters passing out frothy drinks and platters of fruit. "I stay in the same suite every time; I'm so close to the beach, I can smell the ocean."

Yvette was almost six feet and had the slender neck of a dancer. She had silvery hair and wore a black leotard with a red sweater tied around her waist. Even without makeup she was beautiful, with large brown eyes and a wide, sexy mouth. A strand of black pearls encircled her neck and she wore red ballet slippers on her feet.

"I hope I'm not interrupting," Serena replied, suddenly feeling overdressed in her linen dress and crepe jacket. She handed Yvette the package. "I brought you something."

Yvette opened the wrapping and turned over the paperback book. "*Princess Daisy* by Judith Krantz!" Yvette's eyes sparkled. "How did you know I was a fan?"

"I thought you might not have an American copy," Serena said, blushing. "I read an article that said you loved her books."

"I used to devour them like chocolate." Yvette put it on the coffee table and sat in a turquoise armchair, tucking her feet under her. "Tell me about yourself. If we're going to spend so much time together, we must get acquainted."

"I studied English and languages at Amherst." Serena sat opposite her, nervously twisting her silver pen. "I'm fluent in French and Italian."

"Chelsea mentioned that you lived in Paris," Yvette replied.

"My father was the consul general," Serena said, and nodded. "Charles Woods."

"Of course!" Yvette exclaimed. "Your parents held the most intimate salons full of Paris's most interesting people. Your mother looked like a movie star; I convinced her to be in *Vogue* once, talking about being an American in Paris."

"She still has the clipping," Serena replied, wishing they could turn the conversation onto Yvette.

"What a small world." Yvette smiled like a cat. "I think we'll get along very well. Shall I pour us both a cup of vanilla tea and I'll tell you a story?"

"That would be great!" Serena's shoulders relaxed, feeling like she had passed a test. She scribbled some words on her notepad and looked up at Yvette. "Did you always want to work in fashion?"

Yvette poured two cups of tea and added rounded spoonfuls of honey. She furrowed her brow and the lines around her mouth became pronounced. "Goodness, I don't want to talk about fashion, I want to tell you about Bertrand."

"I met Bertrand at this very hotel," Yvette began. "I was younger than you, it was my first assignment. Bertrand was France's literary lion."

"He had already won the Prix Goncourt," Serena said, consulting her notes. "It must have been so intimidating to be in his presence. What was he like?"

"He was thirty and gorgeous," Yvette sighed. "Sharp dark eyes, a firm chin, like a young Marlon Brando. He was promoting his first novel, *The Gigolo*. It was about a male gigolo who saved his wealthy client from an abusive husband. The critics hailed him as a rapturous new voice, but it was the women who really loved him. Every female reader in France imagined him saving her from a life of boredom." Yvette paused, her eyes misting over as if she were drifting back in time. . . .

———

"You look very young to be a senior editor at *Vogue*," Bertrand said. He wore a white singlet and khakis and a silver chain around his neck. He smoked one cigarette after another, grinding them into a glass ashtray.

"I'm Irene's secretary," Yvette admitted. "She got food poisoning at lunch."

"Have you ever interviewed an author before?" Bertrand asked, smiling mischievously. "We can be very demanding. For instance, we can't start until you join me in a glass of chardonnay."

"I don't drink wine in the afternoon," Yvette replied. She was so nervous, she kept twisting her pen.

"Of course you do, you're a journalist." Bertrand poured two glasses of white wine. "Now tell me, what are your goals? Do you plan on running *Vogue,* or are you going to write the great French novel?"

"I'm engaged," Yvette murmured. "My fiancé's family owns a bank in Paris."

"So you are going to make babies and get fat." Bertrand looked at her closely. "That will be a waste of a great beauty."

"I want to be a mother," Yvette replied indignantly. "I love children."

Bertrand paced around the room, his hands in his pockets. "You are right, having children is the only way to gain immortality. We writers try, but it is only our words that will live on. We will become dust in a graveyard. How old are you, twenty-one? Twenty-two? You are too young to devote your life to children. And I bet this fiancé doesn't appreciate you; does he know how to make you come?"

Yvette blushed so deeply she almost fainted in her chair. Bertrand walked over and cupped her chin with his hand.

"I have embarrassed you," he said. "We will talk about something else: art, music, literature."

"I'm here to interview you," Yvette replied, breaking away from his touch.

"Ah, the newspapers and magazines, they make up what they want to hear," Bertrand said, and shrugged. "That I have a mistress in every town, that I was beaten as a child. They don't want to know the real Bertrand Roland; I'd much rather learn about you."

Yvette heard a knock at the door. Bertrand's publicist poked her head in and tapped her finger on her watch.

"I have to interview you," Yvette said, frowning. "Or I'll be fired."

Bertrand waited till his publicist left, then walked over to the table. He picked up a Polaroid camera and handed it to Yvette. "We'll give them what they want."

He stubbed out his cigarette and stripped off his singlet. He unzipped his slacks and folded them on a chair. He looked at Yvette, grinning like a schoolboy. Then he took off his underwear and his socks.

"Take a picture, you'll sell more copies than in the history of *Vogue*."

"I can't do that," Yvette stammered, closing her eyes.

"This morning you were a secretary, now you are a journalist," he replied. "Take the photo."

Serena stood on the balcony, gazing at the glittering coastline. It was late afternoon and beach attendants closed up umbrellas and stacked deck chairs. Women in metallic bikinis slipped on silk caftans and gold sandals and collected their paperback books and suntan lotion. Serena watched couples strolling along the Boulevard de la Croisette already dressed for the evening. They ran down the dock and climbed onto sleek yachts and wide catamarans.

Serena walked back inside, breathing in the scent of dahlias and camellias. The omelets and fresh fruit on the sideboard had been replaced by platters of salmon, bowls of gazpacho, wedges of Brie, and plates of fruit tarts and custards.

Zoe hadn't returned from her afternoon excursion and Serena had the suite to herself. She filled a plate with crusty garlic rolls and plump green olives and settled on a gold velvet armchair. She flipped through her notepad, scribbling notes in the margins.

"I spent the whole afternoon yesterday figuring out who I should fire for messing up your hotel reservation," Chelsea said when Serena answered her cell phone. "I called every hotel from Cannes to Nice, but no one has a room. I even pretended to be Valentino's personal assistant, and the Hôtel du Cap-Eden-Roc informed me that Mr. Valentino knows everything is booked up, and surely one of his admirers has space on their yacht."

"I met a woman in the lobby yesterday," Serena replied. "She let me stay in the guest bedroom in her suite."

"That's wonderful news!" Chelsea exclaimed. "Did you meet Yvette?"

"She's the most elegant woman I've ever seen." Serena nodded. "Like Katharine Hepburn and Lauren Bacall with a touch of Audrey Hepburn. She wore a leotard and tights but she looked dressed for the opera."

"She could as easily have graced the cover of *Vogue* as been the editor in chief." Chelsea sighed like a starstruck schoolgirl. "Tell me about the interview, I want to hear every word."

Serena clutched the notepad to her chest, feeling suddenly

protective. She remembered Yvette's description of Bertrand and the way her eyes clouded over when she talked about him. "We really just got to know each other," Serena said evasively. "We're meeting again tomorrow."

"The whole industry is abuzz; *Harper's Bazaar* and *W* are green with envy. I hope it's juicy," Chelsea replied. "There's nothing like a scandal to sell magazines."

"I can't stay in this suite," Serena said, frowning. "I hardly know Zoe, and it must cost a fortune."

"You have to stay there," Chelsea insisted. "It's the only available lodging in the Côte d'Azur. Take your roommate out for a gourmet dinner and put it on the expense account. You're saving the magazine a fortune and you're going to get the story of the year."

Serena put her notepad on the glass coffee table and walked over to the sideboard. She poured a cup of almond tea, thinking about Yvette. She couldn't wait to sit down with her again and learn more about Bertrand. She pictured Yvette as a young journalist, her silver hair dark and glossy, her papery skin smooth and shiny. She wondered if they did have an affair, if Yvette stripped off her clothes and they made love in his hotel suite.

"You look a million miles away," said Zoe as she entered the room. She wore a yellow tube top and pink miniskirt. She had a red gash on her knee and a purple bruise forming on her thigh.

"Why are you staring?" Zoe asked. "I knew I shouldn't have bought this outfit. I don't have the legs for miniskirts, and yellow makes my skin look washed-out."

"The clothes are fine," Serena replied. "How did you get the cut and bruises?"

"I've had the worst afternoon." Zoe threw her bag on the Aubusson rug and sank into the love seat. "I forgot to put suntan lotion on my neck and got a terrible burn. I almost ran into a group of Japanese tourists on my bicycle and crashed into a wall. Then I let the salesgirl talk me into an outfit that belongs on a prostitute when I really wanted the Lilly Pulitzer belted shirtdress."

"It's a lovely outfit for daytime," Serena said, twisting her ponytail. "Perfect for the beach."

"I don't want to buy clothes for the beach!" Zoe's voice rose and her eyes filled with tears. "I want to dress to eat in elegant restaurants and go to the theater. I want to walk down the street and hear people whisper, 'She has style.'"

"Why don't you shower," Serena replied, afraid that Zoe would dissolve into tears. "I'll lend you a dress and we'll go to the Carlton Restaurant and order chilled prawns and French champagne. My boss insisted I buy you a five-course dinner. Tomorrow we'll go shopping and buy you a wardrobe to rival Victoria Beckham."

"That sounds lovely." Zoe wiped her eyes. She stood up, adjusting her tube top and tugging at her miniskirt. "But I can't eat five courses or I'll never fit into anything in the boutiques. In France clothes only come in one size: zero."

Serena followed the maître d' to a round table next to the floor-to-ceiling windows. The floors were polished marble and the walls were covered in ivory satin. Serena watched waiters in white tuxedos cross the room carrying platters of oysters and baskets of olive bread.

Serena wore a green silk dress and gold sandals. Her hair was piled into a knot and secured with a gold chopstick. She gazed outside at the yellow-and-white awnings and the twinkling lights and felt almost giddy. She was in Cannes, writing a story about one of the most iconic figures in fashion.

"You haven't mentioned that rock on your finger," Zoe said when the waiter had left them with two embossed leather menus.

"I got engaged last week," Serena said, and blushed, gazing at the square diamond glittering under the crystal chandelier. She slid her phone out of her purse and flipped to a photo of Chase wearing a crisp yellow shirt and smiling into the camera.

"I wouldn't dash off to Cannes if I was engaged to him," Zoe said, and whistled.

"Chase is very supportive of my career." Serena slipped the phone back in her purse. She flashed on Chase picking her up to go to the airport, the delicious afternoon sex in her apartment, and a warmth spread through her chest.

"I'd like a stream of sexy boyfriends," Zoe said, her eyes suddenly clouding over. "Marriage seems so complicated."

Serena ordered a Rothschild Cabernet and a half dozen oysters. They talked about Serena's job at *Vogue* and the incredible beauty of the Riviera.

"I could stay here forever." Zoe sighed, tearing apart a baguette. She wore a navy Stella McCartney dress that accentuated her full breasts and small waist. Her bangs covered her eyebrows and her lashes were coated with thick mascara. "The ocean is as warm as a bath and every night the maids leave Belgian chocolates on my pillow."

"Can I ask a personal question?" Serena asked, then hesitated. "How does a twenty-five-year-old girl afford a suite at the Carlton-InterContinental? It must cost more than some precious jewels."

"Should we start with the tomato gazpacho with buffalo mozzarella or the semicooked duck foie gras? They make it with the most delicious cherry juice and a dash of cream." Zoe studied the menu as if it were a math exam.

"I didn't mean to snoop, but the shirts in your closet have someone else's initials," Serena persisted.

Zoe bit her lip as if she couldn't decide what to order. Finally she placed the menu on the linen tablecloth and sighed. "My name is Claudia Zoe Gladding, I'm Malcolm Gladding's daughter."

Serena frowned, trying to remember why that name sounded familiar. She pictured the latest issue of *Time* magazine and the silver-haired man on the cover. He wore a midnight-blue silk blazer with a yellow handkerchief in his pocket. He stood on the steps of the Sydney Opera House, surrounded by long-legged models.

"The head of Gladding House and the eighth-richest man in Australia?" Serena gaped. "I thought you were British."

"I was sent to boarding school in England when I was twelve," Zoe corrected. "My father owns the largest fashion empire in Australia."

Serena frowned. "Why the fake name?"

"My father is retiring and he wants me take over Gladding House." Zoe pierced an oyster with her fork. "My mother is on every best-dressed list in Australia and my father dresses like he's going to dinner with the prime minister. I'm good at business but I can't put an outfit together. How am I going to be the face of Gladding House if I look like a waitress in a fast-food restaurant?"

"I still don't understand," Serena replied. "What's wrong with being Claudia Gladding?"

"The first night at the bar I watched women wearing Courrèges slacks and heart-shaped Chopard watches. I wanted to be that woman—the one who glides effortlessly through a room turning heads and leaving a trail of expensive perfume. I thought the best way was to start from scratch, so I became Zoe Pistachio."

"That's no reason to lie," Serena said, shaking her head.

"My mother and father are always in *The Sydney Morning Herald,* smiling into the camera like movie stars. I wanted the chance to make myself over without it being on page three of the *Daily Mirror.* Haven't you ever wanted to make your parents proud of you?"

"You're a grown woman," Serena said, and shrugged. "I'm sure your parents don't care if you wear the wrong color blouse."

"My father runs a clothing empire, fashion is his religion." Zoe fiddled with her wineglass. "I'm like the child who failed catechism class."

"What does your father say about you being in Cannes?" Serena asked.

"He doesn't know I'm here," Zoe replied. "That's why I need your help; you have to turn the ugly duckling into a swan."

Serena sat in bed, scribbling interview notes on her notepad. Dinner had been delicious. Serena selected the Mediterranean sea bass fillets and Zoe had the organic lamb cutlets and they shared a classic chocolate fondue for dessert. After dinner they sipped amaretto and cream at the Carlton Bar, listening to the pianist and watching movie stars enter the revolving glass doors.

Serena put the notepad on the bedside table and turned off the light. She longed to talk to Chase, but he was probably in a meeting. She thought about her plans for tomorrow: an early-morning run on the beach, shopping with Zoe, and the afternoon spent with Yvette in the Sophia Loren Suite.

The hotel phone rang and she debated answering it. Zoe had

gone to the gift shop to stock up on copies of *Hello!* and *Paris Match*. It rang again and Serena picked up the receiver. Perhaps it was Yvette, rescheduling their meeting, or Chase, anxious to hear her voice.

A male voice came on the line. "Mademoiselle Pistachio, this is Daniel at the concierge."

"Zoe isn't in at the moment," Serena replied.

"Could you please inform Mademoiselle Pistachio her missing suitcase has been located. It was put on the original flight she booked to Milan. It has been rerouted to Nice airport and will arrive at the Carlton-InterContinental in the morning. The airline apologizes for the confusion."

Serena hung up and leaned back against the pillows. Zoe never mentioned she had bought a ticket to Milan. Serena flashed on Milan's runway shows and cutting-edge designs. If Zoe was really interested in fashion she would have kept her reservation instead of coming to Cannes. Cannes was spectacular, but Milan was the center of the fashion world. There had to be another reason why Zoe was in Cannes. Serena slid under the covers, certain Zoe was still hiding something.

chapter four

Serena walked along the promenade, past the shuttered boutiques and cafés. She had run the whole length of the Boulevard de la Croisette, inhaling the sultry morning air. The beach was empty except for a few seagulls and fishermen pushing their boats out to sea. Serena watched the sun inch up the sky and the sea turn from pale gray to a royal blue.

She and Chase used to run together every morning. They loved jogging along the Embarcadero, watching the ferries crisscross the bay. Serena missed his wide smile, the way he wrapped his arm around her waist and kissed her on the mouth before they parted.

Serena's phone rang and she slipped it out of her pocket.

"I'm standing in the most beautiful spot on the Côte d'Azur, thinking about you," Serena said when Chase's name scrolled across the screen.

"I miss you so much; I saw the most stunning roses at Podesta Baldocchi and I have no one to give them to." Chase's voice was tight. "I tried calling you last night; I couldn't sleep. I woke up at five A.M. and jogged to the top of Potrero Hill."

"Is something wrong?" Serena asked.

"I'm not sure," Chase said slowly. "It's about your father."

"My father," Serena said, clutching the railing. Charles had had a minor heart attack during his last term as senator. Since he retired he exercised every day and ate lean meats and fresh fruits and vegetables.

"My friend Cory called me," Chase continued. "He works at the *Chronicle*. He received an anonymous letter saying that your father had a secret second family. He promised he called me first; he hasn't shown it to anyone."

Serena tried to focus, but the Mediterranean became a blur and the yachts sparkled like shining daggers. She sucked in air, feeling it fill her lungs like a hot air balloon.

"Women used to write my father letters all the time when he was in Congress," Serena said, trying to keep her voice steady. "They wanted money or their fifteen minutes of fame."

"The letter was postmarked from France. Apparently the sender accused your father of keeping a mistress and two children while he was consul general in Paris," Chase continued. "If he doesn't acknowledge them, she'll write to every newspaper in the country."

"That's ridiculous!" Serena exclaimed. "We lived in Paris fifteen years ago. Have you seen the letter?"

"I'm going to Cory's office." Chase's voice was flat. "I'll read it myself."

"It's probably written on some old typewriter with all the *P*s missing," Serena said lightly. "With instructions on where to leave a stack of unmarked hundred-dollar bills."

"Try not to worry, I'm sure it's nothing," Chase agreed. "But we should hold off announcing our engagement until I get to the bottom of it."

"What did you say?" Serena demanded.

"I'm about to announce my candidacy," Chase continued. "I can't have a breath of scandal."

"My mother is sending out the invitations to the engagement party," Serena replied. "She booked Harry Denton's Orchestra and McCalls Catering."

"We'll have the engagement party when this blows over," Chase said soothingly. "We need to keep it under wraps for now. Your parents will understand, they were in politics for thirty years."

Serena felt an icy chill fill her veins. "They might understand, but I don't."

"We don't want to call attention to us and embarrass your family," Chase replied. "I'm doing this for us. Trust me; I'll take care of it."

Serena hung up and watched the seagulls peck at the sand. She wished she were in San Francisco, eating breakfast with Chase at Betelnut. She pictured fluffy egg-white omelets and strong black coffee. She and Chase would drive up to her parents' house and they would all laugh about the letter.

When Charles was young he was very handsome, with Serena's blond hair and bright green eyes. He often received fan mail from women who'd seen his picture in the paper. Sometimes he was photographed hugging striking actresses or models at political fund-raisers.

But Charles was devoted to his wife. Serena couldn't count the number of times she'd heard the story of how they met. They were both students at UC Berkeley in the 1970s. Charles was sitting in a tree protesting nuclear power, and Kate was lying on the grass reading a copy of *Fear of Flying*.

"I toppled out of the tree right onto Kate's backpack," Charles would say at a dinner party. "Luckily she carried all of her belongings in that thing—a sweater, textbooks, a peanut butter and jelly sandwich."

"He ruined my sandwich." Kate would smile, smoothing her hair with her hands.

"I had to invite her to lunch," Charles would say, nodding. "It cost me a week's salary."

"How could lunch cost a week's salary?" one of the guests would ask.

Charles would take Kate's hands in his and look into her eyes. "She was so beautiful, I knew I only had one chance to make an impression. We took BART to San Francisco and ate at Ernie's. Filet mignon and roasted potatoes and strawberry pavlova for dessert."

Serena twisted her ponytail, blinking back sudden tears. She turned over her phone and dialed her parents' home number.

"Daddy," she said when Charles answered. "Have you seen Chase?"

"He came over yesterday morning," Charles replied. "We put together a press release; he's going to be the strongest candidate this city has seen in decades."

"Have you talked to him today?" Serena asked.

"I've been on the boat all day. The weather is spectacular, not a hint of fog on the bay," her father said. "Is everything all right? You sound alarmed."

"Chase said his friend at the *Chronicle* received a letter saying you had a secret second family in France," Serena blurted out.

"In France!" Charles exclaimed.

"She threatened to contact every newspaper in America." Serena tightened the grip on her phone.

"Serena," Charles said quietly. "You know that's crazy."

"Of course it's crazy." Serena felt the trapped air leave her lungs. "But Chase said we shouldn't announce our engagement until he figures out what's going on."

Charles was silent and Serena thought they had lost the connection. She was about to call him back when his voice came over the phone. "Chase is being prudent; he's a smart guy."

"How can you say that?" Serena's voice rose. "You're talking about our marriage."

"Politics can get messy," Charles replied. "He'll sort this out and it'll disappear. Let's not worry until there's something to worry about."

Serena kicked off her running shoes and stepped barefoot onto the dock. She didn't know if she was angrier that Chase would suggest postponing the announcement of their engagement or that her father agreed with him. She pictured the two men she loved most—Chase with his wavy blond hair and long thick lashes, her father with his tan leathery cheeks—and tried to stop her heart from thudding in her chest.

Serena walked briskly along the dock, replaying the conversation with her father. He had barely seemed concerned, as if she were reporting a sudden squall that might interrupt a day's sailing.

She remembered interviewing Heidi Klum, just before she split up with Seal. It was Serena's first celebrity interview and she was so nervous she could barely hold her pen.

"A tabloid reported you were holding hands with your bodyguard on a beach in Saint Croix," Serena stuttered.

Heidi plucked a green grape from the platter of fresh fruits and cheeses and shrugged. "That's crazy, I've never been to Saint Croix!"

Serena remembered writing the feature on how Heidi combined her thriving career with a happy family life and Chelsea calling her into her office and throwing a copy of *People* magazine on her desk.

"You're telling our readers Heidi wins the mother of the year award, and *People* says she's fucking her bodyguard," Chelsea said, gritting her teeth.

Serena remembered slinking back to her office and replaying the interview, trying to figure out what she had missed, which words didn't ring true.

Serena jumped onto the beach, digging her feet into the sand. Her mother and father were like matching bookends; they both loved the symphony and James Patterson novels and Belgian chocolate. They walked up to bed at the same time and read the paper aloud to each other on Sundays.

Her father despised politicians who took advantage of their power. He turned off the television whenever he heard John Edwards apologizing for his affair, and disdained David Petraeus and Anthony Weiner. Serena had heard him remark he admired President Clinton's foreign policy but still had trouble shaking his hand.

Serena turned around and ran quickly back to the dock. She wasn't going to let an anonymous letter ruin her day. She'd go back to the suite and eat whole wheat toast and one perfectly poached egg. She'd shower and put on a sundress and explore the Rue

Meynadier with Zoe. In the evening Chase would call and say everything was fine. They'd talk about the mayor's race and their engagement and how much they missed each other.

"*Excusez-moi! Arrêtez, s'il vous plaît,*" a male voice called out.

Serena turned around and saw a man with dark curly hair. He wore a white T-shirt and navy shorts and scuffed leather boat shoes.

"Can I help you?" Serena asked.

"Are you all right?" the man asked in English. "You looked like you were being chased by pirates."

Serena smoothed her hair and tried to calm her breathing. "I'm fine, I just realized I was late."

"Nobody in Cannes worries about time," the man said, leaning against the railing. His arms were tan and he had a thick chest and slender calves. "Even the fishermen aren't in a hurry, they know there will be more fish tomorrow."

"Well, I am late," Serena said, and walked away. Zoe had warned her about locals who tried to capitalize on tourists. He was probably trying to sell waterskiing lessons or hot air balloon rides.

"Wait!" The man ran in front of her, blocking the dock.

"I'll call hotel security if I have to," Serena warned.

The man held out his hand. "You dropped your phone."

Serena took the phone and slipped it in her pocket. She ran down the promenade, past the waiters opening umbrellas at the outdoor cafés, past the salesgirls arranging displays in the boutique windows, not stopping until she entered the revolving glass doors of the Carlton-InterContinental.

chapter five

Serena touched her hair and knocked on the door of the Sophia Loren Suite. She wore a navy-and-white Chloé dress with white sandals. Her ponytail was tied with a silver ribbon and she wore a silver Tiffany heart around her neck. She was freshly showered and her wrists smelled of Givenchy.

When Serena had arrived in the Cary Grant Suite she found a note from Zoe saying she had decided to go on a day trip to Mougins. She hoped they could go dancing tonight at Charly's or Bâoli. Zoe signed the ivory notepaper with a line of smiley faces.

Serena had been too tired and hungry to wonder why Zoe decided not to go shopping. She put blueberry muffins and sliced peaches on a plate and sat on the balcony. Suddenly she remembered her conversation with Chase and her father and started shaking. She left the plate on the chaise lounge and climbed into bed, pulling the feather comforter over her head.

Finally when her teeth stopped chattering and her heart calmed down she stripped off her running clothes and jumped in the shower. She stood under the double jets, looking out the porthole at the Mediterranean. When she was dressed, her cheeks powdered with Chanel blush, her mouth coated with Lancôme lipgloss, she grabbed her notepad and silver pen and marched down the hallway.

"Serena, it is lovely to see you," Yvette said when she answered the door. She wore a red wool dress with gold buttons and black Ferragamos. "I wanted to change into something more comfortable, but I just returned from running an errand."

"Take your time," Serena said as she entered the suite. The sideboard was set with white china and Chopin played over recessed speakers.

"I'll be a minute," Yvette said, disappearing into the bedroom. "I ordered *petit* sandwiches and a selection of teas; help yourself."

Serena poured a cup of cinnamon tea and sat at the bamboo dining table. She gazed at her diamond-and-emerald ring, wondering if Chase expected her to take it off. She blinked, pushing it tighter on her finger.

"Are you all right?" Yvette asked. She wore black cigarette slacks and a red cashmere sweater. "You look like you've seen a ghost."

"I'm still getting over jet lag," Serena murmured. "I can't wait to hear more about Bertrand."

"Bertrand?" Yvette repeated, as if she hadn't thought about him in years. "He has that effect on people. Once you learn about him you want to hear more; it's like an addiction."

"You said last time that's what you wanted to talk about." Serena blushed, suddenly flustered. "I'd love to learn about your career at *Vogue*."

Yvette selected two watercress sandwiches and a mini-éclair

and sat on a pink satin armchair. She nibbled the éclair, blotting her mouth with a napkin, and looked at Serena.

"Yes, let's talk about Bertrand. I didn't see Bertrand again for eight years," Yvette began. "My husband decided we should rent a villa for the summer in Cap d'Antibes. It was a wonderful place; the historic town was full of galleries and bookstores and you could hike for hours and see from Monaco to Nice." Yvette's eyes flickered as if she were watching an old movie. "All the movie stars and celebrities rented villas and there were parties every night. I ran into Bertrand at a soiree given by the American actor Ryan O'Neal. . . ."

Yvette gazed around the starkly modern living room. A conversation pit held plump white sofas, and brightly colored cushions were tossed in front of a granite fireplace. She had never seen so many beautiful people in one place; they all had blond hair and wore white clothing and heavy gold jewelry. She looked out the plate-glass windows at the swimming pool and saw a woman strip off her caftan and jump into the water.

"I didn't expect to see someone like you in this den of iniquity," Bertrand said as he approached her. She hadn't seen him in eight years, but he looked the same. His skin was tan, his hair was slicked back, and he wore white slacks and a white cotton shirt.

"My family is renting a villa in Antibes," Yvette replied, suddenly feeling that the room was overheated. She wore a simple black cocktail dress and black pumps and she clutched a red satin evening bag.

Bertrand looked her up and down as if he were studying an art exhibit. "You haven't gotten fat."

"Why should I get fat?" Yvette bristled.

"You married the bourgeois banker." Bertrand pointed to the large round diamond on her ring finger. "I'm guessing you popped out a couple of *petits enfants,* a little boy who wears sailor suits and a girl who dresses like a princess."

"Camille is six and Pierre is four," Yvette said, blushing. "They are the center of my world."

"Then why are you here?" Bertrand asked. "Consorting with American riffraff."

"My husband is very social." Yvette bit her lip. "He enjoys parties and he is infatuated with Hollywood."

"Most boring people are," Bertrand said. He stood so close she could smell his aftershave. "I prefer one-on-one conversation."

"Then why are you here?" Yvette inched away. She searched for Henri, but he was standing in a corner chatting with two women with beehive hairdos and gold hoop earrings.

Bertrand followed her eyes and then turned back and gazed at Yvette. He drained his scotch and asked the bartender for another.

"I'm looking for new material for my book." He looked at Yvette as if he could see into her soul. "Repressed sexuality, hidden lust, jealousy, marital infidelity."

"Excuse me, I must join my husband." Yvette jumped up and walked toward the fireplace. Her legs suddenly felt wobbly, and she could feel Bertrand's eyes on her back.

Two days later Yvette was sitting in the grand salon, listening to Brahms and reading Anaïs Nin. The villa was set high on the hillside and Yvette could see cypress trees, bright bougainvillea, and the craggy headlands of Cap d'Antibes. She heard a knock at the front door and got up to answer it.

"What are you doing here?" Yvette asked. "I was expecting a delivery boy."

"You said your husband liked entertaining," Bertrand said, grinning like a schoolboy caught skipping class. He wore baggy white pants, a white T-shirt, and a white linen blazer. He held a boater hat in one hand and a lit cigarette in the other. "I thought it would be polite to call on my neighbor."

"Henri went back to Paris yesterday," Yvette said, and instinctively touched her hair. She wore a silk blouse with a wide pleated skirt and a string of pearls around her neck. "He is only here on the weekends."

Bertrand leaned against the stucco and ground his cigarette into the stone pavement.

"I've walked from Juan-les-Pins in this heat, you could invite me in for a drink."

"I don't drink during the day." Yvette shook her head.

"I do," Bertrand said. He strode into the entry, putting his hat on the antique end table and letting out a low whistle.

The villa had high ceilings and rich cherry floors. A series of archways led to the grand salon and everywhere windows looked out on the bay. The walls were covered with framed paintings by Matisse and Monet and a grand piano stood by the window.

"There are perks to being married to a banker." Bertrand ran his fingers over a Tiffany lamp. "We writers have to shit out every penny."

"You must leave," Yvette insisted, crossing her arms. "I cannot be alone with a man."

"Where are Camille and Pierre?" Bertrand asked mischievously, sitting on an upholstered armchair.

"They are at the beach with Françoise," Yvette replied.

"A nanny?" Bertrand raised his eyebrow. He lit another cigarette and flicked the ashes into a glass ashtray. "I thought you wanted to be with your children all the time."

"I do." Yvette knotted her forehead. "But I am afraid of the ocean."

"Why are you worried? Do you think I am going to fuck you in front of the stone fireplace?" Bertrand looked at her with hooded eyes. "I am very traditional, I believe in the marriage vows."

"You've never been married," Yvette retorted. She had followed Bertrand's success over the years. With each new novel he obtained a more beautiful girlfriend; each woman was certain she was the one who would lead him to the altar. He would parade them proudly at movie premieres and society galas only to replace them with a younger, sleeker model.

Bertrand leaned forward and ground the cigarette slowly into the ashtray. He gazed at Yvette, starting at her black satin pumps and traveling up to the diamond solitaires in her ears.

"I didn't come just to see your husband," he said finally. "I have another motive; I noticed at the party you speak very good English."

"My mother's mother was American," Yvette said, and nodded.

"I finished my new novel; it took me two years to wrestle the beast to the ground." Bertrand drummed his fingers on the coffee table. "The English translation of my last novel was terrible, it read like a bodice-ripping romance."

"I doubt that." Yvette smiled. She had read *The Silent Hour* in one sitting. It was the story of a famous opera singer who loses her ability to speak in a car accident and must find a new passion. "I loved it; Allette's real-life tragedy was greater than anything she experienced onstage."

"You see!" Bertrand jumped up and squeezed her hands. "You understand my prose. My publisher said I can choose my own translator; I want you to do it."

"Me?" Yvette pulled her hands away.

"I still have the article you wrote about me," Bertrand continued. "You bared my soul for the world to see and made me a better person."

"It was a silly article written by an ingenue," Yvette replied, shrugging. "I haven't written in years."

"The Americans and British laughed at me," Bertrand persisted. "Consider it your patriotic duty; we don't want them to think the great French author Bertrand Roland is a sham."

Yvette remembered reading a review in *The New York Times* and thinking it was harsh. She recalled the American cover: a curvaceous brunette in a ball gown with a gash across her neck. "I couldn't possibly do it."

"We will work here during the day," Bertrand said, plunging ahead. "While your children play in the garden. It will be completely chaste and aboveboard."

"I have to ask my husband," Yvette wavered, gazing out the window at the gardener clipping hydrangea bushes.

"I should have asked him last night." Bertrand lit another cigarette. "I saw him at Roger Vadim's villa."

Yvette turned to Bertrand and frowned. "Henri took the train to Paris yesterday morning."

"He must have missed it," Bertrand replied. "It was definitely Henri. The model Lauren Hutton was there, they were deep in conversation."

Yvette studied the Oriental rug. When she looked up her eyes were softer and new lines ran across her forehead. "We can start on Wednesday at noon, while Françoise gives the children lunch."

Bertrand's mouth broke into a wide, lazy smile. "You haven't offered me a drink. I'll take a scotch, no ice."

Serena strolled along the Rue Félix Faure toward the Marché Forville. It was late afternoon and shoppers carried shopping bags filled with loaves of fresh bread, ripe red tomatoes, jars of olives, and wrapped fillets of trout.

She had tried to sit on the balcony transcribing her notes. But she kept glancing at her phone, waiting for Chase to call. Finally she changed into a yellow cotton dress and flat sandals, grabbed her purse, and ran down the street. She wanted to explore the old town of Suquet, stroll through the Jardin Alexandre III, and forget that her fiancé insisted they shouldn't tell anyone they were engaged.

Serena entered the covered market, marveling at the selection of fruits and vegetables. There were baskets of raspberries, firm white peaches, sweet plums, and fresh figs. She saw racks of olive oil from Provence, salts from Camargue, and rows of cheeses with handwritten labels.

She pictured the sideboard in the Cary Grant Suite, brimming with fruits and cheeses. But the produce looked so tempting, she couldn't resist filling her basket with juicy pears, tangerines, and bags of white cherries.

"Excuse me, stop, please!" a male voice called as she left the market.

She turned around and saw the man with dark curly hair who had found her phone. "What are you doing here, are you following me?"

"I don't even know who you are." The man caught up with her. He wore a light blue shirt over tan shorts and brown leather sandals. He held up her purse. "You left this at the *fromage* counter."

Serena blushed, taking the purse and placing it in her shopping bag. "Thank you, that's very kind of you."

"Let me guess, you're American," he said, walking beside her.

"From San Francisco." Serena nodded.

"I spent a summer there," the man said as they stood at the corner. "I hated it."

Serena burst out laughing. "Mark Twain said the coldest winter he ever spent was summer in San Francisco."

"Let me guess, you are a famous American actress here for the film festival."

She heard her phone buzz and checked it eagerly, certain it was Chase. She read a text from Zoe saying she had made dinner reservations, and suddenly her eyes filled with tears.

"It's none of your business why I'm here," Serena snapped, running across the road so quickly she narrowly missed a bicyclist. She wanted to find a quiet café or a bench by the harbor. She would call Chase and insist they send out invitations to the engagement party; whatever Chase discovered about her father they would face together.

"Americans say the French are rude," the man said, running ahead of her. He had blue eyes and an angular nose and a small cleft on his chin.

She blushed, suddenly desperate to get away. She grabbed the basket of cherries from her shopping bag and thrust them at him.

"I'm grateful to you for returning my belongings. I really have to go."

Serena crossed the Rue Félix Faure and ducked into the Café Poet. Square tables were covered with starched white tablecloths and a bar held a glistening array of crystal decanters and glass bottles.

She drank a glass of ice-cold lemonade as if she'd spent the last month in the desert. She was about to call Chase when she noticed a young woman sitting on the other side of the restaurant wearing a wide-brimmed white hat with a navy ribbon. Her face was hidden by dark sunglasses and she wore a navy dress and white pumps.

Serena recognized the hat from the Carlton-InterContinental gift shop. She remembered trying hats on with Zoe, giggling that they felt like Julia Roberts in *Pretty Woman*. She looked more closely and realized the navy dress was the Stella McCartney dress she had loaned to Zoe and the white pumps were Serena's own pair of Guccis.

She flashed on the text Zoe sent saying she was taking a bath and made reservations at Côté Jardin for seven P.M. Why was Zoe sitting at Café Poet when she was supposed to be submerged in bubbles?

Serena followed Zoe's gaze and saw an older man wearing a straw hat and a burgundy blazer. He wore suede loafers and a gold Rolex on his wrist. He was leaning forward and whispering to a woman with long chestnut hair and a full pink mouth. She wore a low-cut silk dress and gold espadrilles on her feet.

The man took the woman's arm and led her out of the restaurant. Zoe pushed her chair back and hurried to the door. She waited till the couple strolled down the Rue Félix Faure, and then she turned and followed them.

Serena entered the Cary Grant Suite, slipping off her sandals and feeling the smooth marble under her feet. The air smelled of hyacinths and roses and the French doors were open to reveal the sun setting over the bay.

"You're not dressed for dinner." Serena frowned, seeing Zoe hunched on the ivory silk sofa. She wore a cotton robe and terry slippers. Her eyes were puffy and there were red blotches on her cheeks.

"I ate a bad truffle in Mougins," Zoe said. She didn't look up from her copy of French *Elle*. "I can't go to dinner."

Serena debated whether to tell Zoe she had seen her at the restaurant. But Zoe looked so fragile, like a kitten that had been saved from drowning. Serena stepped onto the balcony and gazed down at the elegant boutiques.

"You're not going to find that je ne sais quoi sitting here." Serena walked back inside. "We're going to put on our sexiest dresses and go shopping."

"The boutiques are closed." Zoe shrugged. "It's after six P.M."

"They put a closed sign on the door but there's always someone inside in case Angelina Jolie makes a night pilgrimage," Serena said. "I'll give you a crash course on Yves Saint Laurent and Dior."

Zoe put the magazine on the coffee table and looked at Serena, her eyes flickering with excitement. "We can pretend we're Audrey Hepburn in *Breakfast at Tiffany's*."

"Get dressed." Serena grinned. "We're going to outshop Katie Holmes and Blake Lively."

Serena and Zoe stepped onto the sidewalk, breathing the warm night air. Serena wore a beige silk dress with spaghetti straps and a wide orange belt. Her hair was tied in a high ponytail and her mouth was coated with shimmering lipgloss.

"I've never seen so many stylish women." Zoe sighed. She wore a snug Lacroix dress and silver stilettos. Her eyes were still swollen and the blotches on her cheeks were hidden by Estée Lauder powder. "I feel like Cinderella's ugly stepsister."

Serena squeezed Zoe's arm. "By the time we're done, you're going to look like a princess."

They started at Bottega Veneta and worked their way through Sonia Rykiel, Chanel, Dolce & Gabbana, and Hermès. The salesgirls were resistant at first, tapping the glass and shaking their heads. But Serena insisted they open the door and spoke in rapid French.

"What did you say?" Zoe asked when the tall, stoic saleswoman at Christian Dior ushered them into the hushed showroom.

"That I'm writing a story on French boutiques for *Vogue,* and Dior is my top choice for the cover," Serena said, and grinned, fingering a red silk blouse with tiny pearl buttons.

Zoe gazed at the rows of summer dresses in bold colors. They were made of the thinnest fabrics and accessorized with vibrant purses, chunky necklaces, colorful scarves, and gold bangles.

"They look gorgeous on the mannequins." Zoe sighed again. "When I wear them I belong in the circus."

"We need to find the right cut and the perfect color," Serena told her. She selected a pale pink dress over a cream-colored satin slip. She paired it with ivory pumps with small bows and a medium heel.

Serena waited while Zoe went into the dressing room. Suddenly she heard stifled sobbing. She stood outside, waiting until the cries turned to hiccups. Then she slowly turned the door handle.

Zoe stood in front of the mirror, wiping her eyes with a tissue. The dress was perfectly cut, accentuating her figure in the right places. The pale pink made her eyes sparkle and her skin look like creamy alabaster.

"Why are you crying?" Serena asked.

"It's my damn allergies." Zoe hiccuped. "I've always been allergic to expensive perfumes. How do I look?"

Serena walked into the dressing room and gazed in the three-way mirror. She handed Zoe another tissue and smiled. "You look like an angel."

"My mother took me to Yves Saint Laurent when we lived in Paris," Serena said as they entered the gold-and-white showroom of Yves Saint Laurent. "She let me pick out her dress to meet the French prime minister. I loved everything: the couture dresses, the long wool coats, the quilted jackets. It's when I decided I had to work in fashion."

"You should buy a dress for your engagement party," Zoe suggested, selecting a floral silk dress. "This would look fabulous with your eyes."

Serena froze, gazing at the colorful fabric. She hadn't told Zoe about Chase's phone call; she kept expecting Chase to text that everything was all right.

Serena held the dress to her neck, imagining standing next

to Chase on her parents' lawn. She saw his brown eyes, his wavy
blond hair, the dimple on his cheek. She pictured cutting their
engagement cake, popping champagne, all their friends clapping
and laughing.

Serena took the dress to the counter and handed the salesgirl
her credit card. "I'll take it."

chapter six

Serena sat on a chaise lounge on the balcony toying with a plate of melon. Her hair was freshly washed and she wore a silk robe and slippers. She poured a demitasse of French press coffee, adding cream and sugar.

She had missed Chase's call while she was in the shower and now his phone went straight to voice mail. She bit her lip and called her parents' home number.

"Darling." Her mother's voice came on the line. "How is Cannes? I haven't heard from you in days."

"It's gorgeous and Yvette Renault is fascinating," Serena replied. "She's the most elegant woman I've ever met."

"When we lived in Paris I wore only the designers she suggested," Kate agreed. "I own my favorite Sonia Rykiel dress because she wrote every fashionable woman must have at least one."

"How's Daddy?" Serena fiddled with her coffee cup.

"Wonderful! We drove to Napa and ate lunch at Bouchon. The sautéed gnocchi with spring vegetables was delicious."

"Have you seen Chase?" Serena asked, trying to ignore the lump that had formed in her throat.

"He was here for hours yesterday," Kate said. "I had to bring turkey club sandwiches to your father's study or they would have starved."

"Did he say why he was there?" Serena asked.

"More campaign ideas," Kate replied. "Your father is like a child in a candy store."

"Is Daddy there? I'd love to say hi."

"He went to get some rib eye steaks," Kate said. "It's such a lovely night, we're going to have a candlelit dinner on the patio. There are advantages to being retired; it feels like we're back in college but with a king-size bed and gourmet cuisine."

Serena hung up, wishing she could call her father, but neither her mother nor her father owned a cell phone. She could talk to Zoe, but she had gone on a day excursion to Théoule sur Mer, grabbing a sausage and a scone as she ran out the door.

Serena walked inside and gazed at the breakfast selections on the sideboard. The Belgian waffles and fresh blueberries that looked delicious an hour ago turned her stomach. She entered her bedroom and stood in front of the closet, debating what to wear for her meeting with Yvette. Suddenly, her legs felt wobbly and she sank onto her bed.

She pictured her mother and father driving in her father's Audi convertible in Napa. Her parents told each other everything, but her father hadn't mentioned an anonymous letter saying he had a secret second family in France.

Perhaps he had said nothing because Chase had already discovered it was false, and the campaign launch and engagement party were going ahead as planned. Serena felt her shoulders relax and the throbbing in her head subside.

She brushed her hair in the mirror, reaching for a blue satin ribbon. She gazed at her reflection and a pit formed in her stomach. What if her father hadn't said anything because there was something he didn't want his wife to know?

"Come in." Yvette opened the door of the Sophia Loren Suite. She wore a red linen dress with a wide black belt and black leather pumps.

"I didn't mean to interrupt your lunch," Serena said, glancing at the room service table set up on the balcony. The table was covered with a pink silk tablecloth and set with white bone china. There was a crystal vase full of peach-colored roses and a carafe of sparkling water.

"Nonsense, you must join me." Yvette motioned for Serena to sit down. "The kitchen makes enough to feed an army."

Serena surveyed the hearts of palm salad with asparagus and green beans, the grilled beef fillet with rock salt and crushed pepper sauce, and the plate of fat *pommes frites*. There were four kinds of mustard and a jar of Heinz ketchup.

"You use ketchup?" Serena raised her eyebrow.

"Bertrand went on a book tour in America and discovered ketchup." Yvette scooped salad onto a porcelain plate. "He insisted it tasted good on everything—eggs, sausages, even filet mignon. I remember the first day he arrived with a picnic basket." Yvette paused, putting her fork down. Her eyes clouded over and she gazed out at the Mediterranean.

"What's that?" Yvette asked, answering the door of the villa. The skies were low and the air smelled like rain. She wore orange-and-white Gucci culottes. Her dark hair touched her shoulders and she wore a gold chain around her neck.

"I brought lunch." Bertrand held up a wicker picnic basket. He wore white slacks and a white T-shirt that was already damp with sweat. He took off his hat and set it on the sideboard, running his fingers through his black hair.

"Our cook makes my meals," Yvette replied, ushering him inside.

"French gourmet food is for sissies," Bertrand said, eyeing the grand salon to see where he should have his picnic. "Cold soups, soufflés, custards. I need red meat, potatoes, vegetables that aren't swimming in butter."

Bertrand laid a red-and-white checkered blanket in front of the stone fireplace and set it with a loaf of crusty bread, wedges of Edam and Camembert cheeses, and slices of roast beef and ham. There was a container of potato salad, a dark chocolate torte, and miniature jars of mayonnaise, mustard, and ketchup.

"What is this?" Yvette picked up the jar of ketchup. She couldn't help but smile, imagining what the owner of the villa would say if he saw the indoor picnic spread out on his hundred-year-old floors.

"Ketchup." Bertrand sliced the baguette and slathered it with mustard. "I discovered it in a minibar at the Beverly Hills Hotel. It is the greatest invention the Americans have made; it can make stale Wonder Bread with bologna taste delicious."

"I would imagine they fed a famous French author better than that." Yvette laughed, perching on an ottoman.

"I couldn't eat at those fucking fancy literary dinners with society matrons hovering over me to see how I held my fork." Bertrand layered the bread with thick slices of ham and cheese. He put the sandwich on a plate and handed it to Yvette.

"I can hardly eat a bite." Yvette accepted the plate and politely nibbled the sandwich. "I had muesli and fresh peaches for break-fast."

"I brought extra slices of chocolate torte for the children." Bertrand made another sandwich for himself, adding pickles and red onions. "I thought they would be playing in the garden."

"Françoise took them to the Picasso Museum in Antibes," Yvette replied, looking out the full-length windows at the dark, oppressive clouds. "It looks like rain."

"Then we will get started." Bertrand nodded, reaching into the picnic basket for a fat manuscript bound with thick rubber bands. "This is for you, work wherever you like. I will sit here and enjoy a glass of claret."

"I thought you were going to read out loud to me," Yvette said, and frowned.

Bertrand burst out laughing. "I never read my work after I finish the final draft; I would rather hang upside down in Fleury-Mérogis and have water dripped on my head."

"How will you know if I do a good job?" Yvette asked, horrified.

Bertrand stood up and walked over to Yvette. She could smell sweat and spicy ground mustard. "You will know if you do a good job." He touched his heart. "You will feel it here. Take your time, we have all afternoon."

Yvette took a long white notepad out of the desk drawer and un-screwed a silver fountain pen. She carefully slid off the elastic bands and began to read. Suddenly the rain came down in steel-gray sheets. There was a bolt of lightning and a loud clap of thunder. Yvette jumped, spilling ink on the page.

"Are you all right?" Bertrand looked at her curiously. He lounged against the fireplace, eating large bites of his sandwich and wiping mayonnaise from his chin with a napkin.

"I'm afraid of lightning and thunder." Yvette shivered as another bolt of lightning lit up the sky. "I have been since I was a little girl."

"You are afraid of many things—the ocean, thunder," Bertrand mused.

"My grandmother was the same." Yvette pulled her eyes from the window. "I inherited it from her."

Bertrand walked to the front door and opened it wide, letting the rain drip onto the wood floor.

"What are you doing?" Yvette demanded, running to close the door.

"There is nothing more beautiful than the elements." Bertrand stood at the entry. "It's like having a first-row seat at the symphony."

Yvette cautiously stood behind him, feeling the rain touch her cheeks. The air smelled fresh and damp. She turned to go back inside when Bertrand grabbed her hand and ran into the front garden.

"What are you doing?" Yvette shrieked. Her heart was hammering so quickly she couldn't catch her breath.

"The lightning is miles away," Bertrand said, grinning. He wrapped his arms lightly around her shoulders. "There's nothing to be afraid of."

Yvette let herself rest against his chest, feeling strangely calm and quiet. Then the sky burst with color and there was a crack of thunder so loud it shook the ground. She put her hands over her head and dashed back to the house.

"Are you crazy?" she demanded when they stood in the grand salon. She had run upstairs and put on a dry sweater and black slacks. She dried her hair with a towel and poured herself a glass of red wine. "We could have been killed."

"Do you know how many people are killed in thunderstorms?" Bertrand took a pack of cigarettes and a lighter from his pocket. "You are in more danger using an electric toaster."

"You're insane." Yvette shivered, gulping the red wine.

"Do you know what it's like to begin a novel? It's like diving into a dark cement tunnel." Bertrand stood so close to Yvette she could almost taste his cigarette. "But when I type 'the end' it is like making love on the top of a mountain with a waterfall roaring behind me."

Yvette blushed, moving away and standing by the window. The rain had turned to a light drizzle and the coastline was enveloped in fog.

"Let's get back to work." Bertrand ground his cigarette into an ashtray. "I promise to behave and not interrupt you."

chapter seven

S erena sat at the round glass table in the Cary Grant Suite, transcribing her notes onto her laptop. She had been working all morning, ignoring the hum of yacht engines and the scent of suntan lotion that drifted through the French doors. She was too consumed by Yvette's story to pause for anything except another cup of coffee and a slice of whole wheat toast with jam.

She had woken up in the middle of the night and called Chase's office. But his secretary said he was at a company retreat at the Bohemian Grove and wouldn't return until Monday. Serena lay back on the Egyptian cotton sheets, thinking of ways to distract herself. She and Zoe could go shopping, get Zoe's hair done, explore *le palais* and the old town.

But when Serena padded into the living room she found a note from Zoe saying she had signed up for a morning tour of Saint-Honorat. Serena studied Zoe's scrawled cursive and frowned. For someone who was intent on learning about style, Zoe spent a lot of time exploring the countryside.

Serena thought about running along the beach but suddenly her legs felt heavy and her head ached. She slipped on a cotton dress, ran a brush through her hair, and sat down at the table to write.

"I keep checking my e-mail and expecting a piece from you," Chelsea said when Serena answered her phone. "I hope you're not spending your days dangling your toes in the Mediterranean and getting your back rubbed by sexy beach attendants."

"I'm typing right now." Serena smiled. "I'll have something to you soon."

"Chanel took out a one-page ad and Dolce and Gabbana wants a two-page spread," Chelsea continued. "They're expecting Yvette to reveal serious dirt about the French fashion industry."

"So far Yvette has mainly talked about Bertrand," Serena replied.

Chelsea was silent and Serena could almost hear her tapping her long French-manicured nails on her polished maple desk.

"Sex and lust is great," Chelsea said. "But they also want to read about Valentino's ego, Givenchy's penny-pinching, and the spectacular rise and fall of the model Anouk."

"I'll get all that." Serena nodded, nervously scanning the words on her computer screen.

"I hope so," Chelsea replied. "Even without paying for your room, this trip is costing a fortune. I read your expense report—two hundred euros for a beach chair on the sand? You could buy a whole chaise lounge set."

Serena hung up and paced around the room. She pictured Yvette in her black cigarette pants and red cashmere sweater talking about Bertrand. Her eyes sparkled and her cheeks filled with color like a young girl with a crush.

What if nothing had happened between them? What if Yvette

translated Bertrand's novel and their friendship stayed platonic? Chelsea's advertisers wouldn't be happy if Yvette's memoir didn't include any torrid sex scenes.

Serena sat on the ivory silk sofa and picked up a copy of *Paris Match*. She remembered reading it religiously at Amherst to practice her French. She loved the glossy photos of celebrities posing in Monaco and Saint-Tropez.

Serena flipped the pages and stopped at a photo of an older man in a straw hat and a woman with luxurious chestnut hair. They were stepping onto a yacht in the harbor, shielding their faces with their hands.

Serena looked more closely and recognized the man's burgundy blazer and the woman's Pucci dress and gold espadrilles. She read the caption out loud: "Australian fashion magnate Malcolm Gladding caught living it up in Cannes, with an unidentified brunette."

Serena pictured Zoe hiding behind a menu at the Café Poet. Why didn't she want her father to know she was in Cannes, and why did she lie to Serena? Serena picked up her phone and dialed Chelsea's number.

"If you're calling to increase your expense account, first I need to see some writing," Chelsea answered. "Give me two thousand juicy words and you can go shopping at Ermenegildo Zegna."

"Have you heard of Malcolm Gladding?" Serena twisted her ponytail.

"I wrote a story about him a few years ago," Chelsea replied. "His wife is Australia's top fashion maven. If she says wear magenta you'll see it at every society gala. I met them at one of Tina Brown's dinners in New York. Laura is lovely in person, quite self-effacing."

"Are they still married?" Serena asked.

"Of course they're married!" Chelsea exclaimed. "He just received an OBE from the queen for his service to Australia. Collette Dinnigan designed Laura's dress, the fabric alone cost ten thousand dollars."

"Okay, thanks." Serena gazed at the photo of Malcolm with his arm around the brunette.

"Are you not telling me something?" Chelsea demanded. "Have you seen Malcolm in Cannes?"

"I don't think so," Serena mumbled.

"Those old buggers think a 'Sir' in front of their name allows them to fuck any woman under the age of thirty," Chelsea replied. "If you run into him I want eight hundred words and a photo. I'll redecorate your office and throw in a Tiffany lamp."

Serena hung up and walked to the balcony. She tried to put herself in Zoe's shoes, but none of it made sense. If Zoe's parents were together, Zoe would want to confront him, not slink around as if she were the criminal.

Serena walked back to the table and sat down at her laptop. Suddenly she couldn't think about Yvette and Bertrand, she kept seeing Zoe with her wide hat and dark glasses like Greta Garbo. She closed the computer and sat on the silk sofa, waiting for Zoe to walk in the door.

"You should have come to Saint-Honorat," Zoe said later when she arrived, dropping her bag on a glass end table and sinking onto a gold velvet armchair. She wore a navy dress with a cream lace collar and a scalloped hem. Her hair was covered by a wide straw hat and she wore beige leather sandals. "I visited the monastery and saw cannonballs made in Napoleon's time. For a short man he had very big balls."

Serena studied Zoe, wondering if she had really gone to Saint-Honorat, or if she had been loitering around the cafés. She twisted her ponytail, wondering how to get Zoe to tell the truth.

"The Cannes Film Festival is almost over," Serena said finally. "It's time I got my own room."

"You can't do that!" Zoe jumped up. "We haven't got my hair done or worked on my French."

"You look lovely," Serena said, and smiled. "You'll do fine on your own."

"But I need a friend." Zoe took off her hat and flung it on the coffee table. "The tour guide almost left me on the island because I didn't understand when we were due back on the boat. We should explore together, go to Nice or Monte Carlo."

Serena handed Zoe the copy of *Paris Match*. "If we're friends, why didn't you tell me your father is in Cannes?"

Zoe gazed at the photo and her cheeks turned pale. She sat down heavily, burying her face in her hands.

"I saw you in Café Poet," Serena continued. "I can help if you tell me the truth."

"Do you promise to stay in the suite?" Zoe asked, her eyes filling with tears. "I don't want to be alone."

"You have to tell me everything," Serena said, and nodded. "Not some half version of the truth."

"I swear," Zoe said. She grabbed her hat and put it on her head. "But not here; let's rent a speedboat and go out on the bay."

"I have work to do." Serena glanced at her laptop on the glass dining table.

"The ocean is spectacular." Zoe ran to the balcony. "We can at least pretend we're having fun."

Serena joined her outside and watched silver and gold speedboats race each other across the water.

"All right." Serena grinned, turning to Zoe. "But you need to wear a lot of sunscreen—you're getting new freckles."

"My mother came from a wealthy family, her father owned one of the biggest sheep stations in Australia," Zoe began.

They sat in the back of a bright red speedboat, leaning against soft leather cushions. Serena felt the sea spray on her cheeks and for a moment forgot her father and Chase and the anonymous letter. She gazed at Zoe in her one-piece bathing suit, her straw hat jammed against her head, and almost believed they were just two young women enjoying Cannes.

"She met my father when they were in their last year at Sydney University. My grandparents were very traditional and they wouldn't let my mother marry until my father could support her. He started designing clothes and began his fashion empire the day he graduated—selling merino wool sweaters from the boot of his car.

"Within ten years he added menswear and accessories and different fabrics. He imported more silk from Asia than any other company and had a line of hugely successful swimwear.

"My parents were crazy about each other. We lived in a mansion overlooking Sydney Harbor, and at night they'd sit on the lawn under my window. My mother would whisper that I was still awake and my father would reply that being in love wasn't a crime. Then I'd hear them kissing.

"When I was ten my mother received a letter threatening to kidnap me if they didn't deliver fifty thousand dollars. Kidnapping threats were quite common; Australia is a small place and the bigwigs are on the cover of every magazine and newspaper. My father was often seen with his arm around the prime minister and my parents entertained movie stars and politicians.

"My mother turned the letter over to the police and they arrested a homeless woman. They assured my parents it was a random threat, but my parents implemented a full security system: a bodyguard who drove me to school, two Doberman pinschers, electric gates around our estate. I was like Rapunzel without the beautiful blond hair.

"When I was twelve my mother had to go to Melbourne for the day. It was school holidays, and I spent all my time practicing gymnastics in the garden. The bodyguard had a bad case of poison ivy so my mother insisted my father didn't go to the office. Even though we had a housekeeper she didn't like to leave me at home.

"I remember it was just after lunch; Betty had made Vegemite sandwiches and strawberry lamingtons. My father came into the kitchen and said he had to run to the warehouse, something about a shipment of silk from Hong Kong that would be returned if he didn't sign off. Betty told me to go outside, and she'd watch me do cartwheels." Zoe's face clouded over and her hands clenched up. She stopped talking and took a long sip of iced tea.

"I was doing the splits when the back gate opened and two men with black masks appeared. One grabbed my hands and the other grabbed my legs and they carried me to their car. Betty didn't say a word, just stood up and walked into the kitchen.

"They drove into the country and left me in a house with a middle-aged woman with blond hair. She fed me sausage rolls and Violet Crumbles and told me not to be afraid. All my parents had to do was deliver two million dollars and I'd be home in my princess bed.

"On the third day the two men appeared and put me back in

the car. They took me to Taronga Zoo and we sat on a bench in front of the penguins." Zoe looked at Serena, her lips trembling. "I always loved the penguins best, they were like live stuffed animals.

"No one came and the men started arguing. The taller man made me get up and we walked back to the car. Suddenly I saw my father running through the turnstiles. He wore a red polo shirt and carried a leather bag. He shoved the bag into the taller man's hands and grabbed my hand. We ran all the way through the zoo until we reached his car. Then he locked the doors and held me so tightly I couldn't breathe.

"Of course it was an inside job," Zoe continued as the speed-boat jumped the waves made by a luxury yacht. "The housekeeper and the bodyguard had been planning it for weeks. I found out later that the police insisted my parents not give in to the demands for ransom. They'd seen too many cases when the father shows up with a briefcase full of hundred-dollar bills and the child is already in a body bag at the bottom of the ocean. My mother wanted to do exactly what the police said, but my father secretly transferred the money and contacted the kidnappers.

"I spent the next six months seeing shrinks, and finally they sent me to boarding school in England," Zoe mused. "My mother was so angry at him for leaving me alone, it took her a year to move back in their bedroom."

"I don't know what to say," Serena said. Her chest felt tight and her stomach turned over.

"Six years of boarding school, four years at St. Andrew's, some very understanding house mothers, and an addiction to Cadbury chocolate," Zoe said, and smiled, scooping up a handful of pea-nuts from the console between them. "I'm almost good as new, but I'm not very good at being alone."

"Why is your father in Cannes?" Serena frowned.

"I moved back to Sydney after university," Zoe continued. "My parents wanted me to live at home but I rented a flat in Darling Point with two girlfriends. My father taught me about Gladding House and my mother put me on her charity boards.

"Last month we traveled to London to accept my father's knighthood. I hadn't seen my mother so radiant in years; she wore a floor-length Collette Dinnigan gown with gold Manolos. My father surprised her with a diamond-and-sapphire pendant from Harry Winston. We stayed at Claridge's and ate at the Savoy and saw a play in the West End.

"My mother returned to Sydney to chair a charity ball, and my father and I were going to travel to Paris and Milan. He wanted to show me the capitals of fashion. I knocked on the door of his suite to go to the airport." Zoe blinked back tears. "He had checked out. He left a note saying he had to take care of something, and I should go back to Sydney without him."

"How did you know he was in Cannes?" Serena asked.

"I hacked into his credit card account and saw he booked a flight to Cannes and reserved a room at the Carlton-InterContinental."

"He's staying in the same hotel!" Serena exclaimed. The speedboat drove close to the shore and Serena could see sunbathers lying on fluffy yellow towels. Children built castles in the sand, filling red plastic buckets with water.

"That's why I checked in under the name Zoe Pistachio. I was going to surprise him, and then I saw him in the lobby with that woman." Zoe's face crumpled and she sipped her iced tea noisily. "My parents are fixtures in Sydney society. They're always photographed on someone's yacht or at someone's beach house. I've never seen my father look at another woman."

"Maybe she works for Gladding House," Serena offered.

"I've been following them for days," Zoe replied. "Morning croissants at the Carlton Bar, dinner at La Palme d'Or. I even saw them in Bouteille—the perfume costs more than gold per ounce. She's so beautiful, she's like a centerfold without the airbrushing."

"You can't snoop around like Nancy Drew," Serena insisted. "You have to ask him what's going on."

"I can't knock on his door and say, 'Why are you shacking up with some bronze pencil when your wife is at the Sydney Opera House donating a hundred-thousand-dollar check to the cystic fibrosis foundation?'"

Serena waited until the driver tied up the speedboat at the dock. She handed him a wad of euros and jumped onto the landing.

"Where are we going?" Zoe asked when they reached the sand.

"I'm a journalist." Serena walked quickly through the throng of bodies. "I make my living asking people uncomfortable questions. Maybe it's perfectly innocent; she's the daughter of an old friend. You won't know unless you ask him."

They reached the boulevard and waited for the light to change. Zoe gazed at the flags flying above the Carlton and turned to Serena. "What if I don't like the answer?"

chapter eight

Serena slipped diamond teardrop earrings into her ears and gazed at her reflection. She had showered and put on a sheer turquoise dress over a lace slip. She tied her hair in a low knot and secured it with a gold pin. She dabbed her wrists with Givenchy and coated her lips with pink lipgloss.

"Are we really going to sit in the lobby bar and wait for them to walk by?" Zoe asked as she appeared at the door of Serena's bedroom. She wore a yellow linen dress with a thin gold belt. Her bangs were brushed to the side and her cheeks were dusted with sparkly blush. "I'll give my father a heart attack."

Serena smiled at Zoe. "You look lovely. I like your hair, and that dress suits you."

"My father is my backgammon partner and the only person I know who can do the *Sydney Morning Herald* crossword puzzle." Zoe turned to the mirror, wrinkling her nose at her reflection. "I can't march up to him and accuse him of having a mistress."

The doorbell rang and Zoe disappeared to the living room. Serena heard her talking to someone and then she poked her head in the door. "It's for you."

Serena frowned, hoping she hadn't missed an appointment with Yvette. She walked into the foyer and saw the door of the suite flung open. Chase stood in the entry, wearing tan slacks and a blue blazer. His hair touched his collar and his cheeks were freshly shaven.

Serena dropped her purse on the cream marble. She picked it up and felt her heart hammer in her chest. She hadn't realized how much she missed Chase, how she'd been living on pins and needles since he called.

"What are you doing here?" Serena asked, standing up and smoothing her skirt.

Chase walked over and kissed her softly on the lips. His white collared shirt was wrinkled and he smelled of Tommy Hilfiger cologne and mint shampoo.

"I remembered I have a date," Zoe interrupted. "I'll see you two later."

Serena pulled away, her cheeks turning pink. "This is Chase."

"I gathered that," Zoe replied, grinning. "He's even better than his photo."

"It's a pleasure to meet you." Chase held out his hand. "Please don't leave because of me."

"I'm meeting a Swiss polo player at La Plage for cocktails," Zoe said as she walked to the door. "He's going to help with my badminton swing."

"Wait," Serena called, following Zoe into the hallway. "You don't have a date with a polo player; you promised you wouldn't lie."

"I promised I wouldn't lie to you." Zoe waited at the elevator. "Your incredibly hot fiancé flew five thousand miles to see you."

"But we were going to sit at the lobby bar and wait for your father." Serena frowned.

"I don't think my father is in any hurry to stop working on his tan," Zoe replied. "We'll do it tomorrow. I have a sudden desire to go dancing at Bâoli. It doesn't get going until midnight, so don't expect me back until late."

Serena watched Zoe step into the elevator and grinned. "I was wrong, you are a true friend."

"I didn't think Chelsea's expense account stretched to this," Chase said, standing in the middle of the living room gazing at the crystal vase of birds of paradise, the sideboard set with gold-inlaid china, the silk curtains pulled back to reveal the twinkling harbor.

"The Carlton-InterContinental messed up my reservation." Serena stood beside him. "I met Zoe and she offered to share her suite. It's a bit over the top."

"It's spectacular." Chase stepped onto the balcony and leaned against the railing. "It suits you, you've never looked so beautiful."

"I thought you were at a retreat at the Bohemian Grove." Serena joined him and gazed down at the Boulevard de la Croisette.

"I stood under a massive redwood tree listening to men wearing suspenders discuss torts." Chase breathed in the sweet night air. "And decided I'd much rather be in the South of France with you."

"That was a smart decision," Serena said, grinning. She wanted to ask Chase about the letter and her father but the night was so beautiful—the sky filled with stars, the yachts bobbing in the harbor, the sound of laughter floating up from the avenue—she didn't want to break the spell.

Chase put his arm around Serena and pulled her close. He

kissed her slowly, running one hand down her back. He reached under her dress and stroked her breasts, gently massaging her nipples.

"You must be starving," Serena said when he released her. "Room service changes the buffet every few hours. There's smoked salmon and cracked lobster and sliced honeydew melon."

Chase pulled the gold pin out of her hair. "I haven't slept in twenty-four hours and I ate rubber chicken and soggy French fries on the plane. I'd love to lie down on a king-size bed with crisp sheets and down-filled pillows."

"No shower?" Serena asked. Her body felt like it was lit by an electric charge, and a warmth spread between her legs.

"Why would I want to shower," Chase whispered, "when we're going to get sweaty."

Chase stood at the side of the bed. He unzipped his slacks and draped them over a chair. He walked over to Serena and unsnapped her bra, his fingers warm and familiar against her skin.

He turned her around, tugging at her panties. He thrust his fingers inside her so quickly she felt like she had stopped at the top of a roller coaster. His fingers worked faster, deeper, pushing her to the edge. She felt the sense of wonderment and then the gasp of exquisite release. He kept his fingers inside her, not satisfied until she gripped his shoulders, waiting for the waves to subside.

"Come here," he whispered, leading her to the bed. She lay on the cotton sheets and watched him peel off his socks. She pulled him on top of her, pressing her fingers into his back. She drew him inside her and arched her body against his chest. He came first, falling against her breasts and burying his head in the pillow until she wrapped her legs tightly around him and let her body split open.

Serena opened her eyes and glanced at the bedside clock. It was almost two A.M. and suddenly she was thirsty. She gingerly moved Chase's arm and slipped on a robe, padding into the living room. She poured a glass of Fiji water and nibbled a chocolate-covered strawberry, feeling deliciously wanton and decadent.

She picked up Chase's blazer to carry it to the bedroom and his plane ticket fell out of the pocket. She reached down and gazed at it absently. Suddenly she saw the date and froze.

Why had Chase said he just arrived when his ticket said his plane landed in Nice two days ago? She put the ticket in his pocket and walked back into the bedroom. She climbed into bed next to Chase and tried to stop her heart from racing.

Serena woke and saw Chase's side of the bed was empty. She remembered him tucking her against his chest, his skin glistening with sweat. Then she flashed on the date on the plane ticket and a pit formed in her stomach.

She jumped out of bed and slipped on a yellow knit dress. She brushed her hair and tied it with a yellow ribbon. She walked into the living room and found Chase eating a triple-decker turkey club sandwich.

"I was telling Chase you should go to Australia on your honeymoon." Zoe sat at the round glass dining-room table, nibbling a piece of toast with honey.

"I woke up starving." Chase wiped his mouth with a napkin. "Zoe was kind enough to order lunch."

"I love watching Americans eat," Zoe said, grinning. "They put bacon on bread and smother everything with mayonnaise."

"We could go to the Marché Forville," Serena suggested. "Buy baguettes and pâté and have a picnic in La Croix des Gardes."

"I'm going to the Casino Croisette," Zoe announced. "I have an appointment with a roulette wheel."

"I'll shower and let you ladies plan the day," Chase said as he stood up, kissing Serena on the cheek.

Serena waited until she heard the shower running and turned to Zoe.

"Why are you gambling in the middle of the day?"

"Because I overheard my father ask the valet for directions to the casino." Zoe stabbed her toast with a knife. "He's never gambled in his life. I can't let him go there with her, she'll make him bet his Rolex or his wedding ring."

"I'd go with you but I need to talk to Chase." Serena twisted her ponytail. She wished she'd told Zoe that Chase insisted they not mention the engagement. She didn't want her new friend to think she was abandoning her.

"I'll be fine, I can practice my French." Zoe smiled, grabbing her wide straw hat and dark sunglasses. "What trouble can I get into at a casino in broad daylight?"

Serena and Chase walked along the harbor, passing rows of sleek chrome-and-glass yachts. Neither of them had said a word since they walked out the revolving glass doors and down the Boulevard de la Croisette. Chase curled his fingers around hers, but there was something about his expression that made Serena uneasy.

"My father would love it here," Serena said finally. "Can you imagine him parking the *Serena* among these yachts?"

"The *Serena* would fit in perfectly," Chase said, then hesitated, drawing an old color photo out of his blazer pocket. He wore tan slacks with a white collared shirt and beige loafers. "I have a photo, it came with the letter."

Serena studied the photo of a man and a woman standing in front of a whitewashed villa. The man had blond hair and green eyes and carried a baby girl in a pink ruffled dress. The woman had long glossy brown hair and wore a white miniskirt and gold hoop earrings. She held hands with a little boy in a powder-blue suit.

"Who are these people?"

"The woman's name is Jeanne Delon, and the children are Giles and Veronique." Chase dug his hands into his pockets. "The man is your father."

"This could be anywhere, my mother might have taken the photo."

Chase turned the picture over and read the faded cursive. "In the garden of Villa Mer, Antibes, 1988."

"That's almost thirty years ago!" Serena exclaimed. "My father wasn't in France then."

"You were two years old," Chase said quietly.

"What are you saying?" Serena's hands shook and her eyes were burning.

"Veronique Delon was born at St. Mathilde's hospital in Nice on February fourth, 1988. Your father's name is on the birth certificate."

"I know my father better than anyone in the world!" Serena sobbed. "He couldn't keep a secret for twenty-eight years."

"Cory's editor is running the story. I made Cory promise to wait until I returned from France."

Serena looked at Chase. "You discovered the birth certificate? You went digging in my father's past without telling me?"

"I had to find out if there was proof," Chase replied.

"Does my father know?"

"I called him yesterday." Chase nodded. "Your father and mother are staying in Napa for a few weeks. A friend lent them his villa, it's very secluded."

Serena pictured her mother in her flawless Chanel suits and Jacqueline Kennedy sunglasses. She saw her slip off her pumps and massage her toes after a grueling day on the campaign trail. She saw her take Charles's hand and lead him upstairs to the bedroom. She heard the sounds of Miles Davis and muffled laughter under the bedroom door.

"I love you more than anything; you are the most breathtaking woman I've ever met," Chase said slowly. "But we need to break off the engagement."

Serena froze. "What are you talking about?"

"Other boys dream of being professional baseball players or astronauts; I've always wanted to be a politician. It's why I went to Georgetown and why I put in these insane hours at the law firm. If we stay together, my career will be over before it starts."

"This will blow over." Serena's teeth chattered and she felt naked in her thin cotton dress.

"Say I lose this election and run again," Chase continued. "My opponent will bring it up in every race from here to the White House. Your father was a two-term U.S. senator with a perfect record, he's fodder for the press."

"You said we were more important than anything, the rest was gravy."

"You wouldn't love me if I quit politics, I'd be half the man I am. The press would keep throwing your father's past in our faces, we'd be miserable. We're young, we can find other people. Trust me, I'm doing what's best for both of us."

"How dare you." Serena felt the rage boil up inside her. "Why didn't you tell me before we made love, before you ate Zoe's triple-decker turkey club sandwich?"

"I wanted to tell you when I arrived." Chase scuffed his shoe on the wood. "But you were so beautiful in that turquoise dress, I missed you so much."

"Get your things out of my suite." Serena pulled the diamond-and-emerald ring from her finger. "Give this to the girl with the perfect pedigree."

"You don't know what I've gone through," Chase begged. "I have to do this, I don't have another choice."

"Leave me alone!" Serena's voice shook. She shoved the ring into his hand and ran down the dock.

"Serena, wait!" Chase called.

Serena turned and saw his face contorted in pain. He strode toward her and for a moment she thought he was going to put his arms around her and say he had panicked, he couldn't live without her.

"It's your grandmother's diamond." Chase pressed the ring into her palm. "You should keep it."

Serena heard the ring clatter on the wood as she ran down the dock. She didn't stop until she had reached the water. Then she collapsed on the planks and buried her face in her hands.

Serena sat hunched for hours, listening to the hum of boat engines. Her throat was dry and every time she pictured Chase, his hands jammed in his pockets, his blond hair touching his collar, her eyes filled with tears.

She heard footsteps, and a man wearing tan shorts and a beige cotton shirt sat on the dock beside her. He had long legs and wore brown leather sandals.

"You dropped this." He held out the glittering engagement ring.

Serena looked up and frowned. It was the man who had returned her phone on the beach and her purse at the outdoor market.

"Why are you following me?" she demanded, turning and gazing at the bay. Suddenly everything seemed too bright: the sparkling ocean, the shiny yachts, the white seagulls skimming the waves. "You can have it, I don't want it."

"It's your grandmother's ring, you should keep it."

"Were you eavesdropping on a private conversation?" Serena seethed.

"I was working on my boat." The man pointed to a small white catamaran. He held out his hand. "My name is Nick."

Serena pictured Chase handing back the ring. She remembered him saying he was doing what was best for them, and warm tears rolled down her cheeks.

"It will get better," Nick said gently. "Time is a great healer."

"You don't know anything," Serena snapped. "You live in a place where palm trees grow in the middle of the avenue and the air smells of Cuban cigars and expensive perfume."

"You think people don't get sick and die because they can dip their toes in the Mediterranean?" Nick raised his eyebrow. "You think heartbreak only exists in cities where people work in skyscrapers?"

"I didn't mean that." Serena gulped. She gazed at the outdoor cafés and elegant boutiques and remembered arriving in Cannes full of excitement and anticipation.

"I didn't hear why you gave your fiancé his ring back," Nick said slowly. His eyes were clear blue and he had sharp, angular cheekbones. "But I bet he wakes up in the morning and wishes he'd found a way to keep it on your finger."

"I have to go," Serena said, and she jumped up.

She ran down the dock to the Boulevard de la Croisette. She walked past the dazzling windows of Chanel and Hermès. She marched through the gold-and-white lobby of the Carlton-InterContinental. It was only when she was in the Cary Grant Suite, drinking a straight shot of vodka, that she realized that the man on the dock still held her grandmother's diamond ring.

chapter nine

Serena sat on the gold velvet sofa nursing her second shot of vodka. She tried to swallow it but the alcohol made her stomach burn. She set it on the glass side table and closed her eyes, letting her misery cover her like a blanket.

She considered ordering room service and watching *Casablanca* or *An Affair to Remember*. But she pictured her office with its narrow view of the Bay Bridge. She saw Chelsea perched on her desk saying she thought Serena valued her career.

Serena walked to the bedroom closet and selected a navy linen dress and a pair of beige pumps. She applied an extra coat of mascara and twisted her hair in a knot. Then she grabbed her notepad and walked down the hall to the Sophia Loren Suite.

"Serena, come in," Yvette said as she opened the door. She wore a black A-line dress and carried a bouquet of pink and red tulips.

"The hotel does a wonderful job with flowers, but it's so satisfying to create one's own arrangement." Yvette walked over to a crystal vase on the cherry sideboard. "I bought these at the market in Rue d'Antibes, they smell heavenly."

"They're lovely," Serena replied, suddenly wishing she'd stayed in her suite. She pictured all the bouquets Chase had sent her—white roses for her birthday, yellow tulips for her promotion, giant sunflowers because he thought they would brighten her desk.

"It's so hot, would you like a lemonade or a glass of iced tea?" Yvette stuck the final bloom in the vase and set it on the dining-room table.

"I'm fine." Serena gulped, trying to stop the throbbing in her forehead. She sat on a peach upholstered chair and flipped to a fresh page in her notepad.

"There's something different about you," Yvette mused, looking at Serena carefully. "You're not wearing that stunning diamond ring."

Serena gazed at her naked finger and instinctively covered it with her other hand. "I hate to wear it to the beach, it gets covered with suntan lotion and sand."

Yvette started to say something and then she flicked a piece of lint from her dress. "Shall we begin? I have so much to tell you."

"Bertrand arrived every day at lunchtime," Yvette began. "He brought roast beef sandwiches and fruit tarts and bags of sweets for the children. Sometimes he brought great bunches of flowers—roses and lilies and daisies—I always gave them to Françoise to take home so Henri wouldn't see them on the weekends. . . ." Yvette gazed at the crystal vase of tulips and her eyes clouded over.

"I'm finished." Yvette put the manuscript on the antique desk.

It was late afternoon and sprinklers played on the lawn outside the floor-to-ceiling window. Françoise had taken the children to Antibes for ice cream and the house was quiet.

"Did you notice these villas smell like rotted wood?" Bertrand asked, sitting in a worn leather chair. He wore khaki pants and a white T-shirt and smoked an extralong cigarette. "The brochures describe them as 'romantic' and 'timeless' and American movie stars rent them for a fucking fortune. But if you're not careful you could be lying in bed and the ceiling might fall on top of you."

"Will you take the manuscript to your editor?" Yvette asked.

"I'll mail it to Edouard at Hachette. He sends it on to Random House in London and Knopf in New York." Bertrand shrugged, grinding the cigarette into an ashtray.

"You trust the French postal system?" Yvette raised an eyebrow.

"If I go to Paris, Edouard will force me to have lunch with bookstore owners and reviewers." Bertrand frowned. "I'll have to eat escargot and drink red wine and listen to them moan about French culture."

"That doesn't sound bad," Yvette said, smiling.

"How am I supposed to write about misery and passion if I'm eating on fine china and sitting on a Louis Seize chair?"

Yvette glanced at the manuscript, bound with a blue ribbon. "I have to go to a dress fitting, I'll take it."

"Does Henri know you go to Paris alone?" Bertrand asked.

"I'm not a prisoner here, I do whatever I want."

Bertrand picked up the manuscript and placed it in Yvette's arms. "In that case, it's all yours. I will give you Edouard's address."

"Are you sure you don't want to read it?" Yvette asked.

"Why would I read it"—Bertrand's dark eyes danced—"when I have complete faith in my translator?"

Yvette pulled out her compact as the train rolled into the Gare du Nord. During the train ride she had reread the manuscript, her stomach becoming a mass of butterflies. She even purchased a pack of cigarettes, hoping to calm her nerves. But she only smoked half a cigarette before she started choking and stubbed it out.

She painted her mouth with red lipstick and brushed her hair until it was a shiny black cap. She wore a red crepe Yves Saint Laurent dress from his latest collection. She paired it with a soft suede purse and patent leather pumps.

Yvette took a taxi to Saint-Germain-des-Prés and entered the brick building. The lobby was carpeted in a green shag rug and the walls were lined with framed book jackets. Yvette saw a photo of Bertrand in his early twenties: his shiny black hair was thick, his stomach was flat, and his eyes seemed to be lit by a fire.

"You must be Yvette." A thin man wearing a dark blue suit appeared from an inner office. "My secretary told me you were here."

Yvette followed him down a hallway to an office with large windows and a polished wood floor. There was a wide cherry desk and floor-to-ceiling bookshelves crammed with books.

"Trust Bertrand to hire a translator who's a beautiful woman," Edouard said, motioning for Yvette to sit down.

Yvette's skin bristled. "I was a journalist before I got married, and I have read all Bertrand's books."

"Bertrand's last book sold more copies in a year than all my other titles combined." Edouard shrugged. "You are not alone."

Yvette stared at Edouard's beaklike nose and gold Cartier watch, and her courage escaped her. She gave him the manuscript as if she were handing over a newborn baby.

"Do you mind if I wait while you read the first chapter?"

"You want me to read it now?" Edouard raised his eyebrow.

Yvette pulled herself up to her full height and tried to stop the nauseated feeling. "Yes, I do."

Edouard sat down and untied the blue ribbon. He set the manuscript on the desk and quickly turned the pages. Yvette glanced at the clock and picked up a copy of *Le Monde*. She read *Paris Match* and *Hello!*, glancing up and studying Edouard's expression. Finally he set the manuscript aside and looked at Yvette.

"It's terrible, isn't it," Yvette blurted out.

"It is true to the manuscript." Edouard sighed, rubbing his forehead.

Yvette let out a deep breath. All the doubts that had been forming over the last month bubbled to the surface. She had transcribed page after page, looking for Bertrand's brilliance. But the plot was too simple, the characters weren't likable, the dialogue was stilted.

"I typed out fifteen pages of notes." Edouard slumped in his chair. "Bertrand returned them with a letter saying I could write the fucking novel, and he'd eat duck *à l'orange* at Tour d'Argent. Two weeks later he sent me a second draft; the only thing he'd changed is he added an *e* to his protagonist's name."

"I thought it was me," Yvette said. "I thought I ruined his story."

"The public won't care, they'll read anything with his photo on the back cover." Edouard frowned. "But the reviewers will skewer him; it will be a bloodbath."

Yvette pictured Bertrand standing in the middle of the garden, protecting her from the storm. She remembered him stripped naked for his photo, exposing himself to the world. She saw him eating ham sandwiches and chocolate cake like a greedy child.

"When does this go to print?" Yvette asked.

"We go to press in August," Edouard replied. "The American and UK editions follow in October."

"Give it to me." Yvette pointed to the manuscript. "I'll have it back to you in two weeks."

"What are you going to do?" Edouard asked, tying the pages with the blue ribbon.

Yvette stood up and clutched the manuscript to her chest. "I'm going to make it a masterpiece."

Yvette stepped out at the Gare d'Antibes and saw Bertrand waiting on the pavement. He wore a white straw hat and clutched a bunch of daisies.

"What are you doing here?" Yvette asked.

"I bribed Françoise into telling me when your train arrived," Bertrand said, and took her arm. "It's almost dark, a beautiful woman shouldn't walk along the streets alone."

"Juan-les-Pins is a resort town, it's perfectly safe." Yvette raised her eyebrow.

"We'll get something to eat on the way," Bertrand said, ignoring her. "I've been working on the new novel all day, I'm starving."

"I ate a sandwich on the train. I should get back to Pierre and Camille."

Bertrand pressed his fingers into her arm. "Two pieces of white bread and a wilted lettuce leaf isn't a meal. We'll have a proper British tea."

They sat in a booth in a teashop on the main street of Juan-les-Pins. The table was covered by a checkered tablecloth and set with blue-and-white ceramic plates. There was a pot of English break-fast tea, a jug of cream, and a plate of warm scones.

"The British don't know fuck about literature, but no one makes better clotted cream," said Bertrand, slathering jam on a peach scone. "How was Edouard?"

"He looked just as I imagined." Yvette smiled, nibbling a digestive biscuit. "Serious and thin."

"Did he make a pass at you?" Bertrand asked.

Yvette burst out laughing. "He read the manuscript and I sat and waited."

Bertrand put his cup down so quickly tea spilled onto the saucer. "He read it while you were sitting there? What did he say?"

Yvette fingered her purse, with the manuscript hidden inside it. She added a spoonful of honey to her tea and stirred it with a silver spoon. She took a sip and looked at Bertrand. "He absolutely loved it."

chapter ten

Serena sat on an ivory love seat and stared blankly at the view. After she left Yvette she deflated like a punctured balloon. She kept expecting Chase to walk through the door or call her cell phone. But she knew that once he made up his mind, he was adamant about following through.

She thought about the things she wanted to ask him: How old was the little boy in the photo? Where were Giles and Veronique now? Was her father going to contact them? She could call Chase, but that would only make the pain last longer. Finally she picked up her phone and dialed her parents' home number.

"Margaret, it's Serena," she said when the housekeeper answered. "Is my father home?"

"Mr. and Mrs. Woods are away," Margaret replied.

"Could you give me their phone number?" Serena grabbed a notepad and pen.

"They didn't leave a forwarding number."

"They must have left a number for emergencies." Serena jumped up and paced around the room.

"I'm sorry, Mr. Woods said they would call for messages."

Serena closed her eyes and wished she were standing in her parents' living room. She pictured the brocade sofas, the lush gardens, the glorious views of the bay. She wanted to smell her mother's perfume and touch her father's magazines and newspapers.

"Tell my father—" Serena stopped. She didn't know what to tell her father: that she was so angry she never wanted to talk to him, that she couldn't eat or think or sleep.

"What would you like to tell him?" Margaret prompted.

"Tell him to call me," Serena said finally, and hung up the phone.

Serena walked outside and leaned against the railing. It was late afternoon and the harbor was alive with activity. Serena saw fishing boats and sailboats with brightly colored sails. She gazed down at her naked ring finger. Then she walked inside, grabbed her purse, and ran down to the beach.

"Excuse me." Serena stood on the dock in front of a small white catamaran.

A man with dark curly hair and blue eyes appeared from the cabin. He saw Serena and his face broke into a smile. "I hoped you'd come back."

"I'd feel terrible if I lost my grandmother's diamond," Serena said, blushing.

"It's a beautiful ring." Nick took it out of his pocket. "Your fiancé had excellent taste."

Serena winced as if she'd been slapped. She slipped the ring in her purse and hurried back along the dock.

"Serena, wait," Nick called after her.

"How do you know my name?" Serena asked, turning around.

Nick ran down the dock to catch up with her. He wore khaki

shorts and a blue cotton shirt and his arms were muscled and tan. "It's inscribed inside."

"You read the inscription?" Serena choked the words out.

"I was hoping I could return it to you," Nick explained. "Keeping someone else's engagement ring is bad luck."

"Well, now I have it," Serena retorted. She bit her lip and softened. "Thank you for finding it."

"I was about to have dinner," Nick said. "Will you join me?"

Serena bristled. "I don't even know you."

"We'll go to Le Maurice, the fish soup is famous." Nick studied her carefully. "If you don't like my company, at least you'll get a solid meal."

Serena twisted her ponytail, trying to remember when she last ate. She wanted to go back to the suite and curl up on the velvet sofa. But she pictured being alone, her thoughts spinning between Chase and her father, and felt a tightness in her chest.

"Okay," Serena said, and nodded.

"I'll introduce you to Maurice; he catches the fish himself. He'll give you the catch of the day."

Le Maurice was perched at the top of a narrow street in the old town. The restaurant had wide windows and a dazzling view of the bay. Fishing nets hung from the ceiling and round tables were set with shiny silverware and sparkling wineglasses.

"Maurice's wife is very meticulous," Nick said, and grinned, putting his linen napkin in his lap. "If she finds a spot on a wineglass she whisks it away and gets you a new one."

An older woman wearing a gray dress approached the table. She carried a basket of breadsticks and a pot of churned butter. She kissed Nick on both cheeks, chattering in rapid French.

"I hope you don't mind me ordering for both of us," Nick said when the woman disappeared to the kitchen. "I've been coming here since I was a child. Isabel used to put extra whipped cream on my berries to fatten me up."

"Your French is perfect, but you speak English without an accent," Serena mused.

"I was born and raised on the Côte d'Azur but sent to boarding school in America," Nick told her as he smeared butter on a breadstick. "My mother wanted me to go to university and become a doctor or an engineer.

"I discovered sailing on the Long Island Sound," Nick continued. "From the moment I tied my first square knot, I was obsessed. I barely passed calculus and physics, but I was the captain of the sailing team."

"Where did you go to university?" Serena asked.

"I didn't." Nick shook his head. "I raced professionally all over the world: South Africa, Australia, the Bahamas. I could sail anything: dinghies, catamarans, keelboats. I competed with the Artemis team for the 2013 America's Cup."

Serena remembered the summer of races in San Francisco, the giant boats flying under the Golden Gate Bridge. The whole city buzzed with excitement and her father spent every moment on the bay.

"The America's Cup was a year ago," Serena said. "Where are you racing now?"

The waitress delivered steaming bowls of fish soup with hunks of sourdough bread.

"I quit last year," Nick said slowly. His eyes were dark and his forehead knotted together. "Sailing is seventy percent skill and thirty percent luck. You need to know when your luck runs out and it's time to walk away."

Nick ate large spoonfuls of soup and looked at Serena. The darkness seemed to have passed and his mouth curled in a smile.

"Are you an actress, should I recognize your face from the movies?"

"I'm a features editor at *Vogue*," Serena replied. "I am doing a story on the former editor of French *Vogue*, Yvette Renault. She's elegant and fascinating and when she talks I never want her to stop."

"You're lucky; being passionate about your work is the best thing in life."

Serena pictured the sixteenth floor of the Transamerica building, the walls lined with glossy *Vogue* covers. She remembered leaving work on Friday afternoons, her Coach bag filled with tear sheets.

She saw Chase pick her up in his silver Fiat and drive to First Crush or Zuni Café. She pictured him drumming his fingers on the steering wheel and explaining the latest polls. She remembered him squeezing her hand and saying, "We won't stop until we reach Pennsylvania Avenue."

"Please excuse me," Serena murmured, dropping her spoon and pushing back her chair.

She rushed out of the restaurant and strode down the hill. She stopped at the bottom and heard Nick calling her name. She kept walking until his voice was swallowed up by the click of her heels on the pavement.

chapter eleven

Serena entered the Cary Grant Suite and saw Zoe sitting on the sofa, eating a bowl of round red cherries.

"It's impossible to stick to my diet when room service keeps replenishing the sideboard." Zoe passed Serena the bowl. "It's like visiting Disneyland without going on all the rides."

Serena shook her head. "I'm not hungry."

"You look like you've been running with the bulls." Zoe eyed Serena's flushed cheeks and messy hair. "Where's Chase?"

Serena sank onto a love seat. "He left."

"I thought I'd find him ravishing you on the sofa like in a Thomas Hardy novel," Zoe replied. "When is he coming back?"

Serena twisted her ponytail, trying to keep her voice steady. "Chase broke off the engagement."

"Chase worships you! He's like one of those biplanes writing 'I love you' in the sky in white curly letters."

Serena stared at the ceramic vase of white roses. If she told Zoe the truth she would have to admit there was no chance the birth certificate was false, the photo was perfectly innocent. No matter how hard she tried, she couldn't imagine her father with a raven-haired mistress and two illegitimate children.

"It's not the right time," Serena said slowly. "Chase needs to concentrate on his career."

"That's absurd! You two were stuck together with Elmer's Glue. You said you were good for his career."

Serena bit her lip and gazed at Zoe. She hated to lie to her friend.

"Maybe later," she said, and shrugged. "Now he has to concentrate on getting elected."

"What are you going to do?" Zoe asked.

"I'm going to give Chelsea the best pieces she's ever read." Serena's eyes flickered. "I'm going to work until I have a corner office with signed prints by Julian Schnabel and 180-degree views of the bay."

"At least one of us has a plan." Zoe slumped against the cushions. "I followed my father all afternoon. I'm in real trouble—he went ring shopping."

"He's married to your mother," Serena said, frowning.

"That's not stopping him from acting like a lovesick teenager." Zoe ate a macadamia nut from a silver bowl. "They were in the casino for hours, playing roulette and drinking kir royales. I've never seen my father drink a mixed drink; he only drinks aged scotch. Then they walked to Van Cleef and Arpels."

"What were they doing there?" Serena raised her eyebrow.

"I stood in a corner like a Russian spy," Zoe sighed. "I heard my father say to the salesgirl he was coming back alone tonight. What if he buys her Elizabeth Taylor's diamond or a priceless jade necklace?"

"I don't think even Malcolm Gladding would buy million-dollar jewelry on a whim," Serena said, smiling.

"I don't want him to buy her a charm of the Eiffel Tower." Zoe's eyes filled with tears. "I want him to go home."

Serena stood up and walked to the balcony. She glanced at the half-moon in the sky and the stars dancing over the harbor.

"Put on something dark and inconspicuous," Serena said. "We're going out."

"Are we going to commit a crime?" Zoe asked. "I heard the food is terrible in French prisons."

"You'll see," Serena replied grimly, walking to her bedroom closet and flicking through a row of black dresses.

"I feel like we're auditioning for *Men in Black Four,*" Zoe said as they strolled down the Boulevard de la Croisette.

They both wore black wool dresses and black pumps. Zoe wore a wide-brimmed black hat and Serena wore her hair in an elegant chignon.

"If I approach my father in public, it will be on the front page of every newspaper." Zoe frowned. "My mother will read it while she eats her Weet-Bix."

"Trust me," Serena said, opening the heavy glass doors of Van Cleef and Arpels, breathing the scent of Chanel No. 5 and lemon polish.

The cherry floors were covered by a white wool rug and the walls were lacquered turquoise. Pinpoint lighting illuminated glass cases filled with emerald teardrop earrings, diamond chokers, and heart-shaped watches.

Serena saw a butterfly with diamond-and-sapphire wings and a whale with a jeweled spout. She stopped in front of a case of engagement rings—emerald-cut diamonds and round solitaires and flawless five-carat stones. She gazed at her naked ring finger and flinched.

"Are you all right?" Zoe whispered.

"I'm fine," Serena said, and smoothed her hair. She took a deep breath and approached a salesgirl wearing a black sheath dress and gold sandals.

Serena whispered to the salesgirl and pointed to Zoe. The salesgirl arched her eyebrows and shook her head. She whispered again and the salesgirl pursed her lips and nodded.

"You wait in here," Serena said to Zoe, leading her into a padded room in the back of the store.

"Please don't do anything I'd regret," Zoe moaned. "I can't afford another six years of therapy."

Serena walked to the front of the store and stood behind a glass case. She heard the tinkle of the doorbell and saw an older man wearing a red blazer and pleated slacks. He had salt-and-pepper hair and wore a gold Rolex on his wrist.

"Can I help you?" Serena asked in French.

"Only if you speak English," the man replied, smiling. "My French makes me sound like a schoolboy."

"We have some unique pieces; this clip is part of the Jules Verne Collection." Serena pointed to a turtle with an emerald shell surrounded by pavé diamonds.

"I want something romantic," the man mused. "Something that says thank you."

The man walked slowly between the glass cases, stopping to peer at a gold ballerina with ruby ballet slippers.

"We keep some of our more important pieces in the back," Serena said. "I'm happy to show you if you follow me."

Serena opened the padded door, her heart pounding. She turned the lights on low and saw Zoe perched on a velvet stool.

"Zoe!" The man's eyes flashed. "What are you doing here?"

"That's my question." Zoe's mouth trembled and her eyes filled with tears. "The last time I saw you you were kissing Mother good-bye in the lobby at Claridge's."

"I can explain." Malcolm sank onto a stool. His cheeks were pale and his tall frame seemed to shrink.

"It's perfectly self-explanatory," Zoe snapped. "Fashion magnate gets knighted and trades in his loyal wife of almost thirty years for a younger model."

"It's not what it seems." Malcolm sighed, rubbing his forehead.

"I've been following you for days—Jet Skiing in the harbor, day trips to Sainte-Marguerite, dancing at Charly's. You're a poster boy for midlife crisis of the rich. Throw in a red Maserati and a floor-length mink for your trollop and you're all set."

Malcolm looked at Zoe and his eyes were like dark wells. "Zoe, I have so much to tell you, we need to go somewhere and talk."

"We can talk here," Zoe retorted. "Serena is my friend."

"Actually, I have an appointment." Serena squeezed Zoe's hand. "I'll see you at the suite."

Serena walked back into the showroom and thanked the salesgirl. She opened the thick glass doors and stepped onto the sidewalk. She pictured Zoe's watery hazel eyes and her father's hunched shoulders. She hurried down the boulevard, hoping she'd done the right thing.

Serena sipped a cup of black coffee and nibbled a piece of dry toast. After she left Van Cleef and Arpels she finally gave in to her grief.

She left a message with Yvette saying she had the flu and crawled under crisp Egyptian cotton sheets.

She pictured eating with Chase at Betelnut, hot air ballooning in Napa, driving along the Pacific Coast Highway. She saw him in his black tuxedo picking her up for the symphony, and wearing his Georgetown T-shirt and carrying a bag of Trader Joe's groceries.

In the morning her head was hot and her skin felt like sandpaper. She wished her mother were there to brew a pot of cinnamon tea. Then she pictured her mother and father: entertaining at their Georgetown town house, reading together in their Presidio Heights mansion, and her heart cracked. She took two aspirin and sank against the down pillows.

Now it was early afternoon and she had finally showered and dressed. She made a plate of cream cheese crepes, fresh sliced mangos, and apricots. But the crepe was too filling and the fruit was too sweet.

Her phone rang and she pressed accept.

"Serena," her mother's voice said. "I'm glad I caught you."

"Where are you?" Serena demanded.

"We're in Napa at a friend's house. It's lovely, with a swimming pool and a vegetable garden."

"Is it true?" Serena's voice shook. "Does Daddy have another family?"

"I'm glad you're away," Kate replied firmly. "This will blow over, but journalists can be nasty. They were hiding in the rosebushes; I had to scare them away with a gardening rake."

"I don't believe it." Serena gulped. "Daddy would never do that."

"This isn't the time to talk about it. I shouldn't use the telephone, one doesn't know who is listening," Kate continued.

"We have to talk about it!" Serena exclaimed, her eyes filling with tears. "I can't think about anything else."

"I have to go. Serena"—Kate's voice grew soft—"your father loves you very much."

Serena hung up and sank onto the ivory sofa. She felt like a little girl on her first day of kindergarten. She wanted to call her mother back and hear her say everything would be all right, it was all a big mistake. She poured another cup of French press coffee and drank it in one gulp.

"Serena!" Yvette answered the door of the Sophia Loren Suite. She wore a black linen dress and her reading glasses were perched on her nose. "I was reading a letter from my son. I'm lucky, my children are excellent letter writers."

Serena entered the living room and sat at the bamboo dining-room table. She wore a white linen sundress and her hair was scooped into a high ponytail and tied with a white ribbon.

"Pierre and Camille live in Paris," Yvette continued. "Lilly married a British doctor and lives in London. I pop over the Channel any chance I get."

"Lilly?" Serena frowned. "I thought you had two children."

"Lilly was a delightful surprise," Yvette mused, folding her glasses and sitting on a pink silk chair. "Let me tell you about the next time I saw Bertrand. It was almost two years after the summer in Antibes. Henri and I were at a cocktail party in Paris and he walked up to me and said I looked fat. . . ."

"I see the life of luxury has finally made you fat," Bertrand said. He wore white slacks and a white button-down shirt and a striped bow tie. He carried a martini in one hand and an unlit cigarette in the other.

"You're wearing a tie," Yvette exclaimed. She hadn't seen Bertrand in many months and her stomach did little flips. She avoided his eyes and glanced at the floor. "And shoes with socks!"

"Edouard dresses me up like a performing bear," Bertrand scoffed. "He even monitors how many cigarettes I smoke. He doesn't want his bestselling author keeling over from a heart attack wearing a singlet and no socks."

"I'm not fat," Yvette said, and blushed, putting her hand on her gently rounded stomach. "I'm pregnant."

Bertrand raised his eyebrow. "I assumed that phase of the marriage would be over by now."

"You're wrong," Yvette snapped. "My husband is a handsome man."

"All wealthy men are handsome." Bertrand shrugged. "Do you know why men kill themselves to get rich? It's not for the big houses or fancy clothes; we're animals, we could live in a cave and walk around naked. It's so we can fuck beautiful women."

Yvette glanced at the men in perfectly cut suits and Gucci loafers. The women had long glossy manes and wore fake eyelashes and bright eye shadow.

"Why are you here?" Yvette asked, watching Henri talk to a woman wearing a red Valentino dress and gold stilettos.

"*Pays de Cocagne* was a bestseller on three continents." Bertrand drained his martini. "*The New York Times* said, 'Roland has touched a nerve that will make grown men cry and women shiver.' Edouard is looking for a seven-figure advance, but they don't give millions to recluses."

"I saw the reviews," Yvette said, nodding.

For weeks after she turned the manuscript in to Edouard she

lived in fear, panicked by what she'd done. She expected Bertrand to appear in a rage demanding to know why she rewrote his novel.

But when the summer ended and she returned to Paris, she grew busy with dinner parties and society functions. She barely thought about the novel until she saw it on the shelves.

She ran down to Shakespeare & Company and bought copies in English. She closeted herself in her bedroom and read it from cover to cover. Then she put it aside and waited for the reviews to come in.

The praise was glorious: *The New York Times,* the London *Observer, Le Monde* said it was a modern classic. Yvette expected Bertrand to call or write a letter and thank her. She even considered stopping by Edouard's office, but she was terrified she would be discovered.

Finally she became pregnant and put it out of her mind. Only, sometimes in the first trimester she had wild dreams: Bertrand demanding she return the original manuscript, Bertrand announcing on television that Yvette was the author, Bertrand knocking on the door of her apartment in the sixteenth arrondissement and smothering her in passionate kisses.

"I have a proposition for you," Bertrand said as he reached into his pocket and brought out a lighter.

"We are leaving for Antibes on Friday."

"Even better," Bertrand said. He lit his cigarette. "I rented a villa in Juan-les-Pins for the summer."

"I'm having a baby in October." Yvette inhaled the menthol scent. "I'll be very busy."

"Knitting booties and folding blankets?" Bertrand moved closer, his arm brushing her shoulder. "Even pregnant women need to stimulate their brain."

"It's none of your business," Yvette replied, feeling her face flush.

"I promise it won't be anything strenuous." Bertrand exhaled a trail of cigarette smoke. "You can work lying on a chaise lounge by the swimming pool."

Yvette had been in the villa for a week when she heard a knock on the door.

"How did you find me?" Yvette asked. She was beginning to show and wore a cotton maternity dress and silver sandals. Her black hair reached her shoulders and was held back with a ceramic clip.

"I bribed my maid, she knows everything." Bertrand put his hat on the end table and strode into the two-story living room. The floors were covered in white shag carpeting and the walls were sheets of glass. There was a mirrored bar and a billiard table.

"Henri's making more money than I thought." Bertrand whistled, glancing at the crystal chandeliers, the large abstract paintings, the white grand piano.

"I'm baking a soufflé," Yvette said, and bristled. "I don't have time to talk."

"You in the kitchen! I've never seen you eat more than a slice of torte." Bertrand burst out laughing. "Tell your au pair to cook, I want you to translate my new manuscript."

"I can't." Yvette shook her head. "I have to prepare for the baby."

"This isn't the Middle Ages," Bertrand said, tapping a cigarette out of his gold cigarette case. "Women lead countries and win wars while they're pregnant."

"I have to prepare the nursery and teach Camille to ride a bicycle and help Pierre with his swimming." Yvette stood up and walked to the window.

"That would overtire you," Bertrand said as he followed her. "My idea is much better. You will work in a comfortable chair with your feet up and I will feed you chocolate parfait."

Yvette turned to Bertrand and could feel his mouth close to hers. She wanted to kiss him so badly it was a physical pain. If she refused his offer she might never see him again, if she said yes she would exist in a state of exquisite torture.

"Will you do it?" Bertrand asked.

Yvette walked to the end table. She handed Bertrand his hat and opened the front door.

"Yes, I'll do it."

chapter twelve

Serena brushed her hair into a knot and secured it with a gold clip. She slipped on a yellow Lilly Pulitzer sundress and gold Manolo sandals. She put her phone and a tube of lipgloss in her purse and walked down the hallway to the elevator.

After her meeting with Yvette, Serena sat at the glass dining-room table, her fingers flying over the keyboard, feeling the familiar rush of excitement. She wrote for hours, flipping between her notes, drinking frosty lemonade, and nibbling green grapes.

When she finally closed her laptop the sun had edged behind the Île Sainte-Marguerite and sunbathers had packed up their beach bags. Serena stood on the balcony inhaling the warm salty air and decided she wanted to hike to the castle or eat scallops at a restaurant by the harbor.

She entered the lobby and saw a familiar figure sitting at the bar. He wore a collared shirt and tan slacks with a leather belt. His dark hair curled around his ears and he wore scuffed boat shoes.

"What are you doing here?" Serena asked.

"I knew you were staying at the Carlton-InterContinental," Nick said, jumping up. "I figured you'd walk through the lobby eventually."

"I need to apologize for leaving you at dinner," Serena replied, suddenly flustered. "I wasn't feeling well."

"You brought me good luck." Nick's eyes sparkled. "I didn't want to eat by myself, so I walked back to my boat. I ran into an American director who said it was exactly what he was looking for. He bought it on the spot, for twice what I paid."

"I'm pleased." Serena nodded, crossing the marble floor.

The lobby was filled with couples drinking predinner cocktails. Serena heard a harpist playing and the sound of ice clinking in cocktail shakers.

"I need to do something nice for you," Nick said, following her to the entrance.

"You found my phone and saved my diamond," Serena replied, walking through the revolving glass doors onto the sidewalk.

"Sailors are very superstitious," Nick said as he put his hand on her wrist. "This is the first good luck I've had in a long time; I don't want to jinx it."

Serena stopped and turned. His hands were rough and he had long fingers with fingernails like half-moons.

"I was about to explore." Serena sighed. "You can show me your favorite places."

Nick's face broke into a smile. He walked to a blue Renault parked at the corner and opened the passenger-side door.

"Where are we going?" Serena hesitated.

Nick walked to the driver's side and squeezed his tall frame into the narrow seat. "Monte Carlo."

———

"Monaco is the second-smallest country in the world after the Vatican," Nick said, his hand poised on the stick shift. "The Grimaldis have ruled the principality since 1297. Prince Rainier and Princess Grace were married in the Cathedral of Monaco in 1956; now they are buried in the crypt."

Serena thought fleetingly of Grace Kelly with her white-blond hair and blue eyes and perfect pedigree. She remembered her parents watching *To Catch a Thief* and herself dreaming of zipping along the Côte d'Azur next to Cary Grant in a white tuxedo. She pictured the honeymoon she and Chase had discussed: Capri, the Amalfi Coast, Monaco.

Nick drove into Monte Carlo and parked next to the harbor. Serena and Nick strolled past the Hôtel de Paris with its creamy white stonework and gray turrets. They climbed the marble steps of the Casino de Monte-Carlo and peeked at the ornate gaming salons.

"The buildings are like birthday cakes," Serena said as she gaped. Even the boutiques and cafés were housed in elegant structures with black tile roofs and gold awnings.

"Follow me," Nick said as he took Serena's hand. "We have to catch the sunset."

They climbed a narrow path that wound above the town. Serena was about to say she needed to catch her breath when she saw a huge stone structure built into the cliff.

"Where are we?" Serena asked.

"You told me to bring you to my favorite place." Nick smiled. "The Oceanographic Museum was built in 1910 by Prince Albert the First. It was run by Jacques Cousteau from 1955 to 1988."

Serena turned to look at the view. The sky was turning purple and the roofs seemed to be dusted with diamonds. White villas perched on cliffs and yachts lined the harbor like strands of a pearl necklace.

"Let's go inside. Wait until you see the shark exhibit."

Serena and Nick walked through a vast room with skeletons of whales hanging from the ceiling. They visited the aquarium, filled with luminous tropical fish and Neptune Grass. Serena saw clown fish and inky moray eels and dazzling sea anemone.

"It's more beautiful than the showroom at Van Cleef and Arpels," Serena murmured, watching a tiger shark glide between pink and white coral.

"I used to come here all the time. When I was eight I decided I wanted to be a submarine captain." Nick grinned, his eyes glinting like a schoolboy. "Once I discovered sailing, I knew I'd rather be cruising over the water."

They walked out into the crisp night air and ran all the way to the harbor. Serena gazed at the yachts lit up like Christmas trees and felt almost happy. Monaco was a jewelry box, filled with wonderful and exotic objects.

"You're smiling," Nick said, glancing at her curiously.

"I thought you were going to drag me into the casino," Serena replied. "Instead I got a history and science lesson."

"I don't gamble; the house always wins," Nick said meditatively. "My father used to teach me random things. He died when I was fourteen. He was in New York on a business trip; his limousine had a flat tire on the way to the airport and he missed his flight. He caught the next one and it exploded over the Atlantic."

"I'm sorry," Serena said quietly.

"He ran out of luck," Nick said. He stuffed his hands in his pockets and walked along the dock. "Luck is everything. If you're not in the right place at the right time you might miss the person you're supposed to spend the rest of your life with."

Serena flashed on meeting Chase in her father's study and fixing his shirt. She remembered the way he plotted their future like a game of Snakes and Ladders. She saw him slide the diamond ring on her finger and whisper they were a great team.

She walked along the harbor to Nick's car. She opened the door and slid into the passenger seat. She leaned against the upholstery and let the tears roll down her cheeks.

Serena walked into the Cary Grant Suite and saw Zoe perched on a love seat, eating a bowl of sorbet. Her hair was softly layered and she wore a red silk dress and taupe pumps.

"Where have you been?" Serena asked. "You changed your hair, it looks gorgeous."

"I feel like Wendy in *Peter Pan*," Zoe said, touching her neck. "But the stylist at Sergio Valente said it brought out my eyes."

"You went to Rome?" Serena raised her eyebrow.

"Rome and Milan and Paris." Zoe licked her spoon. "My father introduced me to Tom Ford and Valentino. When Valentino kissed my hand I almost died—I promised I'd never wear any color besides red."

"Red suits you," Serena said, smiling. "Where's your father's girlfriend?"

"Don't call her that." Zoe shuddered. "She's back in Yugoslavia or Transylvania or wherever *Sports Illustrated* models are from."

"The last time I saw you you looked like you wanted to drive a stake through your father's heart."

"We walked along the beach and he told me everything," Zoe replied. "Then we went back to the Carlton and told Verushka to pack her Louis Vuitton cosmetics case and catch the first flight. After she left he ordered a private jet and we flew to Milan. We had a private tour of Valentino's offices and dinner on Lake Como. Fresh scampi and risotto at an eighteenth-century palazzo in Bellagio. The next morning we flew to Paris and met Tom Ford."

"Chelsea would be jealous." Serena eyed the dress boxes piled on the dining-room table. "Does this mean you're going back to Sydney?"

Zoe's eyes darkened and she put down her spoon.

"My father loves my mother, but it's more complicated than I thought. He's afraid she won't forgive him."

"What are you going to do?" Serena asked.

"You're going to help him," Zoe said. She stood up and smoothed her hair. "He's waiting for us at the Carlton Restaurant."

"How am I going to help him?"

"You'll see." Zoe grabbed her purse. "He'll tell you the whole story."

"Zoe told me so much about you," Malcolm said as he stood up and extended his hand. "It's not often I meet a woman masquerading as a salesgirl at an exclusive jewelry store."

Serena blushed and sat at the round table next to the window. She glanced at her white linen dress and flat sandals and felt underdressed. Other women wore shimmering cocktail dresses with four-inch stilettos and heavy gold jewelry.

Serena remembered the drive back from Monaco, Nick driving too quickly and Serena hunched against the door wishing she hadn't come. She was still too raw, her eyes too quick to fill with tears, to spend time with someone else.

Malcolm put on his reading glasses and consulted his menu. He had salt-and-pepper hair and clear gray eyes and finely lined skin. He wore a light wool blazer and beige slacks and leather shoes with tassels.

"I'm glad you did." Malcolm nodded at Serena. "I hate to see Zoe hurt, it's never what I wanted."

Malcolm ordered lobster rigatoni and chateaubriand and plates of risotto. Serena tasted the fresh tomato and mozzarella salad and realized she was starving. Nick had wanted to stop at a bistro, but Serena pleaded a terrible headache and ran straight up to her room.

"After the kidnapping, my wife wouldn't talk to me," Malcolm began. "She ate her meals in her room and we were only together on public occasions. I slept in the study, spent all my time at the office, made sure I was home at night to be with Zoe."

Malcolm drank the full-bodied red wine and looked out at the harbor. "Laura doubled security on Zoe and wouldn't let her out of her sight. Every time the wind shifted she thought someone was in the house or following her on the street. After four months she said she couldn't take it anymore. She wanted us to move to her parents' sheep farm."

Malcolm paused and cut thick slices of steak. "I was miserable, but I didn't think the answer was to hide at a sheep station in the middle of nowhere. What kind of life would that be for Zoe? She was almost a teenager! She needed to be distracted by boys and clothes and makeup—not listen to the rain on a tin roof and have her schoolwork delivered by a biplane.

"Laura argued that the safety of my family wasn't as important to me as the latest shipment of swimwear and my winter collection." Malcolm's gray eyes flickered. "She was wrong; I'd already made enough money for several lifetimes. I didn't want the kidnappers to win, I didn't want them to take our beloved mansion on Sydney Harbor, Sundays at Doyle's in Watson's Bay, picnics in the Botanic Gardens.

"We saw a therapist and finally agreed to send Zoe to boarding school in Surrey. Laura had cousins there and the name Gladding wasn't anything special.

"I thought things would get back to normal. Laura loved to entertain; we used to have fabulous dinner parties: the prime minister rubbing elbows with Judy Davis and Hugh Jackman and Baz Luhrmann." Malcolm speared a roasted potato with his fork.

"She attended her charity functions and society events. She even moved back into our bedroom so the maids wouldn't gossip, but she wouldn't let me touch her." Malcolm looked at Serena and his eyes were like cut glass. "I hadn't kissed a woman in thirteen years.

"I'm fifty-two years old; I want to travel, see a sunset in Africa, explore the grottoes in Capri. And I want to do it with someone, I want to touch a woman's hair, smell her perfume."

"How am I going to help?" Serena asked. She looked at her plate and realized she hadn't touched the crunchy Mediterranean sea bass or the medley of spring vegetables.

"I bought Laura a beach house in Palm Bay, her own racehorse, a wardrobe of couture clothes, and it didn't change anything," Malcolm said, and pushed aside his plate. "I want to publicly admit that I was wrong, that I should have sold the business, moved to Yarra Yarra or wherever the hell she wanted. I want you to write a feature story for *Vogue* telling her how much I love her."

"You want to apologize to your wife in front of millions of readers?" Serena repeated.

"Laura doesn't wear her emotions, she never has a hair out of place or a creased hemline," Malcolm continued earnestly. "I want to show her I'm willing to bleed in public."

"Do you think it will work?" Serena asked doubtfully.

"I'm too old to learn new tricks," Malcolm replied, leaning back in his chair. "I want my wife back and I don't know how else to get her."

Serena sat in the living room of the Cary Grant Suite watching Zoe unwrap Godiva chocolates.

"I don't even like caramel," Zoe said with a sigh, tossing the wrapper on the coffee table. "I wish room service would stop leaving them on my pillow."

"Do you think your mother will forgive him?" Serena asked.

"It was my idea," Zoe said, unwrapping another chocolate. "I can't bear to think of my parents divorced. My mother might be as stiff as a poker, but I know deep down she loves him."

Serena thought of her own parents, always showering each other with attention. Her father would surprise Kate with a bottle of Dior, tickets to a new play, one perfect orchid. Every morning Kate made Charles two poached eggs just the way he liked them. She made sure his coffee was waiting and his newspapers were neatly folded.

Serena tried to imagine her father sitting at another breakfast table with a dark-haired woman and two small children. She pictured him cutting their toast, pouring their milk, reading them stories.

"I want my parents to be happy." Zoe interrupted her thoughts, tossing the chocolates in the garbage. "And I can't imagine having a stepmother who'd make a perfect villain in a James Bond movie."

chapter thirteen

Serena gazed out the window at the glittering Mediterranean and felt a twinge of excitement. Attendants in crisp white shirts and shorts carried beach chairs and fluffy white towels. Serena watched fishermen push their boats out to sea and yacht captains polish the decks of their floating palaces.

She jumped out of bed, slipped on a cotton dress, tied her hair with a blue ribbon, and took her laptop into the living room. She poured a cup of creamy French roast coffee, cut a ripe peach, and sat down to work on Yvette's story.

Her phone rang and she picked it up.

"Please don't tell me you're sitting on the beach in a bikini," Chelsea's voice came over the line. "San Francisco has been socked in for days. I'm wearing cashmere and drinking hot tea."

"I'm not at the beach." Serena smiled, gazing at the white sand filled with chaise lounges and striped beach umbrellas. "But the weather is gorgeous."

"I knew I shouldn't have become editor in chief," Chelsea sighed. "I answer to bureaucrats in pin-striped suits while my features editor works on her suntan."

"Yvette's story is coming together," Serena said as she glanced at her laptop. "I think you'll be pleased."

"Harry Ames called me, he's worried about you."

"The publisher?" Serena asked.

She had only met Harry Ames once, at *Vogue*'s New York Christmas party at the Carlyle. He kept tapping his fingers on his glass of eggnog, and Serena felt he'd rather be talking to Donna Karan or Ashley Olsen or anyone besides an editorial assistant.

"Someone gave him a copy of the *Chronicle* and he read the story about your father."

Serena clutched the phone so tightly she thought it would break. "I haven't seen it."

"'Retired senator has kept a second family secret for thirty years, his wife and daughter are devastated,'" Chelsea continued.

Serena felt the room tip and sat quickly on an ivory silk armchair. She tried to answer but her throat closed up and her heart raced.

"I told Harry you're staying in a luxury suite at the Carlton-InterContinental sipping Moët and Chandon and eating foie gras." Chelsea paused. "He thought maybe I should send you home and assign someone else to Yvette."

Serena pictured Chelsea in her Hervé Léger dress, perched on the side of her desk. She remembered Chelsea saying if Serena didn't want to go to Cannes, she'd write someone else's name on the Air France ticket.

"I haven't had time to think about anything but Yvette," Serena replied brightly. "She's spilled some secrets that will shock you."

"They better knock the socks off the fashion world or Harry

Ames is going to serve me as lunch to the board of directors." Chelsea was quiet and Serena thought she'd hung up. "You're the best writer I have; don't let me think I've made a mistake."

Serena hung up and sank back against the satin cushions. She was desperate to read the article about Senator Charles Woods, but she didn't have time for self-pity. She had to see Yvette and then she had to sit at her computer and write the best story that ever crossed Chelsea's desk.

"Serena!" Yvette opened the door of the Sophia Loren Suite.

Yvette wore a red linen dress with a wide white hat. Her cheeks were dusted with blush and she wore thick mascara and red lipstick.

"I was visiting a friend," Yvette said as she took off her hat. "She's quite sick, I thought I'd dress up and take her to lunch. There's nothing like eating soufflé and watching the sailboats to lift one's spirits.

"We've been friends for years," Yvette continued, smoothing her hair. "Isn't it funny how much time we waste on men when our female friendships last a lifetime."

Serena took out her notepad and waited while Yvette poured a cup of vanilla tea.

"It's impossible to see that when we're young." Yvette curled up on a peach silk armchair. "We only know desire, the feeling that starts in your loins and makes everything else seem completely unimportant."

"I want you to go to a party with me," Bertrand announced, leaning against the fireplace mantel.

It was late afternoon and Yvette had been working for hours on Bertrand's manuscript. Her back ached and her stomach felt stretched like a balloon.

"What kind of party?" Yvette asked.

"A Hollywood producer is interested in *Pays de Cocagne*. Edouard is in New York and he doesn't trust me to go by myself," Bertrand replied, lighting a cigarette. "He's still angry that I refused to go on a book tour. I wrote the damn thing, do I have to recite it like a fucking parrot?"

"You want me to go to a cocktail party?" Yvette raised her eyebrow.

"Edouard does, he seems to like you," Bertrand said, then inhaled deeply. "Are you sure you didn't sleep with him?"

Yvette felt the baby kick against her cotton dress.

"I'll go." She nodded. "But you have to stop smoking, the smell is making me nauseated."

Yvette stood in front of the mirror in her dressing room, painting her lips with Lancôme lipstick. She told herself she was going to the party because Edouard asked her to, but she knew she wanted to stay close to Bertrand.

Some afternoons after he left she crept up to her bedroom and closed the curtains. She lay on the king-size bed and stroked herself, picturing Bertrand's dark eyes and cocky smile. She touched her nipples and moved her fingers against her wet mound until her body shuddered in long waves. Only when the baby kicked and she needed to go to the bathroom did she get up and splash cold water on her face.

———

"It's a shame your husband is missing the party," Bertrand said as they approached a white villa flanked by palm trees. "He hasn't spent much time in Antibes; is there trouble in paradise?"

Yvette bent down to adjust her heel. She wore a pale pink maternity dress and white leather sandals. Her dark hair curled around her neck and she wore small diamond studs.

"Henri is in London," Yvette said, bristling. "He's in the middle of an acquisition."

"I hear it's raining in London." Bertrand climbed the stone steps. "I hope he took his raincoat."

Yvette stood by the bar, sipping a Shirley Temple. The living room had an oak floor covered with Oriental rugs. Leather sofas were scattered around the room and two afghan hounds slept next to a glass coffee table.

"American women have no fashion sense," Bertrand observed. He wore white linen slacks and a white T-shirt. He held a scotch in one hand and a cigarette in the other.

Yvette gazed at the women in hot-pink miniskirts and platform shoes and wished she'd stayed at the villa. She'd never attended a party without Henri, and she felt suddenly shy and out of place.

Bertrand was swept away by a blond man in a navy silk suit and Yvette examined the array of fruits and cheeses.

"Your husband is very handsome," a female voice said. "I'm sure you'll have a beautiful baby."

Yvette looked up and saw a young woman with blue eyes and straight blond hair. She wore a turquoise miniskirt with a gold chain belt.

"He's not my husband." Yvette blushed.

"Everyone said the French were progressive," the girl said, filling a plate with crackers and duck pâté. "In Ohio you still get a ring before you make a baby."

"I am married but Bertrand is not my husband." Yvette flashed her wedding band. "He is a novelist, we are friends."

"That's the author everyone's talking about," the girl said, glancing at Bertrand curiously. "I imagined him younger, with thicker hair."

"Bertrand is a wonderful writer," Yvette said stiffly, filling a plate with wedges of Edam and slices of melon.

"He has quite the reputation," the girl replied, tossing her blond hair over her shoulder. "If he's not taken, I think I'll say hello."

Yvette watched the girl cross the room and touch Bertrand's arm. She saw Bertrand lean close, his shoulder brushing her breast. She saw the girl flutter long fake eyelashes and whisper in his ear. She saw him take her hand and lead her into the hallway.

Yvette dropped the plate on the side table. She clutched her stomach and ran to the bathroom. She stood in front of the beveled mirror, retching into the pink marble basin.

"You can't go to Paris," Bertrand fumed. "I'm on a fucking deadline. You have to finish translating the manuscript."

"And I'm having a baby." Yvette sat at her desk writing a list for Françoise. "My doctor insists I come in for an appointment."

"You had an appointment last week." Bertrand paced around the living room, clutching his straw hat. "It's not so hard to have a baby; you wait nine months and it pops out."

"Something about test results." Yvette kept her eyes on her notepad. "I'll return in a few days."

Yvette had woken up the morning after the party and knew she couldn't stay in Antibes. Being around Bertrand kept her body in a state of alert. Her blood pressure was raised and the pulsing between her legs was a mix of the most exquisite pleasure and sharpest pain.

She would write him a letter and say the doctor insisted she finish her pregnancy in Paris. He could mail the manuscript and she would complete it in her apartment. The children might be angry that their days at the beach were cut short, but when Henri returned from London he could take them paddle boating in the Bois de Boulogne.

Yvette slept during the train ride, her body filled with a wonderful sense of relief. The train pulled into the Gare du Nord and she gazed out the window, waiting for the conductor to open the doors.

She saw a man kissing a blond woman wearing a short white dress. She pictured kissing Bertrand in public, his smooth cheek touching hers, his hand reaching beneath her skirt.

The couple pulled apart and Yvette saw the man had short brown hair, blue eyes, and a dark suntan. She thrust her face against the glass and saw it was Henri. He wore a short-sleeved shirt and linen shorts as if he'd just returned from vacation.

Yvette's cheeks turned white and her skin felt like ice. She stayed in her seat until the conductor announced the train was leaving. She stood up shakily and descended onto the platform. She walked to the ticket counter and bought a ticket on the first train back to Nice.

chapter fourteen

Serena jogged down the promenade, breathing the scent of hyacinths and bougainvillea. She had woken early and sat at her computer, eagerly transcribing her notes. She didn't stop until the maids knocked on the door and replaced the platters of scrambled eggs and whole wheat toast with grilled vegetables and cold consommé.

She bent down to tie her shoelace and suddenly a camera flashed in her face. She stood up and saw a man with a black Nikon. He snapped another photo and raced down the dock, his camera bouncing against his thigh.

"What do you think you're doing?" Serena demanded, running after him.

She tripped on a plank and fell hard against the wood. She heard yelling and saw a tall man with wavy dark hair holding the camera over the water. The photographer shouted in French and the dark-haired man shoved the camera against his chest.

"Are you all right?" Nick bent down.

"He took my picture." Serena tried to sit up. Her hands were scraped and her knee was bleeding.

"It's not going to do him much good if I have the memory card." Nick grinned, opening his palm to display a small red card.

Serena tried to stand but her knee buckled and she sat quickly on the dock. Nick crouched down and examined her knee. He put her arms around his neck and gently scooped her up.

"Where are we going?" Serena asked.

"You don't want it to get infected," Nick replied, stepping onto the deck of a white catamaran.

Serena leaned against beige cushions while Nick disappeared into the cabin. Her head throbbed and her throat was dry.

"I've never seen paparazzi chase a journalist." Nick returned with a silver first-aid kit. He dabbed her knee with disinfectant and wrapped it in a gauze bandage.

"Don't tell me you're a doctor," Serena said as she winced.

"All sailors know first aid." Nick shrugged. "Are you sure you're not a famous movie star?"

Serena opened her mouth but no sound came out. Suddenly she wanted to go home so badly she couldn't breathe. She wanted to run along Crissy Field with Chase, join her parents for dinner at the Yacht Club, make love on her own cotton sheets.

"You're crying," Nick said, and handed her a handkerchief.

"I'm not." Serena wiped her eyes.

Nick crossed his arms and studied her carefully. He strode across the deck and brought up the anchor. He unfurled the sails, letting them catch in the breeze.

"What are you doing?" Serena asked.

Nick grinned, his blue eyes sparkling. "I'm taking you sailing."

"Are you always a knight in shining armor?" Serena asked, lifting her face to the sun.

They didn't talk until the boat was skimming across the waves, the shore becoming a distant blur. Serena forgot how wonderful it felt to fly across the water, the wind whipping her hair, the salty spray touching her cheeks.

"When I was a kid I found wounded birds and took them home to fix their wings."

"That must have made your mother happy." Serena smiled.

"She complained they carried diseases," Nick replied. "But she never sent them away until they could fly."

Nick tossed the anchor over the side. He disappeared into the cabin and returned with a tray of crackers and cheese and two bottles of sparkling soda.

"No Boy Scout cookies?" Serena asked.

"Are you going to tell me why that photographer was chasing you or do I have to turn you in to the French intelligence agency?"

Serena sipped a bottle of soda and slowly told Nick about growing up in San Francisco and Paris and Washington. She told him how her parents were like doubles partners in tennis, always watching each other's backs.

She told him about Chase and how he had his sights set on the White House. She described the planned engagement party: a twelve-piece band in a white tent on her parents' lawn. She told him about the article in the *San Francisco Chronicle* and Chase unearthing the birth certificate with her father's name on it.

"Your fiancé broke up with you because of an anonymous letter about something that happened almost thirty years ago," Nick said, frowning. He sat on the deck, his long legs spread in front of him, the sun glinting in his hair.

"Yes." Serena nodded.

"I was wrong; he's not going to wake up in the morning and think he made a mistake." Nick's forehead knotted together. "He's going to lie awake at night and realize he's the biggest fool."

Serena trailed her hand in the water as the sailboat eased into its berth. Nick jumped out and conversed with a blond man waiting on the dock. The man waved his arms and spoke in rapid French. Nick nodded and the two men shook hands.

"Who was that?" Serena asked.

"The owner of the catamaran," Nick replied.

"That's not your boat?" Serena raised her eyebrow.

"I'm thinking of buying it with the money I got from my sale," Nick said, grinning.

"The first-aid kit, the crackers and sodas?"

"All boats have first-aid kits and most are stocked with snacks." Nick took her arm as they reached the boulevard. "You looked like you needed to be on the water."

They crossed the boulevard and strolled to the Carlton-InterContinental. Serena stopped at the revolving glass doors and turned to Nick. "Thank you, I had a lovely time."

"I'm not going to let some paparazzi accost you in the lobby," Nick protested, gently propelling her through the doors. "I'm going to escort you to your suite."

They rode silently on the elevator and walked down the hallway to the Cary Grant Suite. Serena fumbled with her key, smelling Nick's scent of suntan lotion and sweat.

"Here." Nick reached into his pocket and brought out a piece of paper. "This is a bill for services rendered."

" 'Found one iPhone, retrieved one purse including wallet and passport, saved priceless diamond, scared away dangerous paparazzi,'" Serena read aloud. "You said I brought you good luck."

"That pays part of the bill," he mused. "I know how you can pay the other half."

Nick leaned down and kissed her slowly on the lips. He put his hand on the small of her back and pulled her close. He ran his hands through her hair, caressing her shoulders.

Serena kissed him back, her body suddenly hungry. She felt his chest against hers, the warmth of his breath, his strong hands on her back.

"I've paid my debt," she said, and pulled away.

"Hardly." Nick grinned. "That's the first of an installment plan."

"I thought we were friends!" Zoe exclaimed.

She wore a red cotton dress with a wide white belt and white sandals. She stormed around the living room, waving a newspaper in the air.

"Of course we're friends," Serena said as she entered the suite. Her heart was racing from Nick's kiss and she instinctively touched her mouth.

"You said friends tell each other everything," Zoe retorted. "I bought all the newspapers in the gift shop to see if there are any pictures of my father, and I found this." She tossed the newspaper on the glass coffee table.

Serena glanced at the *Chronicle* masthead. She scanned the photo of her father in a navy wool suit. She turned the page and saw her mother wearing a Carolina Herrera gown. There was a picture of Serena in her school uniform, and the one of Charles with the brunette and two young children.

"Is this why Chase broke up with you?" Zoe demanded.

"He was afraid the scandal would ruin his chance to be mayor." Serena twisted her ponytail. "Chase's career is very important to him, he's always dreamed of being a politician."

"Why didn't you tell me?" Zoe sank onto the gold silk sofa like a locomotive that had run out of steam.

"I kept expecting Chase to call and say the letter was a fraud."

"And after he came and slept on your Egyptian cotton sheets and you gave your ring back?"

"I never thought he'd end the engagement." Serena's eyes filled with tears. "He said we came first, the rest was gravy."

"What are you going to do now?" Zoe asked quietly, slipping off her sandals.

Serena poured a glass of iced tea and told Zoe about the photographer and Nick and his kiss.

"I shouldn't have kissed him," Serena moaned. Her throat was parched and the tea tasted cold and sweet. "I'm not ready for something new."

"I want a string of sexy boyfriends," Zoe said glumly. "Being in love is exhausting."

"Do you have someone in Sydney?" Serena asked.

"Ian; he's a geologist," Zoe said, and nodded. "We've known each other since the fifth grade. We're sort of engaged to be engaged but I told him we need to wait. I have to save my parents' marriage."

Zoe sifted through the newspapers and suddenly her eyes grew dark. She picked up the paper and quickly scanned the headline.

"Oh God, *The Sydney Morning Herald*." She handed it to Serena. "We're too late."

Serena gazed at the photo of Malcolm helping a luscious brunette into a speedboat. The woman wore a metallic bathing suit and four-inch stilettos and Malcolm wore a short-sleeved silk shirt and a broad straw hat.

"I thought no one had photos except *Paris Match*." Zoe walked over to the sideboard and ate a handful of raisins. "My mother is going to see this with her porridge and stewed apricots. She'll be at her solicitor's office by lunchtime."

"Your parents haven't slept together in thirteen years and they're still married," Serena said as she studied the paper. "She's not going to file for divorce over one grainy AP picture."

"My mother is like the dowager on *Downton Abbey*," Zoe fretted. "Appearances are everything."

"I'm meeting your father in an hour," Serena replied, consulting her watch. "I'm going to write a piece that will make her feel like Olivia Newton-John in *Grease*."

"My parents once dressed up as Olivia Newton-John and John Travolta for a costume party," Zoe mused.

Serena walked over to the sideboard and squeezed Zoe's hand. "Trust me, it'll work."

Zoe's eyes were bright and her lips trembled. "My father looked ridiculous in disco pants."

Serena entered the Carlton Bar and saw Malcolm sitting at a table next to the marble fireplace. He wore a red silk shirt and tan slacks and a gold Rolex on his wrist. His forehead was creased and he sipped a scotch without ice.

"Did you see it?" He stood up. He looked older than when Serena last saw him; his skin was gray and his eyes were dim. "*The Sydney Morning Herald*. They may as well have printed my obituary."

"It was a photo of two people stepping onto a boat," Serena

said as she sat on a blue crushed-velvet chair. "You could have been part of a tour."

"I never wanted to humiliate Laura." Malcolm sighed. "I was so stupid, I thought I could just fade into the sunset."

"That's hard to do when you're head of a fashion empire and one of the richest men in Australia," Serena said, grinning.

"Did Zoe tell you that?"

"I'm a journalist." Serena shrugged. "We're going to use that to our advantage. We're going to put your apology on the cover of *Vogue* and *Harper's Bazaar* and *W*."

"You're going to have to be a magician." Malcolm drained his glass and signaled to the waiter.

"Tell me how you and Laura met," Serena said as she opened her notepad. "Tell me the moment you fell in love with her, when you knew you'd do anything to win her."

"We were in a fashion design class at University of Sydney," Malcolm began. "I noticed her the first day but it took me two months to talk to her. I was a scholarship kid from Newcastle and she was the most elegant woman I'd ever seen: glossy brown hair, big hazel eyes. She wore a strand of pearls and white gloves to class.

"The professor assigned students to work in pairs and create an outfit from scratch. I rehearsed for days how I would ask her to be my partner: with a bouquet of roses, with a slice of pavlova from the university cafeteria. One day I saw her in the hall and I blurted it out.

"She said she didn't even know my name, and she wouldn't trust half her grade to a guy who wore rugby shirts and sneakers and needed a haircut.

"God, I remember the way she waltzed off like a princess,"

Malcolm said, slowly sipping his scotch. "I begged her friend to give me her measurements. I sold my stereo to buy the finest imported Thai silk; I stayed up nights sketching designs. When I was satisfied I scoured the garment district for the best seamstress. I pawned my watch to buy a pair of gold earrings and I delivered newspapers so I could afford a haircut.

"On the day of the presentation, I borrowed my buddy's navy suit and black leather shoes. I stood in front of the lecture hall, trying to see her face. She sat in the back; her skin was like alabaster under the lights. She wore a peach-colored dress and sheer stockings and white silk gloves.

"I unwrapped yards of tissue paper and revealed a dress the color of seashells. It had a heart-shaped bodice and a cinched waist and a full skirt. I paired it with a lace slip and ivory gloves with pearl clasps.

"I remember reciting the words I'd been practicing in front of the mirror: 'Some designers name their collections after movie stars; I call this the 'Laura' after the most beautiful woman I've ever met.'

"I was sweating so badly I wanted to bolt out of there." Malcolm frowned, running his fingers over his scotch glass. "But I knew I only had one chance. I put the dress in the box and gave it to her.

"She said if I was going to give her a gown, I better invite her somewhere to wear it. She had tickets to *Swan Lake* at the Sydney Opera House, and I was going to take her." Malcolm paused, his face spreading into a smile. "Then she told me I better wear socks.

"They say cricket is boring, but ballet takes the cake," Malcolm mused. "But when Laura sat next to me in the dark auditorium, when I smelled her perfume and touched her hair, I knew

I could do anything. I promised myself I'd give her everything she wanted—houses, cars, jewelry, her own damned box at the opera."

Serena waited for Malcolm to continue, but his eyes went dark, as if the film he was watching ended.

"Why did she tell you to wear socks?" Serena asked.

"I borrowed my buddy's suit but I forgot the socks." Malcolm laughed out loud. "The most important moment of my life and I forgot the bloody socks."

chapter fifteen

Serena slipped on her yellow Lilly Pulitzer dress and strapped on white leather sandals. She tied her ponytail with a yellow ribbon and coated her lips with lipgloss. She ate one quick bite of toast with strawberry jam and stepped into the hallway.

"Serena! I'm so happy to see you," Yvette said as she opened the door of the Sophia Loren Suite.

She wore red yoga pants and a black leotard and clutched a paperback book. "I hate insomnia, but reading can be such a gift. I make a pot of tea and curl up with a book and before I know it, it's morning."

"My father gets insomnia." Serena walked into the living room.

The turquoise curtains were pulled back and the bay shimmered like a sheet of glass. The sideboard was filled with platters of warm scones and berries and there was a pitcher of orange juice on the dining-room table.

"Have you read Anaïs Nin? She was born in Paris and was rumored to be Henry Miller's mistress." Yvette curled up on the cream silk love seat, tucking her feet under her. "Her diaries are quite . . . .vivid. It's strange how a staid married woman can meet a man and her whole life can change. . . ."

Yvette smelled Bertrand before she saw him. She entered the ice cream shop in Juan-les-Pins and inhaled his scent of cigarettes and sweat. She turned around and saw him sitting at a table, eating a banana split.

"How do you do it?" he asked. "You have to share your secret with other women."

"What are you talking about?" Yvette blushed, seeing other shoppers glance at her curiously.

Bertrand walked to the counter and gazed at her floral cotton dress with its wide leather belt.

"You keep having babies, but you don't get fat."

Yvette clutched the pint of vanilla ice cream, trying to stop her heart from racing. She hadn't seen Bertrand in two years, since the day she took the train to Paris. When she'd returned to Antibes she discovered Bertrand had left for Hollywood.

She finished translating the manuscript, feeling bold and reckless. She knew Bertrand wouldn't read it and Edouard would say nothing, so she gave Bertrand's dour heroine her own unrequited passion. She turned it in to Edouard like an addict giving up her opium. Then she waited to have her baby, hoping the early-morning feedings, the delirium of sleepless nights, would cure her.

Bertrand sent two dozen lilies when she gave birth with a note written on ivory notepaper. She read the words aloud: "'You have done what I never could, created something perfect.'" Then she folded it carefully and slipped it into her lingerie drawer.

Yvette entered the vast kitchen and put the ice cream in the freezer. She poured a glass of lemonade and sat at the long oak table. Only when Françoise walked in asking about the steaks did she realize she had left their dinner at the ice cream shop.

Yvette saw Bertrand again a week later at the Marché Provençal. It was late morning and she had come with Lilly to buy cut flowers and fresh fruit. Bertrand was standing at a stall, talking to the woman who sold peaches. He walked over to Yvette and inhaled the lilacs and dahlias.

"So this is the infant who made your stomach into a watermelon?"

Yvette glanced at Lilly, whose mouth was full of raspberries. She had dark curly hair and blue eyes like Henri. She wore a pink cotton sundress and sandals with white bows.

"Lilly is almost two," Yvette replied. "You weren't here last summer."

"I was in Hollywood." Bertrand took out his gold cigarette case. "The movie business moves like a glacier. But they give you a mansion and fill it with fine wines and thick steaks and beautiful women. By the time they've ruined your book so you recognize nothing but your name in the credits, you're in a stupor."

Yvette took Lilly's hand and moved to the next booth. The sun was hot and she felt like she might faint. "Are you working on a new book?"

"I'm resting on my laurels." Bertrand blew smoke rings. He wore khakis and a white T-shirt and a straw hat with a black ribbon. "*La Femme* spent sixteen weeks on the *New York Times* bestseller list. I should thank you for the translation, but I had to endure receptions in Los Angeles and New York. I even got invited to the White House. The men in Washington dress like penguins and the women resemble horses."

"I'm glad you won't need my help this summer," Yvette said as she inspected an orange. "I'm busy with the children; Lilly runs me around in circles."

"Is Henri in London, buying banks?"

Yvette's cheeks flushed and she bit her lip. "Henri is in Paris; he will be here on the weekend."

By the time Yvette walked home from the market, she had a terrible headache. Her skin was hot and her throat was dry. She turned Lilly over to Françoise and went to bed.

She stayed in her room for a week, reading D. H. Lawrence and Nabokov. She pictured Bertrand's slick black hair and dark eyes and her body quivered. She wanted him to caress her cheeks, to kiss her lips, to crush her against his chest.

On the eighth day she woke up and her skin felt cool. She glanced in the mirror and her hair was glossy and her eyes sparkled. She slipped on a cotton dress and sandals and ran downstairs to breakfast.

She didn't think about Bertrand until an invitation arrived to a party at Peter Fonda's villa. She knew Henri would be angry if she declined. She put the invitation in Henri's pile of mail and forgot it.

The night of the party, Henri called to say he was delayed in Paris. Yvette glanced at the black Chanel strapless gown and red Ferragamos in her closet. She gazed at the diamond bracelet Henri had given her for their anniversary. She slipped on the dress, teased her hair, sprayed her wrists with Dior, and ran down the oak staircase.

She entered the villa and smelled a mix of perfume and cigarettes. The living room had high ceilings and cherry floors covered by floral rugs. A large abstract painting took up one wall and potted palm trees framed the window.

Yvette saw Bertrand standing next to the painting. He wore tan slacks and a white cotton shirt with a leather belt. He held a martini and talked to a blonde with full breasts and a wide pink mouth.

"Suzy and I were discussing the painting," Bertrand said when Yvette approached. "Suzy admires the artist's use of colors, but I think it's bullshit. Any child can splash paint on a canvas."

Yvette drained her glass of cognac. "I need to talk to you."

Bertrand raised his eyebrow and bowed to the blonde. "Excuse us, we have business to attend to. Where is Henri?" he asked when they stepped outside into the courtyard.

"He was delayed in Paris." Yvette suddenly wanted to slip off her heels and run home. She turned to Bertrand and took a deep breath. "I want you to kiss me."

"What would Henri say?"

"Henri has a mistress on the Rue de la Paix," Yvette replied. "He sees her every Tuesday and Thursday and five days a week during the summer."

Bertrand lit a cigarette and blew slow smoke rings. He paced around the courtyard and turned to Yvette.

"Am I like a pinup in your bedroom—and now that your husband has a woman it is all right to kiss me?" Bertrand stubbed out the cigarette and marched back into the villa. "If you want revenge, go find a pool boy."

The next morning Yvette was reading in the breakfast room when she heard someone knocking. She walked to the entry and opened the front door.

"Wait for me tomorrow at the end of the lane," Bertrand told her as he swept inside. His dark hair was slicked back and his cheeks glistened with aftershave. "I will meet you at one o'clock."

Yvette changed three times before she selected an outfit. She settled on a black lace dress with a wide black hat and black-and-white Gucci pumps. She waited until Françoise took the children to the beach, Lilly bouncing along in her wagon. Then she hurried down the gravel path to the corner.

"You look like you're going to a fucking garden party," Bertrand said, jumping out of a green MG and opening Yvette's door.

"You have a car," Yvette said as she slid onto the leather upholstery.

"Everyone in Hollywood drives." Bertrand shrugged. "It suits me. When I'm bored at a party I can make a quick getaway."

"Where are we going?" Yvette asked.

"If you talk, I'll change my mind. Be quiet until we get there."

"The Hôtel du Cap-Eden-Roc?" Yvette raised her eyebrow as Bertrand pulled down the long drive flanked by stately trees.

The hotel rose before them like a castle. It had a gray slate roof and French windows with thick silk drapes. The courtyard was filled with Bentleys and Rolls-Royces and brightly colored convertibles.

"The staff are good at keeping secrets," Bertrand said, and gave his key to the valet. "Did you know Prince Edward and Wallis

Simpson stayed here after their marriage? Chagall comes every August and never signs a check. He doesn't want anyone to sell his autograph."

Yvette followed Bertrand into the lobby with its Persian rugs and Louis XVI chairs. Glittering chandeliers hung from the ceiling and side tables were filled with crystal vases and Lladró statues.

"You can afford this?" Yvette whispered as they approached the gold-inlaid reception desk.

"I could wallpaper the walls with hundred-dollar bills," Bertrand hissed. "In Hollywood they pay you like a gigolo."

They entered a suite with glorious views of the bay. The living room had creamy marble floors and burgundy sofas. The bedroom had a four-poster bed covered with a red silk bedspread and a signed Monet on the wall.

"Oh," Yvette murmured, admiring the bedside table piled with books, the Tiffany lamps, the silk robes laid out on the bed.

"Did you think I would seduce you in some cold courtyard or against the sink in a guest bathroom?" Bertrand placed his hat on the antique desk. His eyes softened and he took Yvette's hand. "I've waited ten years; it is time to teach you about love."

Bertrand placed the Louis XVI desk chair in the middle of the room. "Take off your clothes and sit down."

"Why?" Yvette asked.

"How can I know how to touch you if I don't study every inch of your body?"

He started by sucking her toes, glancing up to watch her face. When he saw that she was on the brink, he stood up and inserted his fingers inside her. She cried out but he put his other hand in her mouth, letting her bite down on his thumb. She felt the long waves fold in on themselves, carrying her body like a current.

He laid her on the bed and she expected him to enter her quickly, like Henri, breathing hard and collapsing against her chest. But he took his time, touching her, kissing her, stroking her breasts. He made her hold his long, hard length, and then finally he lowered himself inside her and came with the force of a typhoon.

Yvette got up and drank a glass of water. She stood by the window, picturing Lilly's round cheeks, Pierre's serious blue eyes, Camille's pout. Then she crossed the room and lay on the bed. She closed her eyes and put Bertrand's hand between her legs.

chapter sixteen

Serena sat at the wicker table on the balcony, gazing down at the Boulevard de la Croisette. It was early morning and couples clutched folded newspapers and bags of croissants. Serena watched salesgirls unlock boutiques and fill the windows with metallic sandals and silk scarves.

Zoe and Malcolm had gone on a day trip to Monaco and asked Serena to join them. But she wanted to finish the piece on Malcolm and send it to Chelsea. She pictured Chelsea's expression when she received an exclusive feature about Malcolm Gladding and felt a small surge of excitement.

The hotel phone rang and she ran inside to answer it. Every few hours she'd been checking her phone or calling reception, asking if she had any messages. She kept waiting to hear her father's voice, hoping that somehow he could explain the photo.

"Getting hold of you is harder than storming the Bastille; reception wouldn't connect me until I told them I was your doctor."

"You're not my doctor," Serena laughed, twisting her ponytail.

"I did provide necessary first aid," Nick said. "I was wondering if you'd like to have dinner."

"I'm working on two deadlines." Serena shook her head.

"You have to eat," Nick persisted. "We'll go to Vesuvio and order caprese salad and salmon pizza."

"It's tempting," Serena said, smiling. "But room service fills the sideboard with grilled trout and seafood linguine."

"Then I'll join you," Nick replied. "I have to check on your knee; a good doctor makes a follow-up visit."

Serena hesitated, flashing on Nick's wavy dark hair and blue eyes. "Come at eight P.M., I've gotten used to eating late."

Serena stood in front of her closet, choosing between a teal Lanvin dress and a strapless silk Pucci. She finally selected the Lanvin and paired it with diamond earrings and low white sandals. She slipped her hair into a knot and added lipgloss and mascara.

"You're recovering nicely," Nick said when she opened the door.

He wore a yellow sports shirt and navy slacks and carried a pink cake box.

"The chocolate torte is from Isabel," Nick said as he handed it to her. "She said no one makes better torte than Maurice, not even the pastry chefs at the Carlton-InterContinental."

Serena put the cake box on the sideboard and filled two plates with truffle risotto, grilled sole, and Japanese eggplant. She placed them on the linen tablecloth and added a basket of warm baguettes and a pot of herb butter.

Nick sat across from her and they talked about Serena's years in Paris and Nick's boarding school in Connecticut.

"After school I'd stroll down the Rue Saint-Honoré and memorize the clothes in Celine and Dior and Yves Saint Laurent," Serena said, scooping up sautéed baby peas. "I wrote articles for the school newspaper on the latest collections."

"I built a boat and raced it in the school regatta," Nick told her as he sipped a glass of French chardonnay. "I came in last but I was hooked for life. I've sailed through the Strait of Gibraltar and around Cape Horn and across the Tasman Sea."

"Why did you stop racing?" Serena asked.

"The catamarans built for the America's Cup are as tall as skyscrapers with sails as wide as tennis courts. It was the second week of practice and we capsized in the San Francisco Bay. I was under for six minutes." Nick gripped his wineglass. "When I reached the surface, I thought my lungs would explode. My teammate was trapped for ten minutes."

"What happened?"

Nick's eyes dimmed and his jaw clenched. "He died."

"So you quit?" Serena raised her eyebrow.

"I kept going out with the team, but I knew my luck had run out. Other sailors can smell fear; I had to quit to protect them."

"What are you going to do now?" Serena asked.

"Fix up boats, sell them, and buy bigger boats," Nick said, and shrugged. "Maybe I'll lead tours around the harbor."

"Don't you miss racing?" Serena ate the last bite of risotto.

"Sometimes you lose the thing that is most important to you," Nick said slowly, putting his fork on his plate. "But something new comes along that's better than you could have imagined."

Nick poured two glasses of cognac and they stepped onto the balcony. Serena gazed at the yachts blinking in the harbor and felt a warm glow, like a candle trying to ignite.

"It's so beautiful." She smiled. "It's like being inside a jewelry case."

"When I sailed at night, I'd look up at the sky and think it was studded with diamonds," Nick murmured.

He put his arm around her waist and pulled her toward him. He kissed her on the mouth, putting one hand under her chin.

Serena tasted chocolate and wine and butter. She smelled musk aftershave and shampoo. She felt his hand move toward her breasts. His fingers brushed the sheer fabric over her nipples and suddenly she froze.

She pictured Chase's blond hair and yellow Georgetown T-shirt. She remembered how he knew exactly where to touch her. She saw his slow smile when her body reached and shuddered.

Serena pushed Nick away and walked inside. She sat huddled on the sofa as if she'd survived a storm.

"This isn't the right time," Serena said when Nick followed her.

Nick looked at her as if he was about to say something. He walked to the sideboard and cut two slices of chocolate torte. He handed Serena a plate and grinned.

"It's always time for cake."

Serena woke up and slipped on a navy jumpsuit. She brushed her hair into a ponytail and tied it with a white ribbon.

"Whoever said grapefruit tastes better with sugar is mistaken," Zoe said when Serena entered the living room.

Zoe sat at the glass dining-room table, stabbing a grapefruit with a spoon. She wore a white linen dress and Gucci flats. "Room service left the most delicious chocolate torte; I ruined my diet for a week."

"Nick came for dinner, he brought the cake."

"Nick had dinner in the suite?" Zoe raised her eyebrow.

"He's bright and warm and funny," Serena told Zoe as she poured a cup of coffee. "But then he kissed me and all I could see was Chase. It was like playing spin the bottle and ending up with the wrong guy in the closet."

"He doesn't have to run for mayor and wear a Brioni suit to be the right guy," Zoe said. She pushed away the grapefruit.

"I don't have time for men!" Serena exclaimed. "I have to save your parents' marriage and finish Yvette's memoir so Chelsea doesn't put me on the next flight to San Francisco."

"Yesterday we saw the Prince's Palace and the Museum of Napoleonic Souvenirs and ate crepes at Café de Paris." Zoe sighed. "Today my father wants to visit the medieval fortress at Saint-Paul de Vence and the flower market in Nice. He's like a race car zooming around a track. He can't stay still and he's terrified of being alone."

"At least you know where your father is," Serena said, adding cream and sugar. "I haven't heard from my parents in days. I keep expecting my father to call and say it was all a mistake."

"We're the ones who are supposed to be falling in love with the wrong men and making our parents frantic," Zoe said as she tore apart an almond croissant.

"Maybe we're part of the wrong generation." Serena sipped her coffee. "We should have been young in the sixties."

"I could never be as thin as Twiggy." Zoe shook her head. "And the hairstyles were awful."

Serena closed her laptop and dialed Chelsea's number.

"Thank God you called," Chelsea's voice came on the line. "Givenchy is threatening to pull their ad unless they see some copy."

"I haven't finished Yvette's piece yet," Serena replied. "Remember when you said to keep my eye out for Malcolm Gladding? How would you like an exclusive?"

"An exclusive what?" Chelsea asked. "The inside scoop on his winter collection isn't going to sell full-page ads."

"An apology to his wife for not listening to her after their daughter's kidnapping, for running around Cannes with another woman," Serena continued.

"Sir Malcolm Gladding admitting he was wrong?" Chelsea's voice was low.

"Twelve hundred words in black and white." Serena nodded. "He's desperate to win her back."

"When can I have it?"

"I just sent it." Serena's shoulders relaxed.

"This will keep Harry Ames off my back." Chelsea paused and her voice was soft. "Why didn't you tell me about Chase?"

"Tell you what about Chase?" Serena gripped the phone.

"I saw him at Boulevard with Ashley Pearson," Chelsea said. "They were sitting next to each other in a booth."

"Ashley Pearson?" Serena pictured the petite brunette whose great-great-grandfather founded one of San Francisco's first banks.

"They were sharing calamari with lobster stuffing, and they weren't discussing finance."

Serena hung up and sat on a gold velvet armchair. She imagined Chase at city hall, being sworn in as mayor. She saw Ashley in a cashmere dress and pearls, waving at the crowd.

Serena walked to the dining-room table and opened her laptop. She poured a fresh cup of coffee and started typing.

chapter seventeen

Serena closed her laptop and walked onto the balcony. She had been working all day and suddenly she was starving. She wanted to put on a pretty dress and go to a restaurant. She flashed on the fish soup at Le Maurice, the savory smell of herbs and butter and the cozy, intimate tables.

She thought about calling Nick and asking if he wanted to join her for dinner. She pictured his long legs, his wavy hair and easy smile. Then she remembered his mouth pressed against hers, his hands fumbling with her dress. She was going home in two weeks and she didn't want to start a relationship. She'd put on her new Celine tunic dress and eat a plate of seafood pasta by herself.

The doorbell rang as she snapped on a silver necklace. She opened the door and saw a silver-haired man wearing a turtleneck and a tweed jacket. He wore beige slacks and shoes with leather tassels.

"Dad." Serena froze.

"I'm overdressed," Charles said, smiling. "San Francisco was freezing and we just arrived, I haven't had time to change."

"Come inside." Serena's heart raced and her mind whirred.

"You look like you're going out." Charles glanced at Serena's black-and-white silk dress and white patent leather pumps. Her hair was tied in a low knot and she wore a silver bracelet on her wrist.

"I've been working all day." Serena shrugged. "I was going to get some dinner."

"I'll join you," Charles said. "I haven't been in Cannes in fifteen years but I still crave the swordfish at La Plage."

"We can stay here," Serena murmured.

"And miss a date with the most beautiful girl in France? Wait till you try their goat cheese salad."

They sat at an outdoor table under a bright orange umbrella. The table was laid with a white linen tablecloth and large square plates. There was a basket of herb bread and a pitcher of lemon water.

"Your mother and I are staying at the Hôtel du Cap-Eden-Roc in Antibes." Charles buttered a baguette. "She'll join us tomorrow for lunch; tonight I wanted to explain—"

"Maybe we should wait until after dinner," Serena interrupted, suddenly afraid of what he would say.

"I need to tell you," Charles insisted. "It was the summer after you were born. We decided to rent a villa on the Côte d'Azur. I was in Paris on business and I took the train to Cannes. Your mother and you would fly over from San Francisco.

"I stayed at the Carlton-InterContinental and one evening I entered the boutique to buy your mother a present. The salesgirl was a brunette with big brown eyes like a young Brigitte Bardot. She suggested a Hermès scarf and a bottle of Dior perfume.

"The next night I was walking along the Rue de la Feuvre

and I saw the salesgirl huddled on the sidewalk. I asked what was wrong and she started sobbing that she had been fired. The manager discovered her son sleeping in a cot in the hotel kitchen.

"She had no one and nowhere to go. The boy's father was an American producer who got her pregnant and left her. I had just rented a villa in Antibes, the keys were in my pocket." Charles stopped. "I gave her the key and said she and her son could stay there for a few days.

"When I drove to the villa to pick up the key, she asked me to come in." Charles's face turned pale. "You don't know how many times I've played back that afternoon, wishing I'd said I had an appointment. We drank a glass of wine and she started crying that she couldn't find a job or a place to live. I told her she could stay in the villa for the summer." Charles paused. "We ended up in the bedroom; it was the stupidest thing I'd ever done.

"I called your mother and told her we should rent a villa in Portofino. Then I mailed Jeanne a letter telling her to return the key to the estate agent in August." Charles pushed away his plate. "Two months later she wrote back that she was pregnant.

"I sent a monthly allowance and visited four or five times a year. She'd been abandoned once, I couldn't do it again."

Serena gazed at the table and realized the waiter had replaced her goat cheese salad with grilled swordfish and risotto. She scooped up risotto but then she put the spoon on the plate. Her throat was parched and she couldn't swallow. She sat back in the leather chair and waited for her father to continue.

"I didn't want to accept the consulate position, but your mother adored Paris." Charles looked at Serena. "And it was wonderful for you, you grew up so beautiful and cultured.

"One day your mother surprised me with reservations at the Carlton-InterContinental. Kate and I were walking through the lobby when a young girl approached us. She was about thirteen, tall and gangly with blond hair and green eyes. She threw her arms around me and called me daddy.

"God, I remember, it was like watching a train wreck. Jeanne rushed over and removed Veronique from my neck. I saw the realization on Kate's face and my heart stopped. Kate didn't say a word, just entered the elevator. When we got to the suite she demanded I tell her everything.

"She wanted to pack her bags and catch the first train to Paris. She wanted to take you out of school and go back to San Francisco.

"For three days we paced around the suite. On the third night we both fell asleep, too tired to argue. I slept for twelve hours, and when I woke the suite was quiet; I was sure Kate was gone.

"She was sitting at a wicker table on the balcony, eating scrambled eggs. She said we all make mistakes; the test of character is how we behave after they've been discovered.

"I promised to never have any contact, to be the best husband and father and try to make the world a better place." Charles's eyes were moist. "She said she would try to forgive me."

Serena sat on the ivory silk sofa in the living room of the Cary Grant Suite. The curtains were drawn and the lights were dimmed. The room was so quiet she could hear her own breathing.

She had left her father in the lobby and ridden the elevator by herself. She felt fuzzy and nauseated, as if she were snorkeling underwater. She kept replaying her father's words but they were like a jigsaw puzzle with all the pieces jumbled.

She pictured Christmas in Palm Springs and summer in Lake Tahoe. She saw lively dinners around the maple dining-room table and watching old movies in her parents' study. She remembered thinking her family were like three points of a triangle.

She saw her father arrive at the villa, his arms laden with presents, and thought her heart would break. She pictured her father teaching the little boy to ride a bicycle, helping the small girl color a picture. She saw him clean up plates after dinner, eat cake and ice cream in the garden, share a late-night brandy with Jeanne.

She turned off the lights and walked to the bedroom. She unzipped her dress and hung it in the closet. She pulled down the covers and climbed into bed.

chapter eighteen

Serena checked her reflection in the mirror. She hadn't slept and her eyes were large and glassy. She wished she could talk to Zoe, but Zoe and Malcolm had spent the night in Nice. For a moment she thought of calling Chase, but she pictured him sitting in a booth with Ashley Pearson and shivered.

She smoothed her hair, grabbed her notepad, and walked down the hallway to the Sophia Loren Suite.

"Serena, come in! I was just finishing breakfast. Room service prepares the most delicious muesli, I can't get anything like it in Paris."

Yvette wore a black pantsuit with a white leather belt and gold sandals. Her cheeks were powdered and she wore bright red lipstick.

"You're very pale," Yvette said as she ushered Serena into the living room. "I hope you're not coming down with another summer cold."

"I'm fine," Serena replied. "I drank too much coffee and had trouble sleeping."

"I must tell Chelsea what a wonderful job you're doing." Yvette sat at the bamboo dining-room table. "It can be exhausting reliving one's past," Yvette mused. "When we're young we never think we'll grow old, and we don't realize that everything we do has consequences. . . ."

Bertrand rented a room above the ice cream store in Juan-les-Pins and they met there every afternoon. Sometimes Yvette thought he did it to test her. Once she stood at the window and saw Françoise and Pierre and Camille and Lilly enter the shop and she felt nauseated. But Bertrand swore it was the only room available, and the views of the harbor were lovely.

Every morning Yvette sat at her dressing table and planned her day: work in her garden, lunch with the children on the patio, a brisk hike in the afternoon. But then it would be too hot or the children begged to go to the beach with Françoise and she was left alone in the villa.

By noon she was restless and anxious. She'd hastily get dressed and run down the hill to Juan-les-Pins. Often she arrived at the room first and her heart pounded until Bertrand climbed the stairs.

Sometimes he'd be romantic, bringing a picnic of roast beef sandwiches and oranges. Other times he was almost clinical, telling her to take off her clothes and lie on her stomach.

"Sex must be learned," he said when they were both exhausted from an hour of lovemaking. "If I were teaching you how to drive a car I would show you how to steer," he'd say, and then he'd bury his face in her, making her come so violently she couldn't breathe.

They never talked about Henri and they never talked about the end of summer. Yvette lived each day like Alice falling down the rabbit hole.

"Today we are going on an excursion," Bertrand announced.

He wore a white blazer over a black T-shirt and khaki slacks. He carried a straw hat in one hand and a box wrapped in gold paper in the other.

"What if someone sees me?"

"No one will; I bought you a present."

Yvette opened the box and took out a silk Dior scarf and a pair of oversize Gucci sunglasses.

"For me?" Yvette blushed.

"You will be as clandestine as a Russian spy." Bertrand tied the scarf around her hair. "And very beautiful."

They drove out of Antibes and onto the highway. They turned down a long paved drive and Yvette saw a stone mansion with tall white columns. It was flanked by cypress trees and surrounded by acres of lush gardens.

"We cannot stay cooped up like fugitives," Bertrand said as he opened her car door. "We will play tourist and then we will have a picnic in La Roseraie."

They wandered through the mansion with its elaborate crown molding and heavy velvet furniture. Yvette learned that the Villa Eilenroc was built in 1867 by Charles Garnier, the architect of the Paris Opera. Bertrand pointed out the elaborate murals in the Night Salon and the glass cases filled with Flaubert's pens and notebooks.

"*Madame Bovary* was the first book I ever read." Bertrand's face was serious. "No writer has created a greater heroine."

After they had seen the vast kitchen and the antique harpsichord in the music room, Bertrand went back to the car and retrieved a picnic basket. He took Yvette's hand and led her to the rose garden.

"I've never seen so many different types of roses." Yvette inhaled the rich scent.

They sat on the checkered blanket and ate ham and Gouda on pumpernickel bread. There was a jar of dill pickles and a bottle of pinot noir and a raspberry tart.

"Why did you bring me here?" Yvette asked curiously.

"I'm writing a new novel about a Parisian woman whose life is centered around her wealthy husband and children." Bertrand took out his cigarette case. "I want to use you for research."

"Research!" Yvette exclaimed.

Bertrand leaned back on his elbows and blew smoke rings in the air. "Tell me everything about yourself, your childhood, your schooling, your dreams."

"Why me?" Yvette asked, an uneasy feeling forming in her stomach.

"I don't know any other Parisian housewives."

Yvette described her parents' apartment near the Champs-Élysées, summers in Biarritz, skiing in Chamonix. She told Bertrand about her school years at the convent, how she hated math and loved English.

"I always kept a romance novel in my geometry book," Yvette mused. "I'd stay up all night reading Barbara Cartland."

She told him about her parents' long friendship with Henri's family, the wedding at Notre Dame Cathedral, the births of her children.

"Henri was never present at the births, but he arrived in the recovery room with a bouquet of roses and a piece of jewelry: diamond earrings for Camille, a sapphire pendant for Pierre, a ruby ring for Lilly."

She described the apartment on Rue Saint-Honoré that was a wedding gift from Henri's parents, her charitable foundations, the children's activities.

"Camille takes ballet and Pierre has started fencing," Yvette said as she nibbled a piece of tart.

"We eat dinner together before Henri comes home, steak and pommes frites for the children, a piece of fish for me."

"And that's enough?" Bertrand peered at her curiously.

Yvette bit her lip. "It always has been."

After their picnic they drove back to Juan-les-Pins and made love on the low mattress. Bertrand had never been so attentive. Instead of getting up to smoke his cigarettes, he rested his head in her lap, reading pages from *Sentimental Education*. When he dropped her off at the villa, he kissed her tenderly on the forehead.

Yvette threw her purse on the sideboard and ran upstairs to take a bath. It was only after she was reading in bed that she realized she had left the Dior scarf in the entry and Henri would be arriving from Paris in the morning.

She crept downstairs and buried the scarf in her lingerie drawer. She lay awake all night, staring at the ceiling. Finally, at three A.M., she knew what she had to do. She turned over and went to sleep.

"I'm leaving Henri," Yvette announced. "I'm going to rent a villa year-round in Antibes."

Bertrand looked up from his notepad. "He would never divorce you."

"I'll sue him for adultery," Yvette said. "I'll hire a private detective."

She had been thinking about it all weekend. The minute Henri left on Monday after breakfast, she slipped on a cotton dress and ran to tell Bertrand. Bertrand was drinking an espresso and writing at the small desk next to the window.

"A man in Henri's position will say he was visiting a sick friend." Bertrand shrugged. "He'll pay off the detective and send the girl to the country."

"I'll tell him about us," Yvette insisted. "He can sue me for divorce."

Bertrand stood up and put his hands on her shoulders.

"You would lose your children."

"I can't share a bed with him anymore."

Bertrand turned her around and unbuttoned her dress. He caressed her breasts, pushing his thumb against her nipple. He kissed her neck, inhaling her Dior perfume.

"You will say you have feminine problems and need your own bedroom," he said as he reached one hand under her skirt. "Women have been doing it for centuries."

Yvette felt his fingers opening her like a delicate flower. She strained against him, her body wet and hungry. She grabbed his shoulders, waiting for the waves to wash over her.

Bertrand pulled his fingers out before she came. He laid her on the mattress and pulled up her skirt. He entered her quickly and they came together in one long, dizzying thrust.

Yvette rested her head on his chest. She closed her eyes and listened to his heartbeat. She couldn't tell him that she wasn't afraid of sleeping beside Henri; she was terrified of losing Bertrand.

chapter nineteen

Serena entered the Carlton Restaurant and saw her mother sitting at a table on the balcony. Her cheeks were pale but she looked lovely in a pink Chanel suit and beige Ferragamo pumps. Her strawberry-blond hair was brushed into a pageboy and a diamond tennis bracelet dangled from her wrist.

"Serena, I've missed you!" Kate exclaimed, glancing at Serena's floral Ella Moss sundress and white espadrilles. "You look beautiful, what a gorgeous dress."

"Where's Dad?" Serena asked.

"He thought we might want some time alone," Kate said, hesitating.

Kate picked up the menu and studied it carefully. She signaled the waiter and ordered a cup of tomato gazpacho and a watercress salad. She took a baguette from the basket and tore it in half.

"The roasted turbot fish fillet with spring vegetables sounds delicious," Kate said as she buttered the baguette. "But I lost my appetite somewhere over Greenland; we had a bumpy flight."

Kate poured English breakfast tea into a porcelain cup and added a cube of sugar.

"Chase came to see your father before we left," she continued. "They spent a long time in the study."

"How could you live with Dad after what he did?" Serena exploded. "And how could you never tell me?"

"I didn't want you to get hurt." Kate sighed. "What would be the point?"

"Dad had a whole secret life! I have a half sister," Serena spluttered.

"But you don't." Kate's voice was firm. "Because your father promised to never have contact with them again."

"How could you possibly stay with him when he lied to you for fourteen years?" Serena's hands shook and her teeth chattered. She tried to sip her cup of tea but it was too hot and scalded her tongue.

"I wanted to take the train back to Paris and cut your father's suits into little pieces. I wanted to rip the pages from his books and shatter his glasses." Kate stopped, looking at Serena. "But what good would it have done? We had you, we were married."

"People get divorced all the time." Serena's eyes flickered. "Would you want me to stay with a cheating husband?"

The waiter set down two plates of watercress salad with round cherry tomatoes and sliced avocado.

"I imagined life without Charles and it was like cutting out my own heart. I told him what I needed and he agreed." Kate speared a tomato with her fork.

"I don't think I could love someone who did that to me," Serena replied.

"If we all behaved sanely in love there'd be no great literature," Kate said slowly. "It was a long time ago."

"What are you and Dad going to do?" Serena asked. Her eyes were watery and she had a sharp pain in her chest.

"We're going to Africa."

"Africa!" Serena dropped her fork.

"We've always wanted to go," Kate said, and smiled. "And it's the one place we won't be followed."

After lunch they browsed in Yves Saint Laurent and Fendi. Kate picked out a sleeveless cotton dress and a large straw hat. She added ribbed sweaters, two pairs of capris, and loafers in three different colors.

"I've never shopped for a safari, I feel like Meryl Streep in *Out of Africa*." Kate glanced at Serena and paused. "Your father has done great things—helped pass a bill to promote alternative energy, increased funding for schools in California—but he always said you were his greatest achievement." Kate squeezed Serena's hand. "That's all you need to know, let me worry about the rest. You might think I'm weak or old-fashioned, but he's my best friend."

Serena put her mother in a taxi and lingered in front of the Carlton-InterContinental. She didn't feel like walking through the lobby with its gold inlaid floors and uniformed doormen. She didn't want to rub shoulders with women carrying Louis Vuitton bags and men wearing white linen slacks.

She crossed the street and ran down the boulevard. She kept running until she reached the dock. Then she unstrapped her sandals and jumped onto the sand.

Serena hadn't known she wanted to see Nick until she stood in front of the Carlton. Then she pictured him showing her the aquarium in Monte Carlo. She remembered dinner in the Cary Grant Suite and the kiss on the balcony.

"Were you looking for me?" Nick stepped onto the dock. He wore a navy T-shirt and beige shorts.

"I was running on the beach," Serena said.

"In a designer dress?" Nick raised his eyebrow.

Serena glanced at her silk dress and white espadrilles. "How do you know it's designer?"

"I live in Cannes," Nick said, grinning. "Why don't we go somewhere more suitable, like the bar at Bâoli?"

Serena hesitated. "I'm not thirsty."

"You can watch me drink," Nick said, taking her arm. "I've been working on the boat all day."

They sat at a round table close to the sand and Serena watched Jet Skiers jump over the waves. The beach was filled with couples lounging on white beach chairs and children playing with plastic buckets.

Nick ordered two strawberry martinis and a bowl of tiramisu and turned to Serena.

"Let me guess, you were chasing jewel thieves down the beach and they escaped onto a luxury yacht."

"I had lunch with my mother; my parents are in Cannes."

"I thought they were staying at a villa in Napa."

"They came to see me," Serena replied. "Tomorrow they're leaving for Africa."

"I'm guessing they didn't say anything you wanted to hear." Nick frowned.

Serena sipped the smooth vodka and told Nick about her

father meeting the salesgirl at the Carlton boutique years ago, letting her stay in the villa, his indiscretion. She told him how her mother had discovered her father's secret and decided to stay with him.

"While other children were at summer camp I was fishing with the governor of Montana." Serena ran her fingers over her glass. "We hiked the Great Wall of China and sailed down the Nile. I wrote my sixth-grade world history report on my father and I cut out photos of my mother in *Vogue* and put them in a scrapbook."

"None of that has changed," Nick said.

"I always thought we were a team, but my father had another life." Serena's eyes filled with tears. "How could he still love us and keep a secret family?"

"You're beautiful and smart and have a job you love," Nick said. "And you're sitting on one of the most beautiful beaches in the world crying into your tiramisu."

Serena glanced at the sterling silver bowl.

Nick signaled the waiter and grinned. "It's all right, we can order another."

They strolled down the Boulevard de la Croisette and Nick told stories of huge storms off the coast of Africa and great white sharks in Australia.

"It's going to be pretty tame cruising around the Bay of Cannes." Serena smiled, stopping in front of the revolving glass doors of the Carlton-InterContinental.

Nick stood so close she could smell the strawberry martini. She gazed at his tan cheeks and suddenly she wanted to feel his lips on hers, his hand pressed against the small of her back.

"Would you like to come in? The pianist in the bar plays Cole Porter."

Nick glanced at his watch and shook his head. "I have an appointment, I have to go."

Serena entered the Cary Grant Suite and walked into the bedroom. She hung up her dress and slipped on a cotton robe. She curled up in a blue-and-white satin armchair and pictured Nick's dark wavy hair and blue eyes. Maybe she had rejected him too many times and scared him off.

She heard her phone buzz and grabbed her purse.

She read the text: *Would you like to have dinner at Le Maurice tomorrow night? Maurice is making his famous fish soup.*

Serena felt a pinprick of excitement. She picked up her phone and typed: *Yes.*

chapter twenty

"Go online, I want you to see something," Chelsea's voice came over the phone.

"I'm late for dinner," Serena replied, checking her reflection in the mirror.

She wore an ivory lace Givenchy dress and close-toed sandals. Her hair was brushed into a high ponytail and tied with a gold ribbon. She wondered if she was overdressed, if Nick would appear in a T-shirt and khakis. But she fingered the delicate lace and decided she wanted to wear something elegant and sexy.

"Dinner with a man?" Chelsea asked.

"You were the one who said Cannes had more eligible bachelors than any city in Europe." Serena smiled.

"I haven't left the office before nine P.M. in a week." Chelsea sighed. "I eat spinach salad at my desk and wash it down with a green smoothie. Click on *Vogue*. I think you'll be pleased."

Serena brought up the cover of *Vogue* and glanced at the glossy photo of Beyoncé in orange Cavalli. She clicked to the third page and saw a photo of Malcolm and Laura dressed in evening wear and stepping into a silver Bentley.

The headline read, "The Fall of the House of Gladding" by Serena Woods.

Serena scanned the pictures of Malcolm and Laura and Zoe on the ski slopes in Thredbo, Malcolm and Laura on a speedboat in Sydney Harbor, Malcolm and Laura and Zoe being presented at Buckingham Palace.

"It's in the online editions in sixteen countries," Chelsea said. "It will run in the print edition on Monday."

Serena quickly read her own words about the kidnapping, Laura's desire to move out of Sydney, their decision to send Zoe to England. She read about Malcolm's years of misery, his admission that he was wrong, and his plea for Laura's forgiveness.

If I gave Laura the impression she doesn't come first, I've failed as a husband. When we are young we think we can make the world anything we want it to be. As we grow older we realize there are few things we can control and even fewer things that are important. The only two things I can't live without are my wife and daughter.

"Wow," Serena said. She blinked back tears, afraid she'd smudge her mascara.

"I owe you that Aubusson rug and Tiffany lamp," Chelsea replied. "It's a terrific story."

Serena glanced at the clock and grabbed her purse. "I hope it works; I have to tell Zoe."

Serena strode through the lobby and entered a room with marble columns and paneled walls. The ceiling was painted with an intricate fresco and the floors were covered with Oriental rugs.

"I thought I'd find you here." Serena smiled.

Zoe sat in a wing-back chair gazing intently at an ivory back-gammon board. She wore a beige silk dress with pearl buttons. Her hair was curled behind her ears and she wore ruby earrings.

"I won three games in a row," Zoe said. "If I win this game my father will owe me a hundred euros."

"You play for money?" Serena raised her eyebrow.

Malcolm sat hunched in a leather armchair. He wore a navy blazer over a striped shirt and tan slacks. His cheeks were pale and his forehead was creased.

"It keeps the game interesting." Malcolm looked up expectantly. "Serena, it's wonderful to see you."

"Chelsea called," Serena said. "The feature is online."

"I'm so glad!" Malcolm exclaimed. "Can I see it?"

"I left my laptop in my suite," Serena replied. "Chelsea said it would be in the print edition on Monday."

Malcolm jumped up and walked to the entrance. "I'm going to check my computer."

"We're in the middle of a game," Zoe protested.

"Serena can take my turn," Malcolm said, smiling. "You're winning anyway."

Zoe gazed at Serena's lace dress and beige Manolos. "You're wearing a new dress and you smell like Estée Lauder White Linen."

"Nick and I are having dinner at Le Maurice," Serena said, twisting her ponytail.

"My father has been living on aged scotch and pretzels." Zoe sighed. "I can't get him to sit still long enough to eat a steak and grilled vegetables."

"If your mother had seen the photo of your father and the model she would have called," Serena said, frowning.

"My mother is not the kind to scream over an international phone line." Zoe ate a handful of cashews from a silver bowl. "She's the kind who leaves your suitcases packed at the front door."

"My parents are going on safari in Africa; they think they're Meryl Streep and Robert Redford," Serena replied.

"I don't know what my father will do if she doesn't forgive him," Zoe said. "He keeps talking about fly-fishing in Alaska or joining a Buddhist temple in Thailand."

"Maybe I shouldn't go to dinner with Nick." Serena sighed. "I should forget about men and concentrate on my career."

Zoe moved her backgammon piece across the board. "You have to go; you're wearing Givenchy—and I want another slice of chocolate torte."

Serena climbed the cobblestoned street of Le Seurat and saw Nick waiting outside Le Maurice. He wore a tan collared shirt and pleated navy slacks. His hair was damp and he carried a bouquet of yellow and white freesias.

They entered the restaurant and sat at a round table by the window. Serena picked up the leather menu, suddenly feeling out of place. She should be at PlumpJack or Greens with Chase. They would be sharing Bolinas Farms oysters and drinking a Sutter Home zinfandel.

"Let me order," Nick said, touching her hand. "I know everything on the menu."

Serena looked up and saw Nick's warm smile and a small shaving cut on his chin. She felt his hand on hers and the air slowly left her lungs.

She placed her menu on the table. "I'll eat anything except Brussels sprouts."

Nick ordered fish soup followed by roasted sea brim with candied lemon. He selected a niçoise salad and calamari risotto with grilled asparagus tips.

They talked about Nick's summer in San Francisco and Serena's month in Cannes.

"I arrived during the Cannes Film Festival," Serena said. "The hotel mixed up my reservation and I couldn't find a room."

"I've seen paparazzi hide in a public toilet to catch Tom Cruise when he pees," Nick said, and smiled. "For a month, Cannes is the center of the universe. Even the air feels more expensive, as if the movie studios import the oxygen."

"Zoe wanted to crash some of the parties on the yachts," Serena replied. "But I was afraid a Russian bodyguard would throw us into the bay."

"One of my friends attended a party where jungle animals roamed freely on the yacht," Nick said. "A guest fainted when she saw a Bengal tiger."

"That doesn't sound good," Serena said, grinning.

"Especially if she's a famous producer." Nick fingered his wineglass. "When I was a child my mother brought me to the red carpet. I'd stand behind the velvet rope waiting for celebrities. One year I got Harrison Ford's autograph."

"I love French actresses," Serena mused. "Catherine Deneuve always looks so poised, as if she'd never experienced heartbreak."

"You'll have to come back next May." Nick ate his last piece of sea brim. "I'll get tickets to the Palme d'Or and we'll rub shoulders with Tobey Maguire and Keira Knightley."

Nick went to say hello to Maurice in the kitchen and Serena looked down at her plate. Yvette's memoir was almost finished and Serena would be going home. She flashed on her parents' mansion with its large rooms and sweeping views of the bay. She pictured her apartment with its hardwood floors and Pottery Barn furniture.

Why was she sharing seafood risotto with Nick when in a few weeks he'd be sailing in the Mediterranean and she'd be sitting at her desk on the sixteenth floor of the Transamerica building?

She placed her napkin on her plate and pushed back her chair. She grabbed her purse and was about to walk to the door.

"Wait until you see the dessert Isabel prepared," Nick said, approaching the table.

Isabel followed him carrying a silver tray of chocolate profiteroles and fruit tarts with vanilla custard. There were two cups of milky cappuccino sprinkled with cinnamon and nutmeg.

Serena tried to blot out the images of Coit Tower and Fisherman's Wharf. She sat down and put her napkin in her lap. She picked up a peach tart and took a bite. She looked at Nick and smiled. "It's delicious."

Serena and Nick walked out of the restaurant and down the steep hill to the harbor. They strolled along the beachfront and Nick took Serena's hand. She let her palm rest in his, inhaling the sultry sea air.

She gazed at the sleek yachts and saw couples talking and laughing. The women wore shimmering cocktail dresses and gold sandals. The men spoke rapidly and poured bottles of French champagne.

"You look like you're trying to solve the problems of the Western world," Nick said as he glanced at her serious expression.

"Everyone in Cannes knows how to enjoy life," Serena said. "I think I forgot how to be happy."

"I'll show you." Nick stopped and touched her chin.

He tipped her face up to his and kissed her slowly on the mouth. He put his arm around her and pressed her against his chest. He kissed her harder, his lips tasting of peaches and chocolate.

Serena kissed him back, a shiver running down her spine. Suddenly she wanted to feel his mouth on her breasts, his hands in her hair.

"We're creating a spectacle," Serena whispered, glancing at the people standing on the yacht.

Nick looked at her closely. He leaned forward and tucked a blond hair behind her ear. "Then we'll go somewhere more private."

Nick kept Serena's hand in his and she felt her heart racing. She didn't know where they were going but she knew she wanted to be with Nick. She wanted to see his hard chest, watch him take off his shirt and unzip his slacks.

They walked up a cobblestoned alley and into a whitewashed building. A wooden staircase led to the third floor and the walls were pale pink plaster. Serena could smell butter and garlic and fresh baked bread.

Nick fumbled with his key and opened the door to his apartment. The living room had a slanted wood floor and large French windows. There was a floral sofa and a brick fireplace and a bookshelf full of paperback books.

"It's not the Carlton-InterContinental, and most of the furniture belongs to my landlady." Nick grinned. "But if you stand at the window you can see the bay."

"It's lovely," Serena said.

She stood in the middle of the room and suddenly her euphoria vanished. Everything was unfamiliar: the coffee mugs on the counter in the tiny kitchen, the paintings on the wall, Nick's jacket hanging on a peg in the hallway. A shopping bag held a Côte d'Or chocolate bar and a jar of green olives.

"When I saw you running down the dock, I knew I'd never met anyone more beautiful," Nick said, fingering her lace dress. "You carry your heart on your sleeve, and it's luminous."

Nick kissed her slowly, pulling the ribbon from her hair. He turned her around and unzipped her dress. He led her into the bedroom and unsnapped her lace bra. He gently cupped her breast, drawing circles around her nipple.

He reached down and slipped off her silk panties. He plunged his fingers inside her, moving in a slow rhythm. He held her close, watching her bite her lip. He moved his fingers faster, feeling her body rise and fall in one long glorious motion.

Serena rested her head on his shoulders, waiting for the waves to subside. She felt the familiar sense of joy, of giving your body to someone else. She took his hand and pulled him down on the bed.

She slipped off his shirt and unbuckled his belt. She kissed him on the mouth and ran her fingers down his chest. He lay next to her, touching her breasts, her stomach, her thighs. He waited until her body arched and then he opened her legs and pushed inside her.

Serena clung to Nick's back, smelling his musk shampoo. She felt his body working until she forgot about thinking and let herself be carried with him. She heard him moan and then her body opened so completely she couldn't stop. She lay against him, sweaty and gasping for breath.

"You see?" Nick said, and grinned. "It's not so hard to be happy."

Serena stepped out of the shower and slipped on a cotton robe. She slathered her skin with Acqua di Parma lotion and spritzed her wrists with Chanel. She glanced at the mirror above the marble vanity and saw her cheeks were flushed and her eyes sparkled.

She had slept at Nick's apartment and they made love again in the morning. Then they got dressed and ate breakfast at a patisserie by the harbor. After they shared blueberry scones and frothy cappuccinos Nick left to work on the boat and Serena returned to the Carlton-InterContinental.

She wished she could tell Zoe, but Zoe had left a note saying she and her father were taking the train to Saint-Tropez and asking where was her piece of chocolate torte. She signed it with a smiley face and two hearts.

Serena stood in front of her closet, deciding what to wear. She wanted to feel smooth silk or crisp cotton against her skin. She remembered the old movies she used to watch with her parents: Audrey Hepburn singing after she kissed George Peppard in *Breakfast at Tiffany's,* Grace Kelly falling in love with Cary Grant in *To Catch a Thief.*

She selected a turquoise Nina Ricci dress and white slingback sandals. She tied her hair with a turquoise ribbon and grabbed her notepad. Her phone rang and she picked it up.

"Would you like to have dinner tonight on the boat?" Nick asked. "I'll pick up tomato basil pizza and peaches and chocolate éclairs from the market."

"We just had breakfast," Serena giggled.

Nick's voice was low. "For some reason, I'm still hungry."

Serena walked down the hallway and knocked on the door of the Sophia Loren Suite.

Yvette opened the door. "Serena!"

Yvette wore black cigarette pants and a cropped red sweater. She carried a wide straw hat and oversize sunglasses. Her cheeks were lightly powdered and she wore bright red lipstick.

"I had breakfast at La Plage, they make the most delicious egg-white omelets," Yvette said as she walked into the living room and pulled back the turquoise silk curtains. "Sometimes it's lovely to be on the beach early and watch the fishing boats push out to sea."

"I'll have to try it." Serena nodded, sitting on an upholstered chair at the bamboo dining-room table.

"You look luminous this morning," Yvette said, eyeing her carefully. "I was talking to Chelsea, she told me why you're not wearing that stunning engagement ring."

"She shouldn't have done that." Serena's eyes flickered.

"I agree, but editors do talk," Yvette replied. "She was worried about you."

"I'm much better, thank you." Serena bit her lip. She unscrewed her pen and opened her notepad.

"Love is the most interesting emotion," Yvette mused, gazing at the shimmering Mediterranean. "When our heart breaks we think it will never heal, but it can be quite resilient. . . ."

Yvette didn't mention leaving Henri again for the rest of the summer. The last week of August was so hot, they had to keep the windows open. Yvette lay naked on the mattress, listening to children playing on the sidewalk, and wondered what she was doing. Then she would feel Bertrand's mouth on her breast, his hand gently parting her legs. and couldn't imagine being anywhere else.

"I don't know why I let Edouard talk me into going to New York," Bertrand grumbled, reaching over Yvette for his packet of cigarettes. "At least Hollywood has palm trees and the Pacific Ocean. In New York it's impossible to get a taxi and they leave the garbage in the street.

"*Pays de Cocagne* is going to be performed on Broadway." Yvette felt his palm brush her skin. Even though they had just made love she wanted him all over again.

"I'm going to spend six months listening to actors destroy my words," Bertrand moaned. "Americans all sound like cowboys."

"I wish I could come with you," Yvette said. She pictured the long winter in Paris without Bertrand. She saw dinner parties where she had to make sparkling conversation, business functions sitting next to Henri and feeling his thigh pressed against her leg.

Bertrand caressed her nipples. He moved down her body and buried his face between her thighs. He inserted his fingers deep inside her, pressing one hand on her stomach.

He lowered himself into her and came so violently she was afraid the plaster might crack. Then he rolled off and thrust his fingers in her again until she thought the waves would never stop.

Bertrand stood up and walked to the window. He grabbed his singlet from the chair and wiped his brow.

"That's what I'll remember when I'm stuck in a dark theater drinking weak American coffee."

Yvette felt her body shudder and closed her eyes, wishing it were already spring.

It rained all winter and Yvette spent afternoons in Grand Magasins trying on items from their spring collections. She bought Courrèges culottes and brightly colored swimsuits and silver sandals. She imagined strolling along the beach at Juan-les-Pins and making love on the white sand.

She helped Pierre with his math, pinned Camille's hair in a bun for ballet, let Lilly pour the flour into the cake mix. She fixed Henri's martini and listened to him talk about the bank, counting off the days in her head.

Yvette arrived in Antibes in the last week of May and felt like a bird let out of its cage. The villa Henri rented was a small castle with high ceilings and dark wood floors and rich velvet sofas. Yvette ran from room to room pulling back curtains and opening windows like Julie Andrews in *The Sound of Music*.

The second weekend of the summer they were invited to a party by Robert Evans. He had won the Palme d'Or for his latest film and it was the most coveted invitation of the season. Yvette had her hair done at the Carlton-InterContinental and spent the afternoon shopping in Cannes. She wanted to wear something different from all the movie starlets with their gold mesh dresses and platform shoes.

Yvette walked around Robert Evans's villa to the swimming pool and searched the lawn for Bertrand. She saw elegant men and women with bronze skin and heavy gold jewelry. She smelled the sweet scent of marijuana mixed with floral perfume.

"I thought I'd find you here, I saw Henri surrounded by skinny actresses," Bertrand said as he came to stand beside her. He wore a striped shirt and a white blazer. He held a shot glass in one hand and a lit cigarette in the other.

"How was New York?" Yvette tried to keep her voice steady. "Did you acquire an American accent and a love of baseball?"

"I stayed in a place called Greenwich Village, where the women go braless and the men don't cut their hair." Bertrand ground the cigarette into the grass and looked closely at Yvette. "I missed French food and wine and perfume."

Yvette leaned against a marble column and surveyed the scene. A band played soft jazz and couples danced barefoot on the lawn. A few women stripped off their clothes and jumped topless into the pool.

"Do you remember when I first saw you at Ryan O'Neal's party?" Bertrand asked. "I said you didn't belong in such a den of iniquity."

Yvette felt Bertrand's hand brush her back and was almost dizzy. She wanted him to take her into the house and find a spare bedroom. She wanted to unzip her Hervé Léger black dress and slip off her lace panties. She wanted him to fill her up so that the long dry months of waiting would be over.

"I was wrong." Bertrand pulled out a gold cigarette box and tapped out another cigarette. "You proved more wanton than I imagined."

"We could leave now," Yvette murmured, glancing at Bertrand. The sexual energy danced on his skin like an electric current. "I could tell Henri I have a headache and have to go home."

"And miss all the fun?" Bertrand shrugged, gazing at the waiters carrying trays of caviar and foie gras. "There is no rush, we have all summer."

Yvette tried to concentrate on Bertrand's descriptions of Times Square and Fifth Avenue and the theater district. She suddenly spotted Henri walking into the pool house. She excused herself, telling Bertrand she had to use the bathroom.

Yvette stood at the window and saw Henri talking to a small blonde with big breasts and a full red mouth. Yvette recognized Suzy Meadows, a young American actress who wanted to make European art films.

She watched Suzy perch on a billiard table, her skirt playfully arranged around her legs. She saw Henri hand her a drink and put his hand on Suzy's breast. She stood, mesmerized, as Henri unzipped his slacks, fumbled with Suzy's panties, pushed himself against her.

Yvette let out a little gasp and thought she would vomit. She watched her husband's face crumple the way it did before he came. Then she heard him call out and saw him collapse against Suzy's pink cotton dress.

Yvette ran around the garden to the front of the villa. She stumbled into the entry and asked the valet for her coat.

"Where are you going?" Bertrand stood in the foyer, still holding a shot glass.

Yvette turned around but her eyes were blurry and she couldn't focus.

"I'm going home, I have a headache," she mumbled, running down the stone steps to the driveway.

"I'm leaving him," Yvette announced.

It was Monday morning and Henri had returned to Paris. Yvette waited till Françoise took the children to the beach and rushed to Bertrand's new rooms in Juan-les-Pins.

"Let's not spoil our first day together," Bertrand said as he looked up from his morning coffee and newspaper. "We have a real bed, and a hot plate so we can make coffee and fried eggs."

"I saw Henri having sex at the party." Yvette's voice rose. "In the pool house with Suzy Meadows."

"Are you jealous?" Bertrand raised his eyebrow.

"Of course I'm not jealous! I don't need to stay with him," Yvette continued. "I can tell the judge what I saw."

"Henri will say it was dark, you were drinking." Bertrand shrugged. "You mistook him for someone else."

"I saw his face, I saw her blond hair!"

Bertrand took her hand and led her into the bedroom. He unbuttoned her blouse and buried his face in her breasts. "We'll talk about it another time. Let's try out the bed, the old mattress was murder on my back."

Yvette chose a red Yves Saint Laurent linen dress with white buttons. She paired it with gold earrings and Gucci flats. She sprayed her wrists with Dior and grabbed her purse. She was going to tell Bertrand she had made up her mind. Then she was going to see a solicitor and ask Henri for a divorce.

Yvette stopped at the Marché Provençal and bought a basket of strawberries and a carton of eggs and a loaf of French bread. She selected a bunch of purple daisies and a box of chocolate éclairs. She climbed the narrow staircase to Bertrand's room and knocked on the door. Bertrand wore white shorts and a black singlet. His hair was slicked back and he smoked a thin cigarette.

"I was shopping, I brought you some eggs." Yvette held up her shopping bag. She glanced in the room and saw a woman perched on the sofa. She wore a white halter top and a pink skirt. Her blond hair was tousled and she wasn't wearing lipstick.

"Let me introduce you," Bertrand said as he ushered Yvette inside. "This is Suzy Meadows, a delightful young American actress. She is interested in playing Gigi in *La Femme;* we were going over some lines."

Yvette glanced from Bertrand to Suzy, her heart beating like a drum. She saw Bertrand inhale his cigarette deeply, the way he did after they made love. She glanced through the door and saw the sheets to the bed lying in a heap on the floor.

"I forgot I have an appointment, enjoy your breakfast." Yvette dropped the carton of eggs on the wood floor and heard them crack as she stumbled down the stairs.

chapter twenty-one

Serena strolled through the Marché Forville admiring the selection of fruits and vegetables. She filled her shopping bag with endive lettuce, French green beans, and baby peas. She added ripe peaches, a basket of raspberries, and a jar of fresh whipped cream.

She stopped at the patisserie counter and asked for dark chocolate truffles with a cherry filling. She flashed on dinner last night in the Cary Grant Suite. She remembered Nick kissing her while her mouth was full of buttercream and saying if she stayed at the Carlton-InterContinental much longer she'd acquire very expensive tastes.

She bit her lip, thinking about the previous week. Zoe had insisted that Serena share her suite, and so she had canceled her own reservation. After her last session with Yvette, Yvette called and said she had urgent business in Nice. Serena wondered if she was telling the truth or if she needed a break. She remembered Yvette's face when she recounted seeing Bertrand with Suzy Meadows. Her elegant facade cracked and she was suddenly a wife and mother betrayed by two men with the same woman.

Serena wished she could tell Zoe about her feelings for Nick. But Zoe texted that her father hadn't heard from Laura, and she was running out of ways to distract him. She signed up for a four-day excursion to Provence and promised to bring Serena a bottle of perfume from Grasse.

Serena e-mailed Chelsea that she needed more time and allowed herself to enjoy Nick's company. They took a boat to the Îles de Lérins and saw the prison where the Man in the Iron Mask was imprisoned for eleven years. They drove to Monte Carlo and ate blue lobster at the Hôtel de Paris and drank limoncello and lime in the Bar Américain.

They made love in Nick's apartment and in the Cary Grant Suite and in the cabin of the catamaran. Whenever she thought about her father's secret family her eyes misted over and her throat closed up. Nick would sense a shift in her mood and suggest they sail around the harbor. Serena watched Nick at the steering wheel and the tightness in her chest was replaced by a small burst of happiness.

"I brought salad and dessert," Serena said, standing at the door of Nick's apartment.

It was late afternoon and they had decided to spend a quiet evening cooking and playing backgammon. Zoe had taught her the basics and Serena discovered Nick owned an ivory backgammon set.

"Your mailman asked me to bring up your mail." Serena set a pile of envelopes on the wooden coffee table.

"Alec should have been made to retire years ago." Nick wore khaki shorts and a blue T-shirt. His cheeks were freshly shaved and his dark hair curled around his collar. "I feel terrible that he has to climb three flights of stairs. I always think I should ask him to come in and have a glass of water."

"Like the birds you used to rescue when you were young," Serena said, grinning.

"I never believed the bad boy gets the girl," Nick replied. "I'd rather rescue a damsel in distress, like Sir Lancelot and Guinevere."

Serena glanced up and saw his eyes were playful and a smile danced around his mouth. He put the raspberries on the counter and wrapped his arms around her waist. He kissed her slowly and slipped one hand beneath her skirt.

"Then you won't take advantage of me until after dinner." Serena laughed. "I've been writing all day and I'm starving."

"I thought Yvette was away," Nick said, frowning.

"She is, but I have to send Chelsea something," Serena replied. "The advertisers are breathing down her neck."

Serena remembered Chelsea's growing impatience and her demand to see some copy. She pictured her return plane ticket, leaving Cannes, going home alone to San Francisco.

"Then we need to feed you." Nick put a slice of peach in her mouth. He kissed her again and touched her chin. "But I'd be happy to skip dinner and go straight to dessert."

Nick set the round dining-room table with a vase filled with yellow sunflowers and a basket of sliced French bread. He added a pot of olive oil and a jug of raspberry vinaigrette dressing and ceramic salt and pepper shakers.

"I received a postcard from my mother," Serena said as she buttered a piece of bread. "They are on safari in the Serengeti."

"What did she say?" Nick asked.

"That for the first time in thirty years she hasn't worn perfume, that the sky at night is like Space Mountain, that my father is driving everyone crazy with his descriptions of jungle animals."

Serena sipped her wine and thought about her last meeting with her parents. They wanted to take her to dinner at the Carlton Restaurant, but she couldn't imagine sitting on the balcony eating roasted chicken cutlets and braised asparagus. She flashed on the photo of her father with Jeanne and the two children, the family portrait that hung in the Presidio Heights mansion, and knew she had nothing to say.

Serena said she had plans and they had a drink at the Carlton Bar. Charles ordered a bottle of Chateau Rothschild and they talked about the latest Woody Allen movie and the political climate in France.

Serena gazed at her father's green eyes and her mother's strawberry-blond hair and wished they were home in San Francisco. She pictured Sunday dinners at the cherry dining-room table. She remembered eating Niman Ranch steaks and talking about *Vogue* and Chase's run for mayor and the foggy San Francisco summer.

"We'll be home in three months," Kate said when they stood in front of the Carlton-InterContinental waiting for their town car.

"I'll water the orchids," Serena mumbled, furiously blinking back tears.

She watched her father talk to the driver and remembered her first year at summer camp. For months she looked forward to horseback riding and tennis and swimming in Lake Tahoe. But when she stood in front of her cabin and watched her parents drive away, she could barely stop herself from running after the car.

"It'll get easier," Nick murmured, ladling spinach leaves and Camembert and orange slices onto a plate.

"I'm a grown woman and I'm acting like a ten-year-old." Serena put her napkin on the plate and pushed back her chair. "I'm sorry, I'm not hungry."

Nick took Serena's hand and led her to the sofa. He kissed her slowly, tasting of olive oil and sea salt. He kissed her harder, drawing her tightly against his chest. He slipped one hand under her skirt and slid his fingers deep inside her. His fingers moved faster until her tension was replaced by an exquisite release.

He kissed her on the lips. "I told you we should skip dinner and go straight to dessert."

Nick cleared the dishes and Serena set the backgammon board on the coffee table. She knocked the pile of mail on the floor and reached down to pick the envelopes up. She noticed a thick envelope with a San Francisco return address.

"I thought I was the only girl you know from San Francisco," Serena said as she held up the letter.

Nick put the tray of berries and whipped cream on the table and glanced at the envelope.

"It's from the Oracle America's Cup team, they want me to join the crew."

"The America's Cup was more than a year ago," Serena said, frowning.

"They're putting together a team to defend the trophy in 2016," Nick explained.

"Aren't they based in San Francisco?" Serena asked, her stomach doing strange little flips.

"I told them I'm not interested," Nick replied. "I've also been asked by the Emirates team and Luna Rossa."

"You wouldn't consider it?"

"After the Vietnam War, veterans panicked every time they heard a lawn mower or a vacuum cleaner," Nick said, sitting on the floral sofa. "The sound reminded them of choppers flying over the jungle. It's called post-traumatic stress disorder."

She twisted her napkin, trying to think of what to say. She glanced at Nick but he was hunched over and his face was hidden by his hands.

"I'd do anything to be back on one of those huge catamarans, part of a team, winning," he said as he picked up the dice. "But I'm afraid how I would react."

"It was a long time ago," Serena said finally. "You don't know how you'd feel."

Nick threw the dice on the backgammon board. "That's the problem."

Serena entered the Cary Grant Suite and curled up on a gold satin armchair. She had told Nick she had an early-morning deadline and couldn't sleep over. But all evening she had a queasy feeling, as if she'd eaten a bad piece of fruit. Even after she and Nick made love she had the sensation that she had forgotten something important.

She got up and walked to the sideboard. Room service had left an array of midnight snacks: crustless cucumber sandwiches, minipastries, chunks of Brie, and fresh apricots. She remembered when she arrived and was amazed by the pink marble floors, the ivory silk sofas, the spectacular view.

Now it seemed almost normal that her bed was perfectly made and the lotions and soaps in the bathroom replenished. She felt a small stab, like a pinprick, that soon all this would be gone. She'd be back in her apartment on Russian Hill watching *The Good Wife* and eating Whole Foods chicken.

She slipped on a robe and climbed into bed. She closed her eyes and saw Nick's dark hair and blue eyes. She pictured his wide hands and long legs. Her eyes flew open and suddenly she knew why there was a tightness in her chest.

She wasn't upset about leaving the luxury of the Carlton-InterContinental or the beauty of Cannes. She was falling in love with Nick. She turned off the lights and slipped under the covers, wondering how she could make the feeling go away.

chapter twenty-two

Y ou look like the girls at university who drank scotch all night and spent the morning over the sink," Zoe said.

Serena looked up from her copy of *Paris Match*. She had tried to sit down at her laptop, but the words danced on the screen. She finally curled up on the ivory silk love seat with a cup of vanilla tea and a stack of magazines.

"I drank one glass of red wine and went to bed at midnight," Serena said, putting the magazine on the glass coffee table.

"I hope you're not coming down with something." Zoe frowned. "I was stuck on a tour bus for four days, my immune system is shot."

"I think I'm in love with Nick," Serena replied. She wore a yellow cotton jumpsuit and her ponytail was tied with a silk ribbon. She wore no makeup except for clear lipgloss. "At first I thought it was just sex, that time in a new relationship when you can't get enough of each other."

"I don't know actually," Zoe mumbled. "Ian and I never made love."

"You never had sex!" Serena exclaimed.

"There was my roommate's older brother at boarding school," Zoe said, nibbling a croissant. "And the captain of the debate team at St. Andrew's, but Ian and I never got past second base."

"You said he was about to propose." Serena frowned.

"Ian treats me like a porcelain doll. He thinks because of the kidnapping I'm allergic to being touched."

"Are you?" Serena asked.

"There was a man on the tour bus," Zoe said slowly. "He had blond hair and blue eyes and the body of a Greek god. For four days we toured the vineyards in Provence and all I could think about was Gregg ripping off my clothes and fucking me on a bed of grapes."

"You never felt that way about Ian?" Serena asked.

"Ian's idea of fun is exploring rock formations at Bondi Beach," Zoe mused. "He's nice to kiss but I never had the desire to put his hand on my breast."

"I hope you didn't do that on the tour bus." Serena giggled.

"I didn't say a word," Zoe sighed. "I couldn't even sample the French cheeses, I felt like my tongue was taped to the roof of my mouth."

"You have to call Ian and tell him you want a break," Serena insisted. "You can't marry someone you don't want to sleep with."

"I don't want to hurt his feelings." Zoe frowned.

Serena sipped her cup of vanilla tea. "It's better than breaking his heart."

Serena and Zoe strolled along the Boulevard de la Croisette, stopping to look at the boutiques. Serena admired a gold bikini and pictured wearing it on Nick's catamaran.

"You haven't heard a word I said," Zoe said, glancing at Serena curiously.

"I'm sorry." Serena pulled her eyes from the bathing suit. "I'm a bit distracted."

"I asked you about Nick." Zoe wore a green linen Michael Kors dress. Her hair was brushed behind her ears and she wore emerald earrings.

"He's handsome and warm and funny," Serena mused, strolling past Missoni and Chloé and Givenchy. They had decided to distract themselves by going shopping, but every outfit Serena saw—pink Lilly Pulitzer sundresses, white Fendi miniskirts, cotton sweaters at Courrèges—made her think of Nick. She pictured having dinner at Le Maurice, dancing at Bâoli, sharing early-morning croissants on the beach.

"He got an offer to join the Oracle America's Cup team in San Francisco," Serena continued. "I pictured bicycling on Ocean Beach, hiking in Muir Woods, spending the weekend together and knowing I'd see him again on Monday."

"I don't see the problem," Zoe replied.

"He's afraid to race professionally, he told them he wasn't interested." Serena twisted her ponytail. "I realized I didn't want to imagine life without him."

"Have you told him?" Zoe asked.

"I'd spoil our time together and it wouldn't change anything."

"Did I tell you Gregg is a watchmaker in Geneva? He has the most beautiful hands." Zoe stood in front of a patisserie and gazed at the trays of rich desserts. "I know I'm in trouble when I'm not tempted by caramel custard and chocolate marzipan. I'm going back to the Carlton to take a cold shower."

They walked through the revolving glass doors and entered the marble lobby. It was early afternoon and women carried shopping bags filled with gold and silver boxes. Serena saw couples lingering over cocktails and men smoking cigars and reading *Le Monde*.

"Laura sent a letter!" Malcolm rushed toward them. He wore a navy blazer over a red shirt and beige slacks. His cheeks were drawn and there were new lines around his eyes.

"What did she say?" Zoe glanced at the blue envelope covered with Australian stamps.

"I'd like you to open it." Malcolm handed Zoe the letter.

"I can meet you upstairs," Serena suggested.

"We're all going to hear it." He took Zoe's and Serena's arms and led them to the Carlton Bar. "But first we're going to order a round of very dry martinis."

"'Dear Malcolm,'" Zoe began. "'I'm pleased that you surfaced somewhere as pleasant as Cannes. When Zoe said you disappeared from Claridge's I was afraid you had done something drastic. I know life has been difficult. I remember the early years when we held fabulous dinner parties and the house was full of friends and music and laughter.

"'I wish they had gone on forever and now we were doing the things we dreamed of: seeing the Acropolis in Greece, attending Mardi Gras in Venezuela.'" Zoe paused and looked at her father. "I think you should read the rest."

"'I tried to put the kidnapping behind me. If we had seen things the same, our life might be different,'" Malcolm read slowly. "'Your recent apology was quite moving and I ruined some expensive makeup.'" Malcolm paused, his hand shaking. "'If you had written it before I saw the photo of you and that very shapely brunette I might have reconsidered. Please tell Zoe to come home soon; her social calendar is filling up. I'm sure the South of France will treat you well, the French love a man with a title.' "

Serena glanced from Malcolm to Zoe, remembering the dozens of interviews she had conducted. She was always able to say something to break an awkward silence. But Zoe's cheeks were white and Malcolm looked like he'd received a death sentence.

"There's something else in the envelope." Zoe handed it to her father.

Malcolm stared at the picture of himself kissing a dark-haired woman wearing a low-cut red dress and silver stilettos. He saw the Boulevard de la Croisette in the background and the yachts bobbing in the harbor.

Malcolm threw a hundred-euro note on the table and pushed back his chair. He strode across the lobby and entered the elevator.

"What do we do now?" Zoe moaned, scooping up a handful of pistachios and popping them in her mouth.

chapter twenty-three

I missed you this morning," Nick said on the phone. "I had to eat a mushroom omelet and fresh-picked strawberries by myself."

"You're making me hungry." Serena surveyed the glass dining-room table. Her laptop was surrounded by a cup of cold coffee, a plate of crackers, and yellow notepads covered with Post-its. "I've put myself under house arrest. I'm not leaving the suite until I write two thousand words."

"I thought you left because I beat you at backgammon." Nick laughed. "We could have a rematch tonight. I'll make poached cod with stuffed artichokes and we'll play strip backgammon in front of the fireplace."

Serena pictured Nick's small apartment with the slanting wood floors and floral sofa. She saw the wooden bookshelves and the brick fireplace and the wide windows overlooking the bay. She closed her eyes and smelled butter and garlic and cloves.

"It sounds heavenly, but Chelsea already thinks I spend my time eating escargots and drinking dry martinis on the sand," Serena replied.

"Tomorrow night I'm taking you to Z Plage," Nick insisted. "There's someone very important I'd like you to meet."

"I don't know if I can." Serena hesitated. "Zoe is worried about her father, I shouldn't leave her alone."

"You can't leave Cannes without eating at Z Plage," Nick continued. "The fish is roasted in a clay oven and they have fireworks on the beach. We'll bring Zoe one of their chocolate soufflés."

"Breathing salt air sounds lovely," Serena mused. "I could sneak away for a couple of hours."

"I'll pick you up at seven P.M.," Nick replied. "Wear something that's easy to take off, I don't want to fight with zippers and buttons."

"You have to work for your reward." Serena twisted her ponytail.

"I'll work for it." Nick's voice was low. "After I take off your clothes."

Serena walked to the window and gazed at the sparkling Mediterranean. It was early evening and the fishermen pulled their catches to shore. Waiters wrapped up yellow umbrellas and dragged beach chairs across the sand. Serena watched the streetlights turn on and heard the sound of soft jazz.

Her head throbbed and she realized she hadn't eaten anything except one apple and endless cups of coffee. She surveyed the selection of salmon rolls and ham sandwiches, but her stomach felt like it was coated with cement.

Nick didn't know many locals and he hadn't mentioned anyone visiting him in Cannes. Maybe he was talking about an old friend from prep school or a member of the Artemis team. She gazed at the crystal vase filled with birds of paradise and a chill ran down her spine.

Perhaps Nick thought they were having a summer fling and had a serious girlfriend in Paris. Serena imagined a brunette with a chic haircut and bright red lipstick. She pictured her covering Nick with kisses and speaking with an elegant French accent.

Serena stirred cream into a fresh cup of coffee and remembered Nick rescuing her from the paparazzi, finding her engagement ring on the dock. She flashed on their first dinner at Le Maurice, making love in his apartment, sailing on the bay.

Cannes was full of young women who came to meet sexy Frenchmen, suave Germans, gorgeous Swedes. Maybe Nick expected to kiss her good-bye and exchange postcards once a year. Serena sipped her coffee and scowled. It was cold and bitter and even the cream tasted funny.

"You look like you ate a rotten egg." Zoe appeared at the entry. She wore a white linen dress and red Gucci flats. She carried a red Gucci clutch and wore a gold pendant around her neck.

"I haven't eaten anything." Serena sighed, putting the coffee cup on the white saucer. "Why are you dressed up?"

"I was trying to get information out of the concierge." Zoe slipped off her shoes and sat on a royal-blue silk sofa. "I gave him three hundred euros and promised to meet him for cocktails before he gave me my father's key."

"What did Malcolm say?" Serena asked.

"He checked out." Zoe's voice trembled. "His suitcases are gone."

"Where did he go?"

"I tried to hack into his credit card accounts, but he changed the password. He left a note." She fished it out of her purse. "'Dear Zoe, Don't worry about me, do what your mother says.'"

"He can't leave without telling you where he's going!" Serena exclaimed.

"He's getting quite good at it." Zoe walked over to the bar. "Maybe he went to Lithuania to see Verushka."

"You don't believe that," Serena said, frowning. "You know he loves your mother."

"All I know is she told him it's over and he disappeared," Zoe replied. "Honestly, if my parents were children I'd send them to their rooms."

"What are you going to do?" Serena asked.

Zoe poured a shot of scotch and drank it in one gulp. She grabbed her purse and walked to the door.

"I'm going to Nice airport to ask every airline if Malcolm Gladding is on one of their flights."

"I'll come with you." Serena slipped her phone in her purse.

"I'm going alone." Zoe shook her head. "Because if I find him, I'm going to make a scene."

"Serena! It's lovely to see you," Yvette said, standing at the door of the Sophia Loren Suite. She wore a red silk dress with a wide belt and red satin pumps. Her silvery hair fell neatly to her shoulders and she wore large diamond earrings. "I'm glad you could join me for dinner, I was sure you'd have plans."

Serena walked into the pastel living room and saw the dining-room table set with fine white china. There was a basket of fresh bread rolls and pots of whipped butter. Silver domes covered large porcelain plates and Serena smelled steak and mushrooms and roasted potatoes.

"I've been working in the suite all day," Serena replied. "It's nice to take a break."

"I feel terrible that I've been away." Yvette sat on a peach up-holstered chair. "You must be anxious to finish and go back to San Francisco."

Serena gazed at Yvette and thought of the things that had been spinning in her head. She needed to ask someone how to handle her parents, what to say to Nick. But she barely knew Yvette and wasn't comfortable asking for personal advice.

"Did you ever regret telling Bertrand you were leaving Henri?" Serena blurted out. "Do you think if you said nothing, your relationship would have continued?"

"Goodness!" Yvette exclaimed. "I haven't thought about it in years."

"I'm sorry, you don't have to answer that," Serena said, stumbling over her words.

In all their meetings Serena had barely asked questions. Yvette seemed to be channeling some inner voice and forgot Serena was there. When she finished recounting a story she would curl up like a turtle retreating to its shell.

"It's an interesting question." Yvette cut a thin slice of chateaubriand and covered it with sautéed mushrooms. She took a small bite and dabbed her mouth with a napkin. "I didn't see Bertrand again for almost ten years. He moved to Hollywood and wrote screenplays; he was very successful: an Oscar, great success at the box office. He was staying at the George Cinq in Paris and I was editor in chief of French *Vogue*. . . ."

"You must be a big shot." Yvette glanced at the heavy damask curtains, the gilt wallpaper, the Louis XVI chairs. "They only put the most important celebrities in the Royal Suite."

"I have my own steam room and I wash my ass with a gold-plated bidet," Bertrand replied.

His hair was longer and he had permanent dark stubble on his chin. He wore a navy silk shirt and beige slacks and soft leather loafers. "I'm glad you're here."

"You said you wouldn't give the interview unless I came myself," Yvette said, bristling. She wore a red Chanel suit and black leather pumps. Her dark hair was cut in a short bob and she wore a strand of black pearls around her neck.

"I wanted to see you." Bertrand lit a cigarette and sat against ivory silk cushions. "I didn't think you'd agree to a cup of coffee and a croissant."

"Why would you want to see me?" Yvette's eyes flickered and she remembered the last time she saw Bertrand, in the rooms at Juan-les-Pins. She saw Suzy Meadows's blond hair and the sheets crumpled on the bedroom floor.

Bertrand blew a thick smoke ring and looked closely at Yvette. "I want to know how the wife of the bourgeois banker became one of the most powerful women in fashion."

"I'm here to interview *you*." Yvette sat across from Bertrand on a spindly antique chair. She smelled the blend of cologne and cigarettes and her heart beat faster in her chest.

"You know how I feel about journalists." Bertrand shrugged. "You'll print whatever you like: Prix Goncourt winner abandons serious literature to become a Hollywood hack. Tell me about your life; does Lilly still like ice cream?"

Yvette glanced at Bertrand and for a moment she saw them in the room above the ice cream shop in Juan-les-Pins. She pictured Bertrand kissing her breasts, inserting his fingers inside her, filling her with the most exquisite pleasure.

"Lilly is fourteen, she spends all her time on the telephone," Yvette snapped.

"And Henri, how does he feel about his wife being one of the most revered women in France? Does it make his penis very small?"

"That summer in Antibes I took intimate photos of Henri and the actress." Yvette twisted the diamond bird's egg on her finger. "It turns out I was not the only one to capture her without her clothes on. The next year a blue movie surfaced. Suzy claimed she thought it was an art film, but *Lush Meadows* became an instant sensation. I told Henri if he didn't let me go back to work, I'd make my photos public. It wouldn't have made his clients happy that he was romancing a porn star."

"Why didn't you divorce him?" Bertrand asked.

"What would be the point?" Yvette looked past Bertrand to the Paris skyline. She saw the Eiffel Tower and the Tuileries Garden. "We have separate bedrooms; perhaps when Lilly graduates I'll get my own apartment."

"You should have cut off his balls and made them into a necklace," Bertrand said as he stubbed out his cigarette. "He never deserved you."

Yvette poured tea into a Limoges porcelain cup. She sipped it slowly, trying to keep her voice steady. "Tell me about Hollywood; does everyone drive a convertible?"

"I live in a mansion with a swimming pool shaped like an interior organ," Bertrand said as he poured a shot of vodka from a crystal decanter. "I have a fourteen-car garage and my own tennis court. I spend my days trying to stop pimply-faced directors from ruining my lines." Bertrand swallowed the vodka. "But they pay me like an Arabian sheik."

"I'm glad you're happy," Yvette said quietly.

"Remember when I told you men get rich so they can fuck beautiful women?" Bertrand lit another cigarette. His eyes were dark and there were deep lines on his forehead. "I have everything I asked for."

Suddenly Yvette couldn't hold it in any longer. She slammed her teacup on the saucer and jumped up. "Why did you screw that actress? I would have left Henri for you!"

Bertrand walked over to his leather briefcase and removed a magazine. He opened it and handed it to Yvette.

"Do you remember when we met?" Bertrand asked. "I was staying at the Carlton-InterContinental in Cannes and you were a secretary. Your boss got food poisoning and you were sent to interview France's most notorious writer."

"Of course I remember." Yvette blushed, picturing Bertrand stripping off his clothes and insisting she take his photo.

She glanced at the magazine and saw her byline at the top of the page. She quickly skimmed the story about the great success of *The Gigolo* and Bertrand's plans for a follow-up novel. She remembered Bertrand looking like a young Marlon Brando and being so nervous she leaked ink on her skirt.

"I asked you what you wanted to do and you said you wanted to be a mother," Bertrand continued. "If you left Henri he would have found a way to keep the children. I couldn't make you lose the one thing you always wanted."

"I loved you; you broke my heart."

"Everyone recovers from love affairs." Bertrand shrugged. "I took your advice, I decided to have children."

"You have a family?" Yvette started.

"I'm married. Jenny is a television actress, quite pretty if you like skinny blondes. We got married on a cliff in Big Sur, all the guests were barefoot. Sadly, it seems I'm sterile, a bout of chicken pox as a child. I told Jenny I'd give her a divorce, but she enjoys being married to a French screenwriter."

"I'm sorry." Yvette realized her hands were trembling. She opened her notepad and unscrewed her fountain pen.

"God, what I would give to fuck you right now. Did you know that the president of the United States slept on this bed? Two-thousand-count Egyptian cotton sheets and down pillows so soft it's like sleeping on a cloud." Bertrand stood so close she could smell the vodka on his breath.

Yvette sat perfectly still. She wanted Bertrand to pull her up and wrap his arms around her. She wanted him to pick her up and carry her into the bedroom. She wanted to make love until her lips were bruised and her breasts ached and she thought she was drowning.

Bertrand walked to the end table and poured himself another scotch. He swallowed it quickly and sank onto the brocade sofa.

"But I'm married," he said. He glanced at Yvette and his black eyes sparkled. "And you know I take the marriage vows seriously."

"You look beautiful," Nick said as he kissed Serena on the mouth and handed her a bouquet of yellow roses. He wore a blue blazer over a white shirt and beige slacks. His cheeks were smooth and his dark hair was freshly washed.

Serena twisted her ponytail and fingered her Tiffany necklace. She had tried on three outfits before deciding on a Zac Posen silk dress and silver Manolos. She might be overdressed for dinner on the sand, but she didn't want to be outclassed by a supermodel wearing straight-off-the-runway Alexander McQueen and Bottega Veneta stilettos.

Serena followed Nick through the revolving glass doors and

inhaled the sultry evening air. The Boulevard de la Croisette was filled with couples sitting at outdoor cafés. Serena saw maître d's passing out menus and waiters carrying trays of brightly colored drinks.

"V said she might be late," Nick had said as they crossed the avenue. "Rehearsals are dragging on longer than she thought."

"She's an actress?" Serena clutched the roses against her chest. Nick still hadn't told her who was joining them for dinner, and Serena was too nervous to ask.

"V is a dancer, she's been on tour all summer," Nick explained. "When they're home they're supposed to be on holiday, but the choreographer is a slave driver."

"Nick!" a female voice called.

Serena looked up and saw a woman with her hair wrapped in a silk scarf. She wore oversize sunglasses and striped leggings. She had a cotton sweater draped over her shoulders and white loafers on her feet.

"There you are," she exclaimed as she rushed up to Nick and hugged him. "You don't look a day older, and I have to cover my face with foundation. Ballet is such a cruel world; I'm twenty-seven and I'm over the hill."

"You look gorgeous." Nick draped one arm around V's narrow shoulders. "V, I'd like you to meet Serena."

V extended her hand and looked curiously at Serena. She had high cheekbones and a slender neck. Her lips were coated with red lipstick and she wore diamond studs in her ears. "You haven't said a word about her."

"Nick hasn't mentioned you either," Serena stammered.

"Let me guess." V glanced at Nick, a smile hovering on her lips. "You didn't tell Serena that your sister is a principal dancer with Les Ballets de Monte Carlo."

"Nick didn't say he had a sister," Serena replied. Suddenly the Mediterranean sparkled and the boats gleamed on the harbor. She watched the sun glide behind the horizon and felt the air escape her lungs.

"Nick thinks if he tells people his sister is a dancer they won't talk about anything else," V said, and pretended to pout.

"You're not just a dancer, you're one of the most famous ballerinas in Europe. I thought it would be fun to wait until you two met," Nick said, grinning at V. "You're quite capable of talking about yourself."

"I saw you perform at the San Francisco opera house," Serena gushed. "Your Giselle was breathtaking."

"You see," Nick said, rolling his eyes. "You two are going to talk about ballet all night."

Serena glanced at Nick and felt a warm jolt, like a small earthquake. She grabbed his hand and held it firmly in her palm.

"I promise we'll talk about other things after I ask V what it's like to dance under Piers Leon and be the youngest ballerina to ever perform Giselle."

They sat at a round table on the sand and ordered cucumber martinis and mussels in a wine sauce. Nick selected lobster linguine with spinach shoots and a platter of sliced melon and San Daniele ham.

"I haven't smelled butter in so long," V said as she picked up a fresh bread roll. "When we perform we eat the same meal every night. One baked potato, a piece of grilled chicken, and Jell-O for dessert. Other women fantasize about Leonardo DiCaprio, I dream about profiteroles."

"You can eat anything you like," Nick told her as he wrapped a slice of melon in ham. "When we were children you always stole my chocolate cake."

"Now I have to watch every ounce." V tore a piece of bread and popped it in her mouth. "If I eat an extra slice of toast I can't fit into my tutu."

"I thought the fashion world was difficult," Serena said, smiling. "I can't imagine what it's like to be a dancer."

"Serena is a features editor for *Vogue* in San Francisco," Nick explained. "She's in Cannes writing a story."

"You work for *Vogue*!" V exclaimed. "Has Nick shown you Chantal's pictures?"

"Who is Chantal?" Serena asked.

"Nick never likes to talk about Chantal." V shrugged. "I remember when we visited him at prep school, none of Nick's teachers knew his mother was one of the most beloved models in France."

"Chantal lives in Antibes." Nick's voice was tight. "She's retired and she's very private."

Serena looked at her plate, trying to think of something to say. She glanced at Nick but he was hunched over his plate.

"I see an old friend," V said as she jumped up. "Excuse me, I'll be right back."

"I was going to tell you about Chantal," Nick said finally.

"You don't have to tell me anything." Serena's voice shook. "We hardly know each other."

"My mother started modeling after my father died," Nick began. "She wasn't tall enough to do runway, but she had the most beautiful features. She became the face of Lancôme and was on the cover of *Vogue* and *Elle*. She retired a few years ago, she said women should grow old in private." Nick's eyes grew dark and he stared at his plate. "It turned out she didn't have to worry; she was diagnosed with inoperable cancer."

"I'm sorry." Serena froze. Suddenly she felt foolish for being hurt that Nick hadn't confided in her.

"It's one of the reasons I came back to Cannes, I didn't want her to die alone," Nick continued. "I was trying to find the right time to ask you to meet her."

"I would love to meet her." Serena glanced at Nick and her eyes filled with tears. "Your mother was a famous model and your sister is a world-class ballerina. Is there anything else you aren't telling me?"

Nick wrapped linguine around his fork. He ate spinach shoots and sweet baby tomatoes. He took Serena's hand and traced a circle around her palm.

"Maybe one thing," he whispered. "I think I'm falling in love with you."

Serena kissed him slowly, tasting cucumbers and vodka. She closed her eyes and heard the waves lapping against the shore. She kissed him again and felt her heart hammering in her chest.

"Cannes never changes." V sighed, scraping up the last bite of crème brûlée. "I should hang up my point shoes and spend my days playing in the sand."

"It's beautiful everywhere you turn." Serena nodded, gazing at the lights on the Boulevard de la Croisette.

It was almost dark and she could see the coastline from Nice to Monaco. White villas perched on the hillside and pastel-colored apartments lined the narrow streets. She felt Nick's hand on her thigh and a shiver ran down her spine.

Ever since Nick said he was falling in love with her she had been in a heightened state. The melon tasted sweeter, the martini was stronger, the crème brûlée was impossibly rich and delicious. She listened to Nick and V talk about Cannes and his new sailboat and felt like she had been inducted into a secret society.

"I feel like walking," V announced after Nick paid the check. "Let's go to Nick's apartment and play old CDs. I have a box of nineties music—when I was a girl I wanted to be Madonna."

"I always knew I wanted to work in fashion." Serena clasped Nick's hand. "When we lived in Paris my mother took me to the runway shows."

"I used to raid my mother's wardrobe." V nodded. "She collected the most divine outfits from photo shoots: Lanvin, Givenchy, Valentino."

They climbed the three flights of stairs to Nick's apartment. Serena put the bunch of roses in a glass vase and filled the coffeepot. V disappeared into the bedroom and returned with a cardboard box.

"I stash a lot of my things here," she said as she sat cross-legged on the sofa. "We never stay in one city long enough, and I'm too lazy to get my own place. Then I'd have to pay the water and garbage bills and water the plants."

Serena poured three cups of coffee and sat next to V on the sofa. She watched her pull out a stack of CDs and a pile of magazines. V found a copy of French *Vogue* and flipped through the pages.

"Here's Chantal." She handed it to Serena. "Isn't she beautiful?"

Serena gazed at the two-page spread of a woman with large

brown eyes. She had glossy chestnut hair and full red lips. Her eyes were framed by thick eyelashes and she had high cheekbones like Elizabeth Taylor.

Serena looked at the pictures closely and a chill ran down her spine. She glanced at V and saw her untie her scarf. V shook her long blond hair over shoulders and twisted it into a bun.

"She doesn't look like you," Serena said, trying to stop her hands from shaking.

"Nick got her coloring," V said, sipping her cup of coffee. "I take after our father."

"Do you have a picture of him?" Serena asked.

V dug through the box, bringing up programs from *Swan Lake* and *The Nutcracker*. She had a newspaper clipping about the America's Cup and a picture of Nick standing in front of a huge catamaran. Finally she found a yellowed photo of a man and a woman and two children.

"It's the only one I can find." V handed it to Serena. "Dad was always the photographer, so he's never in the photos."

Serena glanced at the photo of a pretty brunette standing next to a man with blond hair and green eyes. She looked more closely and noticed the man's angular cheekbones and dimple on his chin. She opened her mouth to say something, but the room spun and she slid to the floor.

"Are you all right?" Nick stood over her. He held a damp cloth in one hand and a glass of water in the other.

"I'm fine." Serena pressed the cloth against her forehead. She tried to stand up but her legs felt like jelly.

"Why don't you lie down," Nick suggested.

"I should go home, I just remembered I promised Chelsea

another five hundred words." Serena's hands were clammy and she couldn't catch her breath.

"I'll walk back to the Carlton with you," Nick insisted.

"No!" Serena exclaimed, biting her lip. "I don't want to drag you away from V." Serena turned to V. "Could I borrow that copy of *Vogue*? It might be an interesting addition to my story."

"Of course." V gave her a quick hug. "I had so much fun. It's been so long since I stayed up past eight P.M. and talked about anything except pliés."

"I'm coming downstairs." Nick put his hand on Serena's arm. "I don't want you to fall down the stairs."

"Are you sure you're all right?" Nick asked. "You look like you've seen a ghost."

"I must have eaten a bad mussel," Serena replied. "I'll walk it off and be good as new."

Nick wrapped his arms around her shoulders. He pulled her close and kissed her softly on the mouth. He released her, tucking her hair behind her ear.

"I meant what I said at dinner. I know we live in different places"—he looked at her and his eyes were like sapphires—"but I've never felt like this before; we can make it work."

Serena smelled his musk shampoo and wanted to bury her face in his chest. She remembered the yellowed photo and wanted to run as fast as she could. She started walking down the narrow cobblestones and stopped and turned around.

"Why is your sister called V?"

"It's short for Veronique," Nick replied. "When I was a kid I couldn't say her name, so my father gave her a nickname." He grabbed her hand. "You didn't answer my question."

"I didn't know it was a question." Serena turned and ran down the hill.

Serena paced around the living room of the Cary Grant Suite. She had come home and changed into a long-sleeved T-shirt and sweats. She added a cashmere sweater and slippers but she couldn't get warm. She sat on the ivory silk sofa and wrapped her arms around her chest.

She remembered the boy in the photo Chase had shown her was named Giles and thought she had made a mistake. But she flashed on Nick saying when he arrived at boarding school he didn't fit in. Maybe he thought Giles sounded too French and gave himself an American name. She recalled her father's description of the young girl who threw her arms around him at the Carlton-InterContinental and knew she couldn't be wrong.

She picked up the copy of *Vogue* and gazed at the photos. Chantal's eyes were liquid pools and her skin was like honey. She had the kind of beauty that made you forget other women existed.

Serena flipped to the front of the magazine and scanned the Letter from the Editor. She saw Yvette's photo and her spiderlike signature, and the rest of the page blurred. She grabbed her purse and ran down the hallway to the Sophia Loren Suite.

"Serena!" Yvette answered the door. She wore a red silk robe and black slippers. Her silvery hair was smooth and her skin glistened with oils. "It's almost midnight, has something happened?"

"You discovered Chantal, you've known her for years." Serena tossed the magazine on the coffee table. "I want to know every-thing, I want to know the real reason I'm here."

Yvette picked up the magazine. "Where did you get this?"

"From the sister of someone I've become close with." Serena's shoulders shook. "Do you have any idea what you've done?"

"Let me pour you a drink." Yvette walked to the bar and filled two shot glasses.

"I don't want a drink, I want to know how you could let Chan-tal write that letter," Serena raged.

"Chantal didn't write the letter; I did," Yvette said quietly.

"You wrote the letter to the *San Francisco Chronicle*?" Serena demanded.

"Chantal couldn't bear that her children would have no one after she'd gone." Yvette slumped in a peach silk armchair. "She doesn't know I wrote the letter; it was my idea."

Serena picked up the shot glass and swallowed the brandy. "Tell me everything, right from the beginning."

"I met Jeanne at a party at Ralph Lauren's villa. I was already editor in chief of French *Vogue,* but we still spent a month every summer in Antibes. . . ."

"You don't look like you are enjoying yourself," Yvette said, stand-ing next to a dark-haired woman with brown eyes and long eye-lashes.

The villa had high ceilings and polished wood floors. The walls were lined with Picassos and Manets and a white grand piano stood in the corner. Waiters in white tuxedos passed trays of steak tartar and sashimi and julienned vegetables.

"The music was so loud," the woman replied. "I walked down

the driveway to ask someone to turn it down, and the host invited me in."

"Ralph wouldn't let a beautiful woman walk away," Yvette said, and smiled. "It makes his parties more desirable."

"I hardly go to parties, I like to stay home with my children." The woman wore beige slacks and a cream blouse. She lit a cigarette and held it to her lips.

"You should quit," Yvette said. "Smoking's not good for you."

"I've smoked since I was eighteen," the woman said, and shrugged. "It calms my nerves."

"Yvette Renault," Yvette said as she held out a manicured hand. She wore a red Chanel dress and black stilettos. A diamond tennis bracelet dangled from her wrist and she wore black pearls around her neck.

"Jeanne Delon." The woman shook her hand. "I'm sorry, I'm not good at conversation."

"You don't need to be. With your looks, I bet men stick to you like wax paper."

Jeanne gazed at the Picasso and her eyes filled with tears. "The man I love left me."

"What man could be so stupid!" Yvette exclaimed.

"I met Charles when I was twenty," Jeanne replied. "I had just been fired, I had a one-year-old son and no place to live. Charles let us stay at his villa. I knew he was married but I was young and foolish. We became lovers and I ended up pregnant.

"He took care of us and visited the children several times a year. A month ago we ran into him and his wife at the Carlton-InterContinental. His wife gave him an ultimatum, and Charles said he could never contact us again."

"What are you going to do now?" Yvette asked.

"I can stay in the villa, but I need a job." Jeanne lit another cigarette. "I'm not qualified for anything."

Yvette studied Jeanne's high cheekbones and full pink mouth. She saw her luxurious brown hair and the wonderful shape of her face. She felt the same thrill as the first time she saw Naomi Campbell and Christy Turlington.

"Have you ever thought of modeling?" Yvette asked. "You should come to Paris and take some photos."

Yvette gazed at the photo proofs and knew her instincts were correct. The camera captured something that wasn't seen by the naked eye. Jeanne was mesmerizing, like a foal caught in the headlights.

Yvette glanced at the nervous young woman pacing around her office. She wore a cotton dress and white flats. Her nails were too short and her hair needed a good cut. But her features could have been painted by Leonardo da Vinci.

"We will have to do some work." Yvette stood up and walked to the window.

Yvette loved *Vogue*'s large ornate offices on the Rue de la Paix. She loved being able to visit the Louvre at lunch or stroll through the Tuileries Garden. And she loved most that she had to focus on a million details and never had time to think about Bertrand.

"Get you a haircut at Vidal Sassoon, buy a new wardrobe from Escada and Dior," Yvette continued. "Teach you how to do your makeup and change your name."

"Change my name?" Jeanne asked.

"France's next big model has to be called something dramatic and romantic." Yvette tapped her long red fingernails on the Louis XVI desk.

"Chantal!" she exclaimed as if she had found the gold at the end of the rainbow. "We'll name you Chantal."

Yvette took the biggest risk of her career and put Chantal on the cover of *Vogue*. The issue sold more copies than any since Catherine Deneuve burst onto the scene. Women were enthralled that a woman over thirty could still be beautiful. They wanted to know what creams and lotions Chantal used, who did her hair, where she bought her clothes.

Yvette convinced Chantal to move to Paris and her career skyrocketed. Cosmetics companies offered her large contracts; *Elle* and *Bazaar* plastered her on their pages. She became the face of Lancôme and spent a decade as the most desired woman in France.

"Chantal was proud that she earned enough to send Nick to boarding school and Veronique to ballet school," Yvette finished. "She hoped Nick would become a doctor or an engineer and Veronique would be a famous ballerina."

"Why did she retire?" Serena asked.

For a moment she forgot how Chantal ruined her family and was mesmerized by her story. She remembered seeing Chantal in her mother's magazines and thinking she was the most beautiful woman she'd ever seen.

"She didn't want anyone to see her grow old. I remember one day she came into my office and said Lancôme Satin Eye Cream wasn't working; she'd discovered new lines around her eyes. She didn't renew her contract." Yvette fiddled with her emerald ring. "She returned to her villa in Antibes and took up painting and gardening. We lost touch; it was my fault, I was so busy. I ran into her by accident in Nice. I hardly recognized her. She was terribly thin and her skin was like paper."

"Cancer," Serena said.

"She has a few months to live." Yvette nodded. "I insisted we have lunch, and she was so worried about Nick and Veronique. She regretted never telling them the truth about Charles."

Serena heard her father's name and something slammed hard against her chest. "So she decided to rake up the past, ruin my father's career, and destroy my family."

"Chantal did nothing," Yvette corrected. "I wrote the letter to the *San Francisco Chronicle*. Then I saw your byline in *Vogue* and remembered Charles was your father. I met your parents at one of their salons in Paris. I thought if I brought you to Cannes to write my memoir you could convince your father to contact Nick and Veronique."

"But you never mentioned them." Serena frowned.

"I met you and you were so lovely. I saw how Chase hurt you and how hard you worked on my story." Yvette smiled. "I've enjoyed myself more than I have in years. I couldn't bring myself to cause you more pain; I hoped the whole thing would fade away."

"Fade away!" Serena's anger returned in waves. "My parents are hiding out in Africa, paparazzi were chasing me on the beach, my fiancé broke off our engagement!"

"I feel terrible for what I did, I never meant to hurt you," Yvette murmured. "But if Chase couldn't handle that small storm, he would have made a poor husband."

"I know." Serena nodded, and the full depth of her misery enveloped her. She pictured Nick's dark wavy hair and clear blue eyes. She saw his warm smile and the way he tucked her hair behind her ear. How could they possibly be together without causing more unhappiness?

"You didn't tell me how you know Veronique," Yvette said.

"I met Nick by accident; he rescued my engagement ring when Chase broke up with me," Serena said dully. "We explored Monte Carlo and sailed in the harbor and ate fish soup and chocolate torte at Le Maurice. Tonight we all had dinner at Z Plage and he told me he loved me." Serena's eyes blurred. "I thought I was falling in love with him too. What am I going to do now?"

chapter twenty-four

S erena splashed her face with water and patted it dry with a white towel. She covered the dark circles under her eyes with concealer and dusted her forehead with powder. She searched her closet for something to wear, but the new turquoise Pucci wrap, the lace Givenchy she bought for dinner with Nick, seemed to belong to someone else. She selected a cotton jumpsuit and tied her hair with a blue ribbon.

After she left Yvette she wanted to rush to Nick's apartment and tell him everything. But it was past midnight and she was afraid to wake him. She lay in bed replaying the things Nick told her about his father: that he taught him to fly paper airplanes, that he took him to the Oceanographic Museum in Monte Carlo, that they fished together in the harbor.

She remembered Nick describing his father's plane crash, how he believed in luck and being in the right place at the right time. She pictured telling him that Charles deserted him, and a lump formed in her throat. She slipped on a pair of sandals and entered the living room.

"I forgot sex makes you starving," Zoe said. She sat at the glass dining-room table eating a bowl of muesli with strawberries and sliced peaches. She wore a beige linen dress with a wide red belt and ruby earrings in her ears.

"You saw Gregg?" Serena asked.

"I had Skype sex with Ian," Zoe said as she popped a strawberry in her mouth. "It was the hottest night of my life."

"I thought you told Ian you wanted a break." Serena frowned.

"Ian called me," Zoe replied, pouring cream into her coffee. "He met a female geologist in Byron Bay and couldn't stop fantasizing about her. I told him I wanted Gregg to ravish me in the vineyards. We realized we do love each other but we were both horny." Zoe's cheeks turned pink. "The sex was so good, I can't imagine what it's going to be like when we're in the same room."

"Gregg is going to be disappointed." Serena giggled.

"I could never date someone from Switzerland, I'd crave chocolate all the time," Zoe said, and shrugged. "Ian understands me, and when he takes off his shirt it's like Clark Kent becoming Superman."

"What are you going to do?" Serena asked.

"Go home and do normal things: get married, have babies, grow old. Worry about getting fat, never have enough sleep, get into terrible fights." Zoe grinned. "Doesn't it sound wonderful?"

Serena gazed at the shimmering Mediterranean and her eyes filled with tears. She turned away from Zoe and walked to the balcony.

"We'll stay friends; I'll send you a first-class Qantas ticket and give you a tour of the Sydney Opera House," Zoe said. "Please don't cry; I'll start crying and I'll ruin my Estée Lauder foundation."

"I met Nick's sister last night," Serena replied. "She's a famous ballerina with Les Ballets de Monte Carlo. We ate dinner at Z Plage and Nick told me he loved me."

"Shouldn't you be smiling?" Zoe frowned. "You said you were falling in love with him."

Serena paced around the Cary Grant Suite and told Zoe about Veronique's box of old photos, Yvette's letter to the *San Francisco Chronicle,* Chantal dying of cancer. She explained Nick and Veronique had no idea their father was a retired United States senator.

"That's better than one of those blockbuster novels that lists all the characters and how they're related," Zoe said, and whistled. "Charles isn't Nick's biological father, so at least your children will be normal."

"There aren't going to be any children!" Serena exclaimed. "I can't see Nick again. Chantal ruined my family's life, I can't cause everyone more pain."

"Your father had a hand in your family's unhappiness," Zoe mused. "I love my father, but he's acting like a child. He should go back to Sydney and resolve things with my mother, not run off with a supermodel or disappear to a Greek island."

"How do you know he's on a Greek island?" Serena asked.

"I don't know where he is." Zoe's eyes narrowed. "I tried every airline at Nice airport. Then I went to the train station, but there are hundreds of trains leaving Nice every day. What do you want?"

"Nick worshipped Charles; if he discovers Charles abandoned him he'll be devastated." Serena bit her lip. "And I don't know what Nick would say, maybe he'd be like Chase and think it was too overwhelming."

"Put on your lace Givenchy dress and spritz your neck with Dior and go see him," Zoe insisted. "You won't know how he feels unless you tell him the truth."

"I'll think about it." Serena nodded.

"I'm going to Missoni." Zoe grabbed her purse. "They have the most beautiful Chantilly lace panties, and Ian is Skyping tonight at seven."

Serena curled up on the silk sofa, trying to decide what to do. She could pick up flaky croissants and milky cappuccinos and go to Nick's apartment. She pictured sitting on the floral sofa telling Nick the whole story. What if he asked her to leave and told her he never wanted to see her again?

Serena's phone buzzed and she answered it.

"I couldn't wait to call and see how you are," Nick said. "You looked like you were stranded on a dinghy in the middle of a typhoon."

"I slept all night," Serena said as she twisted her ponytail. "I'm much better."

"I wanted to come over this morning, but I have to go to Saint-Tropez," Nick said. "An Italian count is interested in buying the catamaran."

"That's wonderful."

"I'll be back tomorrow night," Nick replied. "We'll drink a bottle of Veuve Clicquot to celebrate."

"I'll keep the champagne flutes chilled." Serena nodded.

"I told you you brought me good luck," Nick whispered. "Ever since we met, everything is perfect."

Serena pressed END and held the phone in her palm. She gazed at the crystal chandeliers and the pink marble floors and the royal-blue silk sofa. She leaned against the satin cushions and did what she had wanted to do since Veronique showed her the photo. She put her head in her hands and cried.

chapter twenty-five

S erena walked to the balcony and gazed at the harbor. It was midsummer and the crowds had thinned. Tourists left for Monaco and Saint-Tropez and Provence. They would wind their way north to Paris, possibly squeeze in Rome or Florence before flying home. Serena flashed on summer in San Francisco, the early-morning fog, the noon sun breaking through and shimmering on the bay.

She used to love stepping out of the Transamerica building at lunchtime and peeling off her wool jacket. She remembered meeting Chase and eating lobster at Fisherman's Wharf. She pictured returning to *Vogue,* eating tuna sandwiches at her desk, going home to an empty apartment and single-serving salads from Trader Joe's.

Her phone rang and she ran inside to answer it.

"I just read your copy," Chelsea announced. "I haven't been this excited since they added the male stripper to *Beach Blanket Babylon.*"

"I'm glad you like it." Serena smiled.

"It's going to set the literary world on fire. Who knew that two of the most beloved books of the twentieth century were written by the editor in chief of French *Vogue*."

"Rewritten," Serena corrected.

"And the sexual chemistry between Yvette and Bertrand is mesmerizing. You've done a wonderful job, I can't wait to read how it ends."

"I'm almost there," Serena replied.

"I showed it to Harry Ames and he was impressed. I may not just redecorate your office; I may get you a promotion." Chelsea paused. "How does senior editor sound?"

Serena gasped. "It sounds wonderful."

"What's your favorite color?" Chelsea asked.

"Green." Serena grinned.

"I'll tell the decorator lime green walls, maybe a framed Seurat behind your desk." Chelsea paused. "It'll be a reproduction; Harry likes to think he's generous, but he is stingy as hell."

Serena hung up and slipped on her sandals. She smoothed her hair and rubbed lipgloss on her lips. She grabbed her notepad and walked down the hallway to the Sophia Loren Suite.

"Serena!" Yvette wore black cigarette pants and a red silk blouse. She had black Gucci flats on her feet and a black pearl necklace around her neck. "I wasn't expecting you."

"Chelsea called," Serena said as she walked into the living room. "She's excited about the piece."

"I'm glad." Yvette nodded. "Have you seen Nick? I thought I could go with you and explain to Nick and Veronique what I did."

Serena's eyes flickered and she felt a sharp pain in her chest. She straightened her shoulders and smoothed her Lilly Pulitzer dress.

"Nick is in Saint-Tropez on business," Serena said. "Chelsea is eager to find out how your story ends. Did you see Bertrand again?"

"Bertrand died a year ago."

"I had no idea," Serena replied. "Was it lung cancer?"

"Bertrand was healthy as a horse," Yvette laughed. "The stupid man got run over by a taxi in New York City. I remember when I received the letter from his solicitor. . . ."

Yvette climbed the stone steps of the office building and rang the doorbell.

"Good afternoon, Madame Renault," the solicitor said, extending his hand. "My name is Laurent Bordeaux, thank you for seeing me."

"It was a beautiful funeral." Yvette wore a black wool Chanel suit and black Ferragamos. "Bertrand would have loved the selection of hymns."

"Not many people know Bertrand was religious." Laurent ushered Yvette into a paneled room with dark walnut furniture. "He was a strict Catholic."

"Your letter said he left me something. I was surprised, I haven't seen Bertrand in years," Yvette said as she took off her gloves.

Laurent handed Yvette a thick envelope. "He asked you to open the letter in my office, he wanted you to read it out loud."

"Out loud?" Yvette frowned.

"He was afraid you'd rip it up and throw it away without reading it." Laurent smiled sheepishly. "He said you weren't pleased with him."

Yvette sliced open the envelope and a check fell out. She picked it up and gasped.

"It's a check for five hundred thousand euros."

"It's the royalties from *Pays de Cocagne* and *La Femme*," Laurent said.

"But why?"

"He explains in the letter."

Yvette slipped on her reading glasses and began to read.

Cher Yvette,

The only good news if you are reading this is you're alive and I'm dead. I can't imagine a world without you, even if you are an ocean away lamenting how I abused my talent and ended up writing Hollywood drivel.

I always knew you rewrote Pays de Cocagne *and* La Femme, *so the royalties belong to you. Spend it on a Hermès bag or a vacation. You should go to California and stay at the Beverly Hills Hotel; I think you'd like it.*

I was telling the truth when I said I didn't read my work when I was finished, but the minute the reviews came in for Pays de Cocagne *I knew something was amiss. All Edouard's society galas and literary functions ruined me. I couldn't write about poverty and despair when I was plump as a Christmas turkey. I couldn't describe lust and longing when all I had to do was tap my cigarette and women lined up to fuck me.*

I suspected you rewrote some passages, so I read the whole bloody thing. What an amazing book you wrote. The heroine was pure, the hero handsome and callous and greedy but with a heart of gold. You created literature worthy of Flaubert and Stendhal and I took the credit.

A hundred times I strode into Edouard's office to tell him the truth. But you had your children, your wealthy husband, your apartment on the Rue Saint-Honoré. The only thing that separated me from the line cook at the Crillon was my pen and the page. Authors are a narcissistic bunch, and I was worse than the rest. From the age of twenty-five I was petted like a prize pony; I couldn't go back to being a nobody.

I was going to take the money and retire to Majorca, but Edouard brokered another deal without seeking my permission. I had to ask you to translate La Femme. *If it failed after the spectacular success of* Pays de Cocagne *it would have been a disservice to Edouard and all my publishers.*

I finally went to Hollywood, where everyone drives shiny convertibles and harbors dark secrets. No one would have cared if I said my books were written by my dead grandmother during a séance. In Hollywood, art is what children do in elementary school.

Last month I flew in a single-engine plane to Yosemite. The engine failed and we had to make a crash landing. I sat on the runway and knew I had to tell the truth. I couldn't lie under the earth for a thousand years with my name on your books.

I want Edouard to publish new editions of Pays de Cocagne *and* La Femme *with your name on the cover. I have written a foreword explaining the circumstances and left it with my solicitor. I loved you since the day we met at the Carlton-InterContinental in Cannes. If only I had been a better man or you had been a lesser woman, we could have made it work.*

Yvette sat in the salon of her apartment on the Rue Saint-Honoré and reread the letter. She imagined what it must have been like for Bertrand, knowing he was a sham. She saw his proud black eyes, his slick dark hair, and felt her heart would break.

She flashed on their first tryst at the Hôtel du Cap-Eden-Roc in Antibes. She pictured the elegant suite, the four-poster bed, the red velvet bedspread. She remembered how he taught her to delight in his touch and make love with abandon.

She took the check out of her purse and tore it into small pieces. She tossed them into the fireplace and sank into a brocade arm-chair. She took off her reading glasses and let the tears roll down her cheeks.

Serena sat perfectly still, waiting while Yvette collected herself. Yvette's cheeks were white and her shoulders sagged. She suddenly looked old and tired.

"Are you going to republish his books?" Serena asked.

"I can't deprive France of one of its idols," Yvette replied. "You will tell the story in my memoir. Maybe readers will believe me and maybe they will think I'm a bitter scorned lover." Yvette laughed softly. "People write strange things in their autobiographies.

"You asked if I was sorry I told Bertrand I loved him," Yvette continued. "We do extraordinary things for love; if we didn't there would be no great books."

"That's what my mother said, when she justified staying with my father," Serena replied.

"Perhaps we heard it at the same cocktail party." Yvette smiled. "If you love Nick, you have to tell him."

"That's none of your business," Serena said tightly.

"I know you are furious with me," Yvette replied. "But if I hadn't brought you here, you would never have met Nick."

"Nick thinks life is about luck," Serena said, fiddling with her pen. "That you meet the right person if you're in the right place at the right time."

"Real love doesn't happen often, and when it does you have to embrace it." Yvette looked at Serena and her eyes were dim. "After all, what else is there?"

chapter twenty-six

Serena ran along the beach, inhaling the salty air. She forgot how good it felt to fill her lungs with fresh oxygen and feel the sand under her feet. She gazed at the seagulls skimming the waves and the tightness in her shoulders relaxed.

She had stayed up all night thinking about Chantal and her father's secret family. She pictured Charles and Chantal strolling along the shore while Nick and Veronique played in the sand. She saw them eating family dinners in the villa and sharing ice cream cones in Juan-les-Pins.

She stood on the balcony watching the morning sun glint on the bay and knew she had to get out of the Cary Grant Suite. She strapped on her running shoes and ran past the street vendors selling fresh coffee and chocolate croissants. She jogged down the Boulevard de la Croisette and didn't stop until her calves burned and her forehead was covered in sweat.

Her phone buzzed and she reached in her pocket to answer it.

"Darling, I'm thrilled to hear your voice," her mother's voice came over the line. "I was worried I wouldn't get a connection."

"Where are you?" Serena squinted into the sun.

"Dakar," Kate replied. "Don't be alarmed, but your father is spending the night in the hospital. He had an incident on safari."

"An incident?" Serena started.

"He swears it was nerves but they're calling it a minor heart attack," Kate replied. "I told him not to get too close to the water buffalos but he wouldn't listen."

"Should I come there?" Serena asked.

"Fly halfway around the world to hear your father complain about hospital Jell-O?" Kate laughed. "Don't be silly. They're pumping him full of drugs and he'll be good as new in a couple of days." Kate paused and her voice was soft. "I'm calling to see how you are. Your father and I are worried about you, we wish this nightmare never happened."

"I'm wonderful." Serena gulped, gazing at the fishing boats bobbing in the harbor. "Chelsea is so pleased with my story I'm getting a promotion."

"How exciting!" Kate exclaimed. "I can't wait to tell Charles."

"Tell Dad to do what the doctors say." Serena blinked away tears. "And send me a picture, I've heard Dakar is beautiful."

"All I've seen is a hospital waiting room with Formica floors and vinyl chairs." Kate sighed. "But I made Charles promise we'd go to an outdoor market. I've always wanted a sarong."

Serena hung up and jogged back to the Carlton-InterContinental. She walked through the marble lobby and paused in front of the gift shop. She gazed at the elegant mannequins dressed in white Courrèges slacks and mesh Lanvin sweaters and suddenly knew what she had to do.

Zoe was right; she needed to tell Nick the whole story. She'd go to his apartment and wait for him to return from Saint-Tropez. She'd stop acting like a victim and buy something that made her feel glamorous and sexy.

She entered the gift shop and sifted through racks of designer dresses and Italian shoes. She selected a green Chloé dress and a pair of gold Manolos. She added a Pucci scarf and a thin gold belt. She carried the box to the elevator and pressed the button.

"Serena," a familiar voice called.

She turned and saw Malcolm striding through the lobby. He wore a red blazer and tan slacks and a wide straw hat. He held hands with a woman wearing a beige linen dress with a wide silver belt. She wore low heels and carried a soft leather clutch.

"I'm glad I found you, I've been looking for Zoe," Malcolm said.

"She's shopping on the Rue d'Antibes," Serena said, trying not to stare at the woman. "She's flying home to Sydney tomorrow."

"I'm glad we got here in time. I'm being rude." Malcolm took off his hat. "Serena, I'd like you to meet my wife, Laura."

"I can't believe you flew to Cannes without telling me," Zoe fumed. "I could be sitting on a Qantas 747, about to land at Kingsford Smith Airport by myself."

Serena looked from Zoe to Malcolm to Laura and couldn't help grinning. She remembered Zoe's face when she appeared in the lobby and saw her parents holding hands at the elevator. Zoe's cheeks turned pale and she spilled her boxes all over the marble floor. The concierge hastily picked them up while Zoe demanded to know what Malcolm and Laura were doing in Cannes.

They sat at an outdoor table at the Carlton Restaurant sipping strawberry martinis. Malcolm ordered pan-fried scallops with truffled mashed potatoes and artichokes flavored with parsley and garlic and Parmesan cheese. There was a basket of baguettes and pots of herb butter and olive oil.

"We wanted to surprise you." Malcolm grinned. He looked like a different man from the one who had disappeared after reading his wife's letter. His gray eyes gleamed and he kept one hand draped over Laura's shoulder.

"I spent three days trying to tracking you down," Zoe said, and glared at her father. "You can't crisscross the globe as if you were driving to the Blue Mountains."

"I won't be sorry if I don't see the interior of a first-class airplane cabin for a while." Malcolm nodded, piercing a scallop with his fork. "But I had to try to win your mother back."

Laura spoke for the first time. "I spent almost two decades being angry at your father." She had smooth brown hair and hazel eyes and finely lined cheeks. She wore freshwater pearls around her neck and a heart-shaped Chopard watch on her wrist. "He didn't build Australia's biggest fashion empire by sitting back and doing nothing. I finally understand he doesn't listen to anyone else."

"Then why are you here?" Zoe frowned.

"I didn't think Malcolm could do anything that would change my mind," Laura said, and sipped her martini. "But he pulled off something extraordinary."

"After I left you and Serena, I went up to my suite and stood on the balcony," Malcolm recalled. "If I had been younger, I would have climbed on the railing and thrown myself on the Boulevard de la Croisette. Instead I poured a scotch and reread the article Serena wrote. I hardly recognized the young man who sold his stereo and pawned his watch to create a dress. Can you imagine having the confidence to think if you turned up with a box full of tissue paper you could win the girl of your dreams?

"I finished the bottle of scotch and the idea came to me. I gathered my passport and took a taxi to the airport before I could change my mind. I remember the flight attendant saying I looked like I had a fever. She gave me a blanket and tucked me into one of those enormous first-class cocoons and I slept the twenty hours to Sydney.

"When I woke, we were circling the airport and I realized what I had done. The funny thing was that though I was sober, I didn't regret it. I grabbed my carry-on bag and took a taxi straight to Gladding House.

"It took me two hours to dig up the original design of the 'Laura'; we keep all our designs in a library on the third floor. I slipped it in my briefcase and drove to the garment district. Mei-ling's shop looked the same as it did almost thirty years ago. One tiny room with a sewing machine and a table filled with fabric and buttons and zippers.

"The girl at the counter was Mei-ling's daughter; she said Mei-ling had retired five years ago. I begged her and finally she brought her mother downstairs. I told Mei-ling what I wanted but she said her arthritis was too painful. I insisted I'd pay her anything. She pointed to my wrist and said, 'My son would love your pretty gold watch.'

"I handed her my Rolex and drove to the western suburbs to meet a man who imports the finest Thai silk. I showed him the color swatches and two hours later he called and said he found a match.

"While Mei-ling was sewing the dress, I went to David Jones and bought a pair of white silk gloves and sheer stockings. I stopped in the men's department and bought a plain black suit, and then I picked up a pair of tickets to *La Sylphide* at the Sydney Opera House.

"I hadn't been that nervous since I waited at the Taronga Zoo with the kidnappers' ransom. I knew if Laura saw me, she'd ask me to leave. I bribed my housekeeper to tell Laura that a delivery-man needed her signature, and I waited in the entry.

"You should have seen her face when she walked down the stairs. She was the same glorious girl who tried to brush me off in design class.

"I handed her the box and said, 'Some designers give their favorite collections to museums or galleries. No one should ever wear the "Laura" except the woman it was designed for, the most beautiful woman I've ever met.'"

"What happened to the original dress?" Serena broke in.

"It was destroyed in a fire at the dry cleaner's years ago," Laura answered, twisting her wedding band. "I fell in love with the young man in my design class with the bad haircut and borrowed suit because he was larger than life. I still don't agree that staying in Sydney was the best thing after the kidnapping, but I understand his reasoning.

"The young Malcolm wasn't going to let a couple of thugs dictate our lives. I saw him as being selfish, but his only crime was believing he was invincible. The same man showed up at my door yesterday; I would have been foolish not to let him in."

Malcolm held Laura's hand tightly. He leaned forward and kissed his wife on the lips. "And this time I was wearing socks."

"But why are you in Cannes?" Zoe asked. Her eyes were wide and her skin was blotchy, as if she had eaten bad shellfish.

"Malcolm showed me a picture of a white stone church perched on a cliff in Antibes," Laura said. "We decided to renew our vows."

"You're doing what?" Zoe's mouth fell open.

"We're getting married." Malcolm smiled, eating the last scallop. "And we'd like you and Serena to be bridesmaids."

"I can't believe I'm going to walk my mother down the aisle," Zoe moaned.

Malcolm and Laura had gone to Antibes to meet the priest and Serena and Zoe took the elevator to the Cary Grant Suite. Zoe tossed her purse on the sideboard, slipped off her sandals, and collapsed on an ivory silk love seat.

"I thought you'd be thrilled they're back together," Serena mused.

"I haven't seen my mother so happy since her thirty-fifth birthday. Dad hired the Sydney Opera Company to perform *Otello* in Centennial Park." Zoe paused, her eyes misting over. "That was before the kidnapping, when everything he did was perfect."

"Some couples can make it through anything." Serena pictured her mother sitting at her father's bedside at a hospital in Dakar. "I think they'll be fine."

Zoe walked to the sideboard and popped a strawberry in her mouth. She studied her reflection in the gilt mirror and tucked her hair behind her ears.

"I thought I'd be the next bride in the family," Zoe said, sinking onto the love seat. "At least it will be an excuse to buy a fabulous lace dress and eat chocolate raspberry fondant cake."

chapter twenty-seven

Serena walked along the Boulevard de la Croisette, inhaling the scent of rich cigars and exotic perfume. It was early evening and couples sat at outdoor cafés, sipping aperitifs. Serena watched waiters set round tables with starched white tablecloths and sterling silverware and flickering candles.

All afternoon she had wanted to call Nick but she was afraid to pick up the phone. She was afraid he would sense the uncertainty in her voice and knew she had to tell him in person. She slipped on her new Chloé dress, strapped on the gold sandals, and twisted her hair into a bun. She spritzed her wrists with Dior and pushed through the Carlton-InterContinental's revolving glass doors.

The closer she got to Nick's apartment, the more nervous she became. She pictured telling him about her father, and her stomach rose to her throat. She climbed the cobblestone street to his building and stopped at the entrance.

"What are you doing here?" a male voice demanded.

Serena turned around and saw Nick striding up the alley. He

wore a navy cotton shirt and khaki slacks. He clutched a brown shopping bag and a bunch of purple irises.

"I wanted to surprise you." Serena smiled. "How was Saint-Tropez?"

"I sold the catamaran and couldn't wait to come home and celebrate," Nick replied. "I stopped at the Marché Forville and bought fresh trout and white truffles and heirloom tomatoes. I got blackberries and whipped cream for dessert and a bottle of pinot blanc. I ran into Yvette Renault; I hadn't seen her in years but she recognized me right away." Nick stopped and his eyes were like sharp stones. "She said she was sorry she wrote the letter, she was only trying to help Chantal. She had no idea we knew each other, and it was such a tragic coincidence." Nick gripped the shopping bag tightly. "I didn't know what she was talking about and she grew flustered and said she thought you told me everything."

"I was going to tell you tonight," Serena said quietly.

"You think I wouldn't want to know that the man I called my father wasn't at the bottom of the Atlantic Ocean but lives in a mansion in San Francisco?" Nick raged. "That he wasn't a commodities broker specializing in Africa and South America but a United States senator?"

"How do you think I felt when Veronique showed me a photo of my father with his arm draped around Chantal?" Serena felt the bile rise to her throat.

Nick was about to say something and he turned and gazed at the glittering ocean. He sucked in his breath and took Serena's hand.

"Let's not give the whole neighborhood a performance, let's go sit on the dock."

Serena walked down the alley, listening to her heels click on the cobblestones. She felt Nick's hand in hers and felt a small stirring of hope. But when they reached the dock, he put the shopping bag on a bench and stuffed his hands in his pockets.

"How could you not tell me?" Nick demanded. "Do you know what it was like hearing it from Yvette?"

"It's a minefield; I didn't want to explode any mines," Serena said as she sat on the bench and gazed at the harbor. The sun had set and the water was an inky black. Lights flickered on yachts like fireflies dancing in the dark.

"My mother kept a calendar in the kitchen with the dates when he'd be home," Nick said. He paced up and down the dock, kicking the wood with his shoes. "He sent me postcards with little reminders: Practice your tennis; you're a gifted player. Study your math; it will serve you later in life.

"When he was home we did everything together: watched polo matches in Monte Carlo, flew in a single-engine plane down the Côte d'Azur."

"My father always wanted a boy," Serena murmured, flashing on Charles and Chase planning Chase's campaign. She pictured them sitting at the large oak desk in his study, surrounded by charts and spreadsheets.

"Once I asked my mother why he traveled so much," Nick mused. "She described the diamond mines and rain forests he visited; I pictured him wearing a fedora like Harrison Ford in *Raiders of the Lost Ark*." Nick's eyebrows knotted together. "When his plane crashed I was devastated. The funeral was in the abbey in Antibes; my mother said my father wouldn't have liked a big fuss. I wore a new suit and my mother wore a black silk dress. I'd never seen anyone so beautiful or so sad. Now I know why she was sobbing; it was because he never wanted to see us again."

"Do you think this is easy for me? Imagining Sunday dinners

at the Carlton Restaurant?" Serena couldn't stop shaking. "Picturing my father consulting the wine menu while the maître d' compliments him on his beautiful children."

Nick stopped pacing and turned to Serena. His eyes were dark and his voice was low.

"You must hate us."

"I don't know what I feel," Serena admitted. "But it hurt so much I didn't want to cause you the same pain. We were having so much fun." Serena stopped. She wanted to tell Nick she was falling in love with him, but the words stuck in her throat.

"There's nothing worse than being lied to. If you don't have complete honesty in a relationship you have nothing." He gazed at Serena and his voice was like ice. "I guess you're good at that in your family, your father is a pro."

Serena sucked in her breath as if she'd been punched. She hated Nick saying terrible things about Charles, but she didn't know how to defend him. She sat on the bench, fiercely blinking back tears.

"I need to be alone," Nick said, grabbing the brown shopping bag. "Keep the flowers, I bought them for you."

Serena listened to Nick's footsteps echo on the dock. She watched couples stroll along the shore, laughing and holding hands. She remembered the first night when they made love and Nick told her it wasn't hard to be happy. She clutched the bunch of irises, tears spilling down her cheeks, and thought he was wrong.

chapter twenty-eight

M y parents' renewal of their vows is turning into the society event of the season," Zoe mused, flipping through a
French *Elle*.

Serena and Zoe lay on the balcony of the Cary Grant Suite,
rubbing their skin with Acqua di Parma suntan lotion. Zoe wore
a Betsey Johnson bikini she bought for a Skyping session with
Ian. Her skin was lightly tan and she wore Dior sunglasses and
Tory Burch sandals.

Serena adjusted her black two-piece and gazed at the coastline. It was early afternoon and blindingly beautiful: the sea was
a clear blue flecked with diamonds. The Îles de Lérins glittered
on the horizon and yachts lined the dock like a collection of precious jewels.

"After the ceremony, there will be a reception at the Hôtel du
Cap-Eden-Roc," Zoe said as she rubbed suntan lotion on her arms.
"My father is flying in the cream of Sydney society: Hugh Jackman, Cate Blanchett, Hamish Blake. Then my parents will sail
to Portofino and spend two nights at the Hotel Splendido. Then
they'll fly to Venice and take the Orient Express to Budapest. My

mother is at Chanel buying her trousseau and my father is at Harry Winston commissioning a five-carat diamond wedding ring."

"You sound like you don't approve." Serena frowned.

"I think it's wonderful," Zoe said, and grinned. "I've never seen my mother so excited. Yesterday we chose favors at Tiffany: silver bracelets with charms shaped like yachts. This morning we did a trial makeup run and this evening we're sampling entrées: duck *à l'orange* and chateaubriand and roasted sea bass. When Ian and I get married, we'll go to a pub and have fish and chips."

"No, you won't," Serena replied.

"My mother is already considering renting out the Sydney Opera House for the reception, and Ian hasn't even proposed." Zoe sighed. "Did you know they're not sharing a room until after the ceremony? My father reserved the Presidential Suite for their wedding night. It has a personal chef and a swimming pool."

"Will your father still retire?" Serena looked up from her copy of French *Vogue*. Ever since she saw Nick she hadn't been able to concentrate. She barely ate and her skin felt like paper. She desperately wanted to call him but there was nothing she could say. Every time she pictured his drawn cheeks her stomach clenched.

"He'd drive my mother crazy rattling around the house." Zoe shook her head. "I'm relieved; I wasn't ready to take over a global company. I'm going to be Head of European Accessories."

"What's that?" Serena shielded her eyes from the sun.

"I made it up." Zoe beamed. "I've been buying things on our day trips: silver earrings in Grasse, an antique brooch in Provence, the sweetest gold locket in Mougins. We're going to devote a section of every store to unique accessories and I'm going to go on buying trips to France and Italy and Spain."

"There's nothing like creating your own dream job." Serena grinned.

"There has to be perks to having your father own the company. You don't look happy for someone who was just named senior editor of *Vogue*," Zoe said, and hesitated. "Have you heard from Nick?"

"I don't think I will," Serena replied slowly. "I seem to pick men who run away at the hint of trouble."

"Nick isn't like Chase," Zoe insisted.

"Maybe Nick was upset because I didn't tell him the truth or maybe he just couldn't handle the situation. In either case he's gone." Serena stopped as if she'd run out of air. "I should stop thinking about him."

"Nick probably needs some time," Zoe replied. "Men are like puppies, they need to crawl into a corner and lick their wounds. He'll appear at the Carlton-InterContinental tomorrow with two dozen pink roses."

"We said some terrible things." Serena bit her lip. "And I never told him I loved him."

"You need some distraction," Zoe insisted. "Let's get out of these swimsuits and go buy our bridesmaids dresses."

"Your mother said we could wear whatever we like," Serena said, shrugging. "I thought I'd wear my Givenchy lace dress."

"There will be photographers from every major newspaper," Zoe said as she jumped up. "My father wants everyone in the fashion world to know he's not still slinking around with twentysomething models. You have to wear something fabulous, you're representing *Vogue*."

Serena imagined Chelsea's expression when she heard that Serena was a bridesmaid at Malcolm and Laura Gladding's wedding. She pictured wearing a gorgeous silk Armani gown or an elegant Jacqueline Kennedy dress.

She slipped on her sunglasses and smiled. "All right, but I'm not wearing purple, it makes my skin look washed-out."

Serena stepped into the Dior boutique and gazed at the mannequins wearing kelly-green slacks and cream-colored cashmere sweaters. The store was full of fall fashions: floor-length skirts in orange and magenta, close-toed shoes with jeweled heels and brightly colored pashminas. There were racks of long wool coats and cropped jackets and knit dresses.

"I love autumn fashions." Zoe sighed, fingering a purple jersey dress. "You don't have to suck in your stomach all the time."

Serena gazed at a pair of suede ankle boots and flashed on the *Vogue* offices in September. Everyone wore knee-length skirts and wool sweaters and the latest shoes and boots. There was a ripple of excitement, like the start of a new school year, and endless discussions about the new black and the perfect handbag and this year's fall coat.

"Fall is my favorite season in San Francisco." Serena admired a burgundy dress with a wide black belt. "The fog disappears and the view is spectacular. You can see from Berkeley to the Farallon Islands."

"I've always wanted to visit," Zoe said, slipping her foot into a leather loafer. "San Francisco has the best sourdough bread and world-famous chocolate. You can teach me how to eat Chinese food and ride a cable car."

Serena pictured the crowded streets of Chinatown and the stalls selling sticky noodles and wonton soup. She saw the tall buildings in the Financial District and men and women carrying Starbucks Frappuccinos and warm danishes. She pictured the lobby at *Vogue* full of women wearing sheer stockings and four-inch stilettos.

She saw her office with its narrow view of the bay and a shiver of excitement ran down her spine. She imagined being sent to New York for Fashion Week or to the runway shows in Milan. She pictured interviewing Anne Hathaway and Michelle Williams and Blake Lively. She saw herself going to gallery openings and industry galas and introducing herself as senior editor at *Vogue*.

Serena fingered a coral-pink cashmere sweater and recalled Yvette saying the best thing about being editor in chief was never having time to think about Bertrand. She remembered always seeing Chelsea's light on in her office when she went home at the end of the day.

She would throw herself into her work and not think about Nick. She would stay busy with production meetings and photo shoots and copy deadlines. She would pretend it was a holiday romance and let it fade like a summer tan.

"When I arrive in Sydney it will be spring," Zoe said glumly. "I'll have to worry about tan lines and flabby arms all over again."

"You look beautiful." Serena gazed at Zoe's smooth brown hair and large hazel eyes. Zoe wore a white lace dress with a pleated skirt. She wore Prada sandals on her feet and small ruby earrings in her ears.

"At least I'm not wearing polka dots anymore." Zoe grinned. "You've taught me some fashion sense."

"I haven't done anything." Serena shook her head. "You have an innate sense of style, you just had to stop listening to the wrong people."

They entered Dior's bridal salon and gazed at the rows of ivory satin dresses and silk sheaths. The walls were covered in pale blue silk and the carpet was a thick white wool. Glass display cases held velvet slippers and diamond tiaras and long lace veils.

"Can I help you?" A tall saleswoman approached Zoe. She wore a navy dress and her blond hair was pulled into a tight bun. "You're going to be the most beautiful bride. You have the perfect figure for our new line of dresses and your hair would look fabulous with a princess tiara."

"I'm not the bride," Zoe replied, a blush spreading across her cheeks. "I was looking for bridesmaids dresses."

"Your friend is lucky to have such a gorgeous bridesmaid." The salesgirl nodded at Serena. "You'll both look stunning in the wedding photos."

"The saleswoman said I was beautiful," Zoe said as they left the boutique. She clutched a bag that held a teal-blue satin dress with spaghetti straps. She had selected silver sandals and a diamond choker. "That's the first time a salesgirl hasn't looked at me as if I'm chewing gum and don't belong in her store."

"You're going to make your parents very proud," Serena said, and nodded. She had sifted through racks of chiffon dresses but nothing excited her. Finally she settled on a pale pink dress with a satin bodice. She bought beige slingback sandals and an ivory satin clutch.

"I could have tried on dresses all day," Zoe continued. "Did you sample the mini-éclairs and the puff pastries? And the champagne was heavenly; I felt like Victoria Beckham."

Serena saw a man walking down the street and froze. He had Nick's wavy brown hair and wide shoulders. He turned around and Serena saw he had brown eyes and stubble on his chin. She dropped her bag and her purchases scattered on the sidewalk.

She didn't want to go back to nights alone with tear sheets and photo proofs. She wanted to drink white wine and eat mussels with Nick. She wanted to hold hands on the beach and smell his musk shampoo. She wanted to lie on his narrow mattress and taste the salty sweetness of his lips.

"Are you okay?" Zoe asked. "You look like a wax figure at Madame Tussauds."

Serena crouched down and picked up her bag. She smoothed her hair and tried to smile. "I'm fine; I drank too much champagne."

chapter twenty-nine

I feel as nervous as I did when I was twenty-two," Laura said, sitting on a stool in the small room at the back of the church. "We got married at Saint James Church in Sydney. Malcolm wore a gray morning coat and a yellow-and-white striped tie. I thought he was the most handsome man I'd ever seen."

Serena gazed at Laura's smooth brown hair and immaculate makeup and smiled. It had been an intoxicating day and Serena felt caught up in the excitement of the wedding.

A white Bentley had picked Serena and Zoe up at the Carlton-InterContinental and delivered them to the Hôtel du Cap-Eden-Roc. Serena glanced around the lobby with its Louis XVI chairs and delicate tapestries and remembered Yvette's descriptions of the hotel. Every surface was filled with crystal vases, and tall French doors opened onto lush gardens. Serena smelled the scent of roses and bougainvillea and polished wood.

A uniformed valet escorted them to the Presidential Suite and drew back brocade curtains. The view stretched down the whole coastline and Serena could see Nice and Cannes and Monaco. She stood outside and heard birds chirping and watched fishing boats glide out to sea.

They spent the morning getting their makeup done and eating a brunch of fluffy egg-white omelets, buttered scones, and strawberries and mangoes and pomegranates. Laura kept flying to the door and exclaiming over the array of cards and blue Tiffany boxes.

"You look beautiful," Serena said as she admired Laura's gray Oscar de la Renta dress with its small waist and flared skirt. She had paired it with jeweled Stuart Weitzman pumps and a satin Chanel evening bag. She wore an amethyst around her neck and diamond solitaires in her ears.

"I had forgotten weddings are so much fun," Laura said as she sipped a crystal flute of champagne. "Zoe is taking things so seriously. She went to talk to the priest about his reading; I think he's actually afraid of her."

Serena smiled. "Zoe is very excited."

"She's becoming more like her father every day," Laura replied, picking a piece of lint from her skirt. "She's turning into a wonderful young woman, I couldn't be more proud of her."

"She's very happy the way things turned out," Serena said slowly.

"You'd think at our age we'd get over the emotional drama and leave it to your generation." Laura sighed, fluffing her hair. "Zoe told me about your parents, and I read it in *Paris Match;* I admire your mother."

"You admire her?" Serena raised her eyebrow.

"It's wonderful to love someone so much you'd stand by them through anything." Laura applied coral-pink lipstick. She glanced in the oval mirror and blotted her lips.

"I hadn't thought about it that way," Serena said, frowning.

"Love is messy and painful, but once you find it you have to hang on to it." Laura turned to Serena and smiled. "Because really, what else is there?"

Serena stood in the front of the church, gazing at the pews filled with men in linen suits and women wearing silk cocktail dresses. She felt Zoe poke her rib and suppressed a giggle.

The church was one tiny room with stained-glass windows and stone floors. The aisle was covered with a red carpet and strewn with yellow and white roses. Roses were everywhere: filling the entry in great tubs, packed in tight bunches on the altar. Zoe kept whispering there were so many flowers she felt like she was suffocating.

Serena glanced at Zoe and felt a warmth spread through her chest. She had never seen her friend look so radiant. The teal dress fit her perfectly and she wore a pink Cartier Panthère watch. Her cheeks were dusted with gold powder and she wore teal eye shadow and thick mascara.

"I saw Russell Crowe and Nicole Kidman," Zoe whispered. "I'm going to faint."

"You can't faint," Serena hissed. "They're about to start the ceremony."

Serena watched the priest appear from the vestry. Malcolm wore a gray morning coat with tails and a yellow tie. His salt-and-pepper hair was freshly cut and his gray eyes sparkled. Laura stood beside him clutching a bunch of yellow daisies. She wore white silk gloves and a small white hat.

Serena heard the church door open and saw a tall figure standing in the back. He wore a navy sports jacket and a white shirt and tan slacks. She looked more closely and recognized Nick's wavy dark hair. She put her hand to her mouth and gasped. Nick caught her eye and held it. Then he smiled and slid into a pew.

Serena walked outside and stood in the church garden. Guests milled around the steps, congratulating the bride and groom. Malcolm and Laura and Zoe posed for photographers and a flower girl littered the lawn with rose petals.

She leaned against the stone wall, gazing at the view. The church was high above Antibes and all Serena could see was blue. She glanced around, hoping to find Nick. He had left before the ceremony ended and she wondered if she had been hallucinating.

"I had to get out of there quickly," a male voice said behind her. "I was about to be trampled by paparazzi trying to get a shot of Miranda Kerr."

Serena turned and saw Nick walking toward her. His cheeks were smooth and his blue eyes sparkled.

"The Gladdings are well known in Australia," Serena replied. "They have a lot of prominent friends."

"It was a beautiful ceremony," Nick said as he stood beside her. His hair was freshly washed and he smelled of musk shampoo. "I almost cried at the reading."

"Why are you here?" Serena asked in shock.

"Zoe invited me."

"Zoe invited you to her parents' wedding?" Serena raised her eyebrow.

"I was on the America's Cup team, I'm sort of a celebrity." He slipped his hands in his pockets and his eyes flickered. "That's not why she invited me; she thought I'd want to see you."

Serena's heart skipped a beat. Her stomach did little flips and her throat was dry. "Do you?"

Nick touched her chin. "More than anything."

Serena felt his mouth on hers. He pressed against her, running his hands through her hair. He pulled her close and circled her waist with his hands.

"We have a lot to talk about." Nick pulled away. "But my invitation said the ceremony is followed by a reception with a five-course dinner and the finest French wines. Why don't we celebrate the bride and groom and talk later. I've never been to a wedding that didn't serve dry chicken and warm beer."

Serena saw Zoe motioning her to join her in the white Bentley. She grabbed Nick's hand and ran to the car. She leaned against him, listening to Zoe chatter about hymns, and felt Nick's hand curl around her palm. She wanted to say something but she sat perfectly still, afraid to break the spell.

Serena entered the Salon des Lérins and gasped. The ballroom had been transformed into a scene from *A Midsummer Night's Dream*. The walls were covered with pale green silk and the room was scattered with trees. Tables were covered with gold tablecloths and filled with ceramic bowls of peaches and grapes and berries. Ballet dancers dressed like fairies posed on marble pedestals and there was an ice sculpture of a fawn.

"How did they do this in three days?" Serena gazed at the green and blue pinpoint lighting, the tall urns of red and white and pink roses, the gold filigree chairs.

"It helps to have an unlimited budget—wait until you see the wedding cake." Zoe grinned. "Oh, God, it's my turn to give a toast."

Serena sat next to Nick and saw Zoe take the stage. She watched her friend smooth her hair and gingerly tap the microphone.

"I never thought I'd walk my mother down the aisle. Thank God she's too old to have babies; I'd be useless in the delivery room." Zoe paused while people laughed. She glanced at her notes and squinted at the crowd. "If a parent's job is to teach their children, my parents get an A plus. They taught me to be independent and hardworking and loyal, but most important, they taught me about love.

"Twelve years ago I was kidnapped and my parents thought they lost the most important thing in their lives. Now I know how they felt, because recently I thought I lost what I valued most: my family. But tonight we are here together, celebrating with our dear friends. They showed me with love you can accomplish anything, and I hope I have a marriage that lasts as long and brings joy to so many people." Zoe paused. She looked up from her notes and her hands were shaking.

"They taught me something else." Zoe grinned, her shoulders relaxing. "If you want people to fly halfway around the world at a day's notice, you better throw a great party. May I introduce the one and only Sir Elton John!"

"How did you get Elton John to sing at your parents' wedding?" Serena asked when Zoe joined them at their table.

The room had erupted in applause and waiters popped bottles of Dom Pérignon. Malcolm wiped his eyes with his gray handkerchief and Laura twisted her new five-carat diamond ring.

"He's staying at the Hôtel du Cap-Eden-Roc; I ran into him in the lobby." Zoe guzzled the champagne. "We met when my father received his knighthood, we all had tea with the queen. He loves Violet Crumbles and he has the coolest collection of glasses. We're going to carry them at the store."

"I'd like to propose a toast," Nick said as he raised his champagne flute. "To a fairy-tale wedding and two beautiful bridesmaids." Nick leaned forward and kissed Serena on the lips. "I'm the luckiest guy in the room."

"I'm sorry I disappeared, it was so much to take in," Nick said later, leaning against the glass railing. "I was out of my mind, I felt like my whole childhood had been obliterated."

They had nibbled caviar and duck pâté and Russian foie gras. They ate lobster soufflé and lamb medallions with stuffed red peppers. They watched Malcolm and Laura glide across the dance floor and saw Zoe standing on the side, holding back tears. After the first dance, Nick grabbed Serena's hand and led her to the balcony.

"I know." Serena nodded. She gazed at the glittering lights of the Côte d'Azur and wished they could talk about selling Nick's boat and her promotion at *Vogue*.

"I walked for hours in the hills and then I went home and drank a bottle of scotch."

"Where did you see Zoe?" Serena asked.

"She came to my apartment," Nick replied.

"She shouldn't have done that," Serena murmured. Suddenly the breeze picked up and she wrapped her pink pashmina tightly around her chest.

"She said I shouldn't be angry at you, you were hurting as much as me," Nick replied. "Then she said you might have forgotten to tell me something."

"What?" Serena asked.

"That you were falling in love with me."

Serena looked at the stars forming constellations in the sky. She gazed at the moon glinting on the sea. She felt Nick tuck her hair behind her ear. He gathered her in his arms and held her against his chest.

"Let's go," he whispered.

"They're about to serve cake," Serena mumbled. Her head buzzed from the champagne and she felt like there was an electric current coursing through her body.

Nick took her hand and ran through the ballroom and into the hallway. They ran through the ornate lobby and down the stone steps. They ran over the lush green lawns until they reached the driveway.

"Where are we going?" Serena slipped off her sandals so she could keep up with him.

"I didn't leave my car with the valet." Nick grinned. "It cost a fortune."

They hopped into his blue Renault and drove fifteen minutes to Cannes. Nick parked at the bottom of the alley and they ran over the cobblestones to his apartment. They raced up the stairs and Nick opened the door.

Serena took a deep breath and glanced around the room. There was an empty bottle of scotch and an uneaten slice of pizza. The curtains were closed and the air was warm and dank.

Suddenly she thought she shouldn't be here. She pictured her father and mother in the drawing room of the Presidio Heights mansion. She saw the photo of Chantal and Charles at the Antibes villa. She turned to the door but Nick caught her hand. He slipped one hand under her dress and touched the soft silk of her panties.

Serena bit her lip and froze. He slipped off her panties and stroked her thighs. He moved his fingers slowly, thrusting them inside her until her body became liquid and she clung to his shoulders. He moved faster and she felt the pleasure well up and tip her over the edge. She felt the waves wash over her and the breath leave her chest.

"Come here," Nick whispered. He entered the bedroom and unbuttoned his shirt. Serena fumbled with his belt and unzipped his slacks. She lay on the bed and pulled him beside her. She opened her legs and wrapped her arms around his back. He plunged into her, picking up speed and carrying her with him. She felt the explosion, the long, endless shuddering, and burst into tears.

Nick pulled her close, waiting for her breathing to subside. He tucked her against his chest and whispered, "I told you there were some things better than cake."

chapter thirty

Serena opened her laptop and clicked on her to-do list. She twisted her ponytail and scrolled down the page. She poured a cup of black coffee and walked to the balcony.

She had spent the night in Nick's apartment and in the morning they ran along the beach and ate crepes at Z Plage. They talked about Yvette's story and Serena's promotion and the count who bought Nick's boat. They talked about Veronique's summer tour and the Cannes Film Festival and their favorite types of fondue. They sat with their hands entwined and talked about everything except their parents and the fact that Serena was leaving in two days. Then Nick had to leave for an appointment and Serena returned to the Carlton-InterContinental.

She walked back to the glass dining-room table and glanced at the computer screen. Serena had one more meeting with Yvette and the memoir would be complete. She glanced at the smartly dressed flight attendants and smiling travelers on the Air France site and wished she felt anything but dread. She pictured Nick's broad chest, his lips on hers, and shivered.

Her phone rang and she answered it.

"How's my little girl?" a male voice asked. "I was expecting you to say hello in French."

"Dad?" Serena asked. "Where are you?"

"At the Hilton in Dakar. Your mother is punishing me for giving her a scare by traipsing around the outdoor markets. We're going to need a camel to carry home all the knick-knacks."

"How are you feeling?"

"I told the doctors it was nothing," Charles replied. "Anyone's heart would race if you saw a herd of water buffalo bearing down on you. He won't let me go back on safari; we're flying home to-morrow."

"To San Francisco?" Serena asked.

"We're hoping you'll be home soon." Charles paused. "Unless you've fallen in love with some European playboy and are stay-ing on the Côte d'Azur."

Serena clutched the edge of the desk. "I booked my ticket, my flight arrives on Saturday."

"Kate will be thrilled, she's already planning a dinner party," her father replied. "All she talks about is Niman Ranch steaks and Bolinas endive lettuce and Sonoma goat cheese. I caught her looking at photos of Just Desserts raspberry cheesecake on the hotel computer."

"I miss Peet's coffee and Lappert's strawberry ice cream." Ser-ena smiled.

"It's going to be all right," Charles said quietly. "Everything will get back to normal."

Serena gazed at the pink marble floors and the striped silk sofas of the Cary Grant Suite. She glanced at the sleek white yachts in the harbor and the Île Sainte-Marguerite shimmering on the horizon. She shut her laptop and nodded. "I know."

"I'm starving," Nick said over the phone. "I'm picking you up for lunch."

"I have to edit two chapters before I meet Yvette," Serena replied, glancing at her laptop. "I barely have time to eat a crustless cucumber sandwich."

"The lunch special at Vesuvio is salmon pasta with niçoise salad and caramel flan," Nick insisted. "V is going to join us; I told her everything."

Serena's heart beat faster. "What did she say?"

"V is a ballerina, she wraps her toes in bandages every night," Nick said slowly. "She's the strongest woman I know."

"She still wants to have lunch with me?" Serena asked.

"She'd do anything for Vesuvio's calamari pizza," Nick told her. "And she thinks you have beautiful eyes."

"Okay." Serena nodded. "What time should I meet you?"

"I'm in the lobby, I'll be upstairs in five minutes."

"When I was young my father was my hero," V mused, peeling the crust off a piece of pizza. "He bought tickets to Les Ballets de Monte Carlo for my eighth birthday. I wore a red velvet dress and gold slippers and a satin bow in my hair. He wore a black tuxedo and a white tie. We drove in a town car and had box seats; it was one of the best nights of my life."

They sat at an outdoor table at Vesuvio, sharing a pizza topped with calamari and sun-dried tomatoes and green olives. There was a platter of salmon linguine and a green salad with anchovies and peppers. Serena was afraid V would be devastated, but she gave Serena a quick hug and spread butter on a crust of bread.

"As I grew older, I became obsessed with ballet and didn't spend as much time with him. Every night I knelt next to my bed and prayed I'd become a ballerina." V stopped and her face clouded over. "I'm lucky, my wish came true."

"I'm sure if Dad knew you were a ballerina he'd be proud," Serena said awkwardly.

"In ballet there's always something you crave: the principal role in *Romeo and Juliet* or to be the guest ballerina at the Kirov. I've learned to appreciate what I have." V looked at Serena. "Now I have a sister, or at least a friend."

"I'd like to be friends," Serena said, and nodded, sipping her sparkling water.

V ate a bite of pizza and grinned. "You have the best taste in clothing, and I bet we're the same shoe size."

The waiter replaced their plates with bowls of coffee-flavored gelato and caramel flan. They shared a bottle of chardonnay and Serena began to relax. V told stories about dancers purposely tripping other dancers at rehearsal and shrinking their leotards so they thought they had gained weight.

"Ballet dancers are the most competitive people I've ever met," V said as she licked gelato off her spoon. "Sometimes they'd replace your point shoes with a smaller pair while you slept."

"In racing we worked as a team." Nick finished his glass of chardonnay. "The best part about sailing was always knowing someone had your back."

"I would have loved to see you race." Serena nodded.

"Grant Simmer came to see me this morning," Nick said. "He's the manager of the Oracle America's Cup team."

Serena put her spoon down. "He came to Cannes to see you?"

"He kept calling, so I agreed to meet him." Nick shrugged. "They've almost finished putting together the team for the 2016 Cup. They've got the best sailors from Australia and New Zealand and a new state-of-the-art training center in San Francisco."

"What did you say?" Serena felt a shiver run down her spine.

"When my father died I thought life was all about luck—when your luck ran out you had to change direction," Nick began. "I was wrong; life is about finding what you're passionate about and embracing it. I told him yes."

"What about the huge catamarans?" Serena asked. "You said they tip over too easily and they're impossible to steer."

"They're not racing them anymore, they've designed a smaller, lighter boat." Nick touched her hand and his eyes flickered. "I couldn't think of a reason to turn him down."

Serena pictured having picnics at Golden Gate Park and buying sunflowers at the Flower Mart. She saw candlelit dinners in her apartment and weekend trips to Muir Woods. She pictured Nick on the hull of a catamaran, racing against the wind.

"Where am I going to stash my stuff when I'm on tour?" V interrupted. "I'm going to have to behave like a grown-up and get my own apartment."

"When do you leave for San Francisco?" Serena asked.

Veronique had gone to soak her feet, and Nick and Serena strolled along the dock. It was early afternoon and waves lapped against the shore. Serena saw seagulls skim the water and sail-boats tip gently in the breeze.

"In two weeks; I can't wait to test the new catamaran." Nick's eyes sparkled. "It's going to be the best-designed craft in America's Cup history."

"I'm glad you're joining the team." Serena smiled. She wore a yellow-and-white cotton dress and her hair was tied with a yellow ribbon. She wore silver Gucci sandals and a silver Tiffany locket around her neck. She felt Nick's hand on her back and felt young and happy.

"I have to make sure my mother has everything she needs," Nick said, squinting into the sun. "I'd like you to meet her."

"You want me to meet Chantal?" Serena gulped.

"I told her everything," Nick replied. "I said I'd bring you to the villa."

Serena felt her stomach rise to her throat. She pictured the dark-haired beauty in the photograph, the elegant model on the cover of French *Vogue,* the young shop assistant who ruined her parents' marriage.

"When?" Serena asked.

Nick took her hand and led her to the Renault. "Today."

They drove down a gravel driveway and stopped in front of a whitewashed villa flanked by wide palm trees. Serena saw a garden filled with pink rosebushes and tall birds of paradise. There was an olive tree and clusters of bougainvillea and beds of purple and white pansies.

"My mother adores her garden." Nick opened Serena's door. "She used to spend all her time with her roses."

"Nick, you're here!" a woman's voice floated through the entry.

"I'm sorry it's dark, the light hurts my eyes. Pull back the curtains, I want to meet Serena."

Serena walked through the tile entry and entered a living room with plaster walls and wood floors. The furniture was draped with cotton sheets and the floors were covered by faded Oriental rugs. There was an antique desk and a burgundy velvet day bed filled with silk cushions.

"I hate turning the salon into a sickroom, but I can't climb the stairs to the bedrooms," Chantal said, waving her hand. "At least I can smell the roses in the garden; did you see my English lavenders? They smell like Elizabeth Taylor's White Diamonds."

Serena peered into the dark and saw a woman reclining on a brocade sofa. She had a long face with brown eyes and dark eyelashes. She wore a pink housedress and white slippers on her feet.

"Gia made fresh scones and Earl Grey tea. She's pleased to have young people to feed; I can hardly eat a bite." Chantal gazed at Serena. "You look like Charles, I always imagined you did. I was very angry with Yvette for writing the letter." Chantal paused. "Nick told me how happy you've made him, and now I'm glad Yvette went behind my back."

Serena turned to Nick, trying to think of something to say. She glanced around the room at the ceramic vases filled with flowers and the paintings on the walls. There was a series of Monet's haystacks and a Matisse in a gold frame.

"I know what I did was wrong, but when you're young and scared you use what you have," Chantal said slowly. "In the beginning I think Charles enjoyed his French family. Veronique was a beautiful child and Nick was always so serious, like a little man." Chantal wetted her lips with a glass of water. "Later I sensed Charles wanted to be somewhere else. I'd catch him with his newspapers in his lap, staring into space. Except when he was with Nick; those two were like a couple of pirates! Always out on a boat or fishing on the dock, they'd come home with more fish than I could cook in a week.

"I'm telling you this because in his way Charles wanted to do the right thing. When I saw him with his wife at the Carlton-InterContinental I knew it was over. They were like a bride and groom on top of a wedding cake.

"I thought it would be best for Nick to go to boarding school." Chantal paused. "At first I got daily letters that he had no friends. Then he wrote that he changed his name from Giles to Nick and joined the sailing club. Finally the letters stopped and I received a monthly postcard." Chantal smiled. "I knew he was happy.

"Veronique was easy, she always loved the ballet," Chantal mused. "The day she got accepted at the Ecole des Ballets de Monte Carlo, I knew she was going to be famous.

"Then Yvette handed me my brilliant career and I had money and furs and diamonds," Chantal said as she reclined against the cushions. "After I got sick, I was afraid my children would be orphans. I should never have lied to them about Charles being dead." Chantal looked at Nick. "It's hard to imagine your children as adults, and even harder to stop protecting them."

Serena gazed at Chantal's translucent skin and remembered the luxuriant hair and elegant cheekbones in the photographs. She pictured the bright blue eye shadow and the eyelashes that went on forever. She wanted to ask Chantal a dozen questions, but then she pictured her mother in her Chanel suits and wanted to escape the salon and breathe fresh air and sunshine.

"Please stay for dinner, Gia is making grilled halibut and baby peas and green beans from the garden," Chantal said. "I'll take a nap, you two can explore Juan-les-Pins. Bring back a vanilla flan and a carton of strawberry ice cream."

"We don't have to stay," Nick said.

Chantal fell asleep and Nick and Serena strolled in the garden. Serena heard birds chirping and saw the white sand beaches of Antibes far below them. She glanced at Nick and saw his eyes were moist and his cheeks were drawn.

"Of course we'll stay." Serena squeezed his hand. "When have I said no to flan and ice cream?"

They drove into Juan-les-Pins and parked at one end of the main street. Serena saw the newsagent and the patisserie and thought nothing must have changed in thirty years. She glanced above the ice cream shop and saw a bay window overlooking the harbor.

"Bertrand Roland kept a room here," Serena said, pointing to the brick building. "He and Yvette were lovers. Yvette told him she was going to leave her husband, and when she found Bertrand with another woman, she was devastated.

"I asked her whether she was sorry she told Bertrand she loved him; if she hadn't their affair may have continued," Serena said earnestly. "But she said if you find true love you have to do anything to keep it."

"My mother is sorry for what she did," Nick said quietly. "She never meant to hurt your family."

"Having an affair with a married man was probably not the way to go about it." Serena blinked back sudden tears. She turned away from Nick and hurried down the street.

"Serena, wait!" Nick called. He caught up with her and grabbed her hand. "I can't turn back the clock and erase what happened between our parents, but it doesn't change the way I feel about you. I know I said I don't believe in luck, but that's not true. The luckiest day of my life was the day I found your cell phone. You're gorgeous and intelligent and when I'm with you I feel like I can do anything." Nick paused and kneeled on the cobblestones. "Serena, will you marry me?"

Serena put her hand to her throat. She couldn't catch her breath and her legs felt like jelly. She had sat across from Chantal and wanted to run out of the villa. Now she looked at Nick's clear blue eyes and wanted him to wrap his arms around her.

"I know it's sudden, but I fell in love the night we had dinner at Le Maurice. You're braver than you know, and together I'm not afraid of anything." Nick reached into his pocket and pulled out a dark green velvet box. He opened it and displayed a yellow diamond flanked by two amethysts.

Serena looked at the velvet box with the gold letters that spelled SHREVE and gasped. She remembered trying on her mother's earrings and rings as a child. Kate's jewelry case was filled with identical green boxes with the same gold lettering. Shreve & Co. was San Francisco's oldest jewelry store and every woman in Presidio Heights wanted a green velvet box with the scrawled gold signature.

"Where did you get that ring?" Serena whispered.

"My mother has a stunning jewelry collection." Nick smiled. "She was going to leave it all to Veronique but she told me to pick my favorite pieces. I can have it reset if you don't like it."

"Shreve is my father's favorite jewelry store; he bought my mother a new piece for every anniversary." Serena pulled her hand away. She turned and started walking down the street.

"Where are you going?" Nick ran after her.

Serena stopped and took a deep breath. She looked at Nick and thought her heart would crack. "I need some time to think, I'm going to catch the bus to Cannes."

"I'll drive you." Nick grabbed his car keys.

Serena shook her head and bit her lip. "I'll be fine, go have dinner with your mother."

chapter thirty-one

Serena spooned honey into vanilla tea and added warm milk. She wrapped her white cotton robe around her and paced around the living room of the Cary Grant Suite. Ever since she caught the bus back from Antibes she'd been trying to distract herself. She read French *Vogue* and *Paris Match*. She turned on the television and watched *To Catch a Thief* in French with English subtitles. She made herself a plate of lobster ravioli and baked squash and didn't eat a bite. She poured a shot of aged cognac but couldn't swallow it.

Every time she closed her eyes she saw her father entering the Shreve store on Post Street in San Francisco. She pictured him selecting the flawless diamond and asking the salesgirl to wrap it up. She saw him slip it in his overnight bag after Kate had done his packing. She saw her mother kiss Charles good-bye at the airport, wishing him a safe trip.

Her parents' marriage survived the last fifteen years because they made an agreement to forget the affair ever happened. How would her mother feel if she were reminded of it on a daily basis? She pictured introducing Nick to Kate and her stomach turned over. She saw Veronique with her blond hair and green eyes and knew her mother couldn't possibly welcome the product of Charles's infidelity.

Serena thought about Nick and how close Chantal said he'd been with Charles. How would Nick feel if Charles refused to acknowledge him? She pictured awkward meetings at the yacht club or family dinners at the Presidio Heights mansion. Perhaps Nick would grow jealous of her relationship with her father and stop loving her.

Then Serena pictured turning Nick down and her heart pounded. She imagined running into him at Whole Foods or on the Marina Green. She saw him with his arm draped around a tall brunette or a petite blonde and she felt faint.

Serena stood on the balcony and gazed at the yachts twinkling on the harbor. It was almost midnight and the bay was still. She heard muffled laughter on the Boulevard de la Croisette and a European sports car gunning down the avenue. She walked inside and picked up her phone.

"If you're calling to thank me for the upgrade to first class, you're welcome," Chelsea's voice came over the line. "I can't wait to have the finished memoir in my hands."

"I was calling for a favor." Serena wrapped the robe tightly around her waist. "I wonder if you could ask Harry if there are any positions open in New York."

"You hated New York, you said even the coffee baristas were rude and in summer it's so hot you could fry an egg on the sidewalk."

"I've reconnected with a college boyfriend." Serena crossed her fingers behind her back. "It's getting serious and I don't want a long-distance romance."

"You just got a promotion," Chelsea protested.

"I know it wouldn't be senior editor," Serena said. "I'd take anything."

Chelsea hesitated. "I'm sure Harry could find something, but you wouldn't have your own office and your name on the masthead."

"It doesn't matter." Serena clutched the porcelain teacup. "I really need to be in New York."

"I'll see what I can do," Chelsea said slowly. "I'm disappointed, I didn't think you were the type of woman who put a man before your career."

Serena placed the teacup on the glass coffee table. She sat on the ivory silk sofa and tucked her legs under her. She closed her eyes and let the tears roll down her cheeks.

"Serena!" Yvette opened the door of the Sophia Loren Suite. She wore a red linen dress with a cropped black jacket and a wide gold belt. Her hair lay smoothly behind her ears and she wore diamond earrings and a black pearl necklace.

Serena touched her hair and adjusted her skirt. She had been nervous about seeing Yvette but she couldn't leave without saying good-bye. She had slipped on a crisp black Donna Karan dress and Prada pumps and knotted her hair in a low bun. She drank a cup of espresso and marched down the hallway to the Sophia Loren Suite.

"You look like you haven't slept a wink." Yvette gazed at Serena. "You must have so many last-minute things to do; what time is your flight?"

"Not till this evening." Serena glanced at her watch. "I didn't want to leave without saying good-bye."

"I know this has been difficult for you." Yvette perched on a peach upholstered chair. "I'm not proud of myself, but we do what we think is best for the people we care about." Yvette paused and picked up a parcel from the bamboo dining-room table. "I have enjoyed our talks so much; I brought you a present."

"For me?" Serena took the package and slipped off the gold ribbon. She undid the silver wrapping paper and turned the book over. "It's a signed first edition of Bertrand's *The Gigolo*," Serena gasped. "It must be worth a fortune."

"Sotheby's auctioned one copy off last year for ten thousand dollars." Yvette smiled. "Bertrand would laugh, he always called *The Gigolo* literary porn."

"I can't take this." Serena handed it back, thinking how angry she had been at Yvette for writing the letter to the *San Francisco Chronicle*, for blurting the story out to Nick.

"I can't undo the damage I've caused, but I can show you how grateful I am. Writing the memoir has brought me such joy." Yvette pressed the book into Serena's hands. "You made Bertrand come alive."

"I met Chantal," Serena said slowly. "She was very weak but still beautiful."

"You met Chantal!" Yvette exclaimed. "She didn't tell me."

"Nick took me to the villa. Then he asked me to marry him," Serena replied.

"What did you say?" Yvette asked.

Serena stood at the French doors and gazed at the harbor. It was midmorning and the Mediterranean was like a sheet of glass. White clouds drifted across the sky and pink and white villas climbed the hillside like icing on a cake.

"I'm taking a position at *Vogue* in New York." Serena turned around. "Long-distance relationships never work."

"I see." Yvette looked at Serena quizzically. "Chantal told me Nick joined the Oracle America's Cup team in San Francisco; he must really love you."

"Chelsea offered me a wonderful opportunity in New York." Serena bit her lip. "I couldn't pass it up."

"I remember when Bertrand left for Hollywood," Yvette mused. "He said everyone gets over love affairs, but I didn't believe him." Yvette walked to the sideboard and filled a plate with cantaloupe and honeydew and wheat toast. She added a strip of bacon and a pot of strawberry jam and sat at the dining-room table.

"Now I think he was right. I can hardly remember the way my heart used to pound when I smelled Bertrand's cologne. He always smelled of aftershave and cigarettes, I used to think it was the sexiest scent in the world." Yvette sighed. "For years whenever I saw a man wearing a white straw hat, I couldn't catch my breath. If I heard Bertrand's name in conversation, I felt a throbbing between my legs. But time heals most things; it's been almost thirty years and I'm learning how to be happy." She ate a bite of melon and looked at Serena carefully. "The fruit is delicious, please help yourself."

"Look what I have!" Zoe exclaimed, entering the living room of the Cary Grant Suite. She wore a red Marc Jacobs shirtdress with a wide leather belt. She carried a Louis Vuitton overnight bag and clutched a brown paper sack.

"How was the wedding breakfast?" Serena asked, moving around the living room collecting her books and magazines. Her flight left in four hours and she was almost packed. Her Coach suitcase stood at the entry and her laptop and notepads were stacked on the dining-room table.

"I just saw my parents off on the yacht, they were like a couple of teenagers," Zoe said as she drew a round object out of the paper sack. "It's Bono's egg timer. He's staying at the Hôtel du Cap-Eden-Roc and he sat next to us at breakfast. I asked for his autograph but he didn't have a pen. He gave me his egg timer; he eats the same breakfast every day: a four-minute egg, porridge, and an orange. Isn't that the sexiest thing you ever heard?"

"I wonder if Ian would think so." Serena laughed.

"Ian thinks Bono is one step below God. We're taking a walking tour of Bono's favorite Irish pubs next summer." Zoe scooped up a handful of macadamia nuts from the silver tray on the coffee table. "How's Nick? The last time I saw you, you and Nick were slow dancing to 'Candle in the Wind.'"

Serena dropped a copy of French *Elle* on the side table. "Nick told me you went to see him at his apartment. You shouldn't have done that."

"Someone had to, you two were like Romeo and Juliet." Zoe ate a cluster of raisins. "I hated that play. I always wanted to shake Romeo and say don't drink the hemlock, Juliet's only sleeping."

"Nick is joining the Oracle America's Cup team and moving to San Francisco." Serena sat on the royal-blue velvet sofa. "He asked me to marry him."

"What did you say?" Zoe demanded.

"He gave me a yellow diamond in a green Shreve jewelry box. It was part of Chantal's jewelry collection." Serena twisted her ponytail. "Nick didn't realize the ring was a present from my father. Shreve is San Francisco's most renowned jewelry store; my father shops there all the time."

Zoe's eyes grew wide and she fiddled with her silver charm bracelet. "If you don't like the ring, tell him you want to pick one out yourself. I was just at Van Cleef and Arpels drooling over the two-carat diamond solitaires."

"My parents survived the affair by pretending it never happened. Can you imagine how hurt my mother would be if I wore Chantal's ring?" Serena frowned. "Situations like that would arise all the time. Nick and I would be a walking reminder of my father's secret family.

"Nick worshipped Charles when he was a boy," Serena continued. "How will Nick feel if Dad refuses to acknowledge his existence? Chase and I used to have dinner with them twice a week; can you imagine Nick and my parents sharing a Napa Valley chardonnay and Bolinas Farms oysters?"

Zoe stood up and walked to the sideboard. She gazed at the platters of cucumber sandwiches and deviled eggs and puff pastries. She turned and glared at Serena.

"You're treating your parents like newborns in the neonatal ward. When your mother decided to stay with your father she knew it wasn't going to be easy. The affair ended fifteen years ago! If Kate hasn't forgiven him, they'll never last," Zoe raged. "And Nick can take care of himself. He's faced thirty-foot waves in the Tasman Sea; he can survive your father's cold shoulder." Zoe strode back to the sofa. "Stop thinking you're protecting everyone else and admit you can't handle it. If you want to run away, go ahead, but don't blame anyone else."

"I don't know what you mean." Serena's voice was tight.

"I mean"—Zoe grabbed her paper sack and slung her Louis Vuitton bag over her shoulder—"you sound just like Chase. I'm going to Skype Ian, I'll see you later."

Serena sucked in her breath as if she'd been punched. She stared at the blue Mediterranean, trying to stop her heart from racing. She watched wooden fishing boats row to shore and silver speedboats fly over the waves. Finally she stood up and walked to the dining-room table. She picked up her phone and dialed Chelsea's number.

Serena left her suitcases with the concierge and ran through the revolving glass doors. She glanced at her watch and strode quickly down the Boulevard de la Croisette. The car taking her to the airport would arrive in fifty minutes. She clutched her soft leather purse and walked faster.

She climbed the narrow cobblestones to Nick's building and rang the doorbell. She treaded a small circle on the sidewalk, waiting for Nick to let her in. She slipped in the entrance behind an old woman and ran up the three flights of stairs. She knocked on the door and listened for Nick's footsteps. Finally she gave up and ran into the street.

She thought of asking Isabel at Le Maurice where Nick was, but it was late afternoon and the restaurant was closed. She stood at the top of the alley and gazed at the glittering ocean. She saw the wide yachts lining the dock and the seagulls clustered on the shore. She took off her sandals and ran down the hill to the sand. She ran faster, scouring the small fishing boats and sleek catamarans.

"What are you doing here?" Serena asked.

Nick sat on the dock with his legs dangling into the water. He wore rolled-up khakis and a navy T-shirt. His hair stuck to his shoulders and he had light stubble on his chin.

"I'm thinking of buying a boat; it might be rushing things to join the Oracle team," Nick said slowly. "I should stay in Cannes and be close to Chantal and Veronique."

"That's a shame," Serena said as she sat next to Nick and swung her legs over the dock. She wore a floral Pucci dress and silver leather sandals. Her ponytail was tied with a yellow ribbon and she wore diamond studs in her ears. "You'll miss the wedding of the year in San Francisco. The ceremony is going to be at Saints Peter and Paul Church, the San Francisco Boys Chorus is going to sing 'Ave Maria.' The reception will be held in a tent at the Palace of the Legion of Honor. Stanlee Gatti is providing the flowers and Michael Mina is doing the catering: Morro Bay abalone and Liberty Farms duck breast and king crab tortellini. The Fundamentals are going to perform and Sam Godfrey is baking a six-tier chocolate mousse wedding cake."

"Who's getting married?" Nick asked.

Serena took a deep breath. Her arms shook and her mouth trembled. "We are, if the offer you made earlier is still available."

"What are you saying?" Nick's voice was low.

Serena stood up and smoothed her skirt. She shielded her eyes against the sun and glanced down at Nick.

"Ask me again," she whispered.

Nick kneeled on the dock and took Serena's hand. He reached into his pocket and took out a red leather jewelry box with CARTIER printed in gold letters. He opened the box and displayed a solitaire diamond ring in a white gold setting.

"Serena, will you marry me?" Nick asked.

"Where did you get that ring?" Serena gasped.

"I thought if by some wonderful stroke of luck I got to ask the question again, I should have a new ring." Nick smiled. "One without any history."

Serena felt the air rush from her lungs. Nick hadn't given up. Even when she turned him down he believed in them enough to buy a new ring.

"Yes, I'll marry you." Serena nodded.

Nick slipped the ring on her finger and wrapped his arms around her waist. He kissed her slowly, tasting of mint toothpaste. He held her tightly, running his hands through her hair. He finally released her, gripping her hand as if he were afraid she'd disappear.

"I love you," Nick said, and tucked a blond hair behind her ear. "It might not be easy, but together we can accomplish anything. We're a team."

"There's someone I need to call." Serena fished her phone out of her purse and scrolled down the screen. She found the number and pressed call.

"Serena! How wonderful to hear your voice. We were about to check out and leave for the airport; I bought you the most fabulous sarong hand sewn by African villagers," Kate's voice came over the line.

"I'm glad I caught you," Serena replied, gazing at the shimmering coastline.

"Is anything wrong? Charles told me you're arriving on Saturday," Kate replied. "I can't wait to see you, I'm going to book us facials at Joseph Cozza on Maiden Lane. Africa is fascinating, but it's so humid; my skin feels like paper."

"Everything is perfect." Serena paused. "I'm in love, I'm getting married."

"Getting married!" Kate exclaimed. "That's very sudden. The Côte d'Azur can be so seductive, are you sure it's not a holiday romance?"

"He's everything I wished for. He's handsome and smart and kind and he makes me happy." Serena felt the warm sun on her back and her shoulders relaxed. She took a deep breath and squeezed Nick's hand. "I can't wait for you to meet him."

acknowledgments

First and always, thanks to my wonderful agent, Melissa Flashman, and my brilliant editor, Hilary Rubin Teeman. A thank-you to Hilary's terrific assistant, Alicia Clancy; my amazing publicist, Katie Bassel; and the great team at St. Martin's Press: Jennifer Weis, Jennifer Enderlin, Lauren Jablonski, Elsie Lyons, and Bethany Reis.

Thanks to the wonderful blogger Andrea Peskind Katz for the support and friendship, and a special thank-you to Jane Hanauer and the staff at Laguna Beach Books. And a big thank-you to my family—my husband, Thomas; my children, Alex, Andrew, Heather, Madeleine, and Thomas; and my daughter-in-law, Lisa—for bringing me so much joy.

1. Do you think Serena should have taken the assignment in Cannes right after Chase proposed, or should she have stayed in San Francisco to help Chase with his mayoral campaign and plan the wedding? Would their relationship have turned out differently if she didn't take the assignment?

2. Zoe lied to Serena at the beginning of their friendship. Serena forgave her and agreed to continue the friendship. If you were Serena would you have done the same thing, or do you expect honesty from your friends at all times?

3. Describe Kate's relationship with Charles. How do you perceive Kate as a woman? Do you respect the decisions she made or disagree with them?

4. Of all the relationships in the novel, which one resonates the most with you and why?

5. Do you think Serena was correct in keeping what she learned about their past from Nick? Would you have done the same thing, and if not, what would you have done instead?

6. At one point, Bertrand says to Yvette, "If only I had been a better man or you had been a lesser woman, we could have made it work." What did he mean, and how do you feel about his words?

7. Yvette and Kate have similar views on love. What are they, and do you agree with them?

8. What are your thoughts on Chantal? Do you have any sympathy for her either when she was very young or now that she is dying?

9. Do you think Zoe put too much time and effort into keeping her parents together when she should have been pursuing her own life? Why or why not?

10. Location plays a big part in the story. Cannes seems idyllic—the food, the hotels, the beaches. What is your favorite holiday destination and why?